Beulah Marie Dix

Soldier Rigdale

Beulah Marie Dix

Soldier Rigdale

ISBN/EAN: 9783337105372

Printed in Europe, USA, Canada, Australia, Japan

Cover: Foto ©Andreas Hilbeck / pixelio.de

More available books at **www.hansebooks.com**

SOLDIER RIGDALE
by
Buelah Marie Dix

SOLDIER RIGDALE

"As if he knew the place and held he had the right to come there."

Soldier Rigdale

·HOW HE SAILED IN THE "MAYFLOWER"·
·AND HOW HE SERVED MILES STANDISH·

BY

Beulah Marie Dix

AUTHOR OF "HUGH GWYETH: A ROUNDHEAD CAVALIER"

WITH ILLUSTRATIONS BY REGINALD B. BIRCH

New York
THE MACMILLAN COMPANY
LONDON: MACMILLAN & CO., Ltd.
1899

Contents

v

Contents

List of Illustrations

SOLDIER RIGDALE

CHAPTER I

PLAYING WITH POWDER

WITH the approach of sunset, the wind that all day had ruffled the waves to white edges died down, till there was left on the water only a long, heaving motion, that rudely swayed the old ship *Mayflower*. One moment from her broad deck could be seen the steel-like gleam of the fresh-water pond on the distant beach; the next moment, as the ship rolled between the waves, the shore presented nothing but solid sand dunes and shrubby pine trees. But always overhead the sky, athwart which the yards, bulging with the furled sails, were raking, remained the same,—a level reach of thick gray that, as twilight drew on, seemed to brood closer over earth and ocean.

How those yards seesawed up and down with the rolling of the ship, and the mastheads, they dipped too, quite as if they might pitch down upon a body! Miles Rigdale, standing with legs

craftily planted and head thrown well back, stared
and stared at their measured movement till, dizzy
with the feeling that the great spars were tottering
loose, he was glad to straighten his aching neck
once more.

"Did you see a goose, all roasted, flying for your
mouth?" Francis Billington called from the waist
of the ship, where he perched jauntily upon the
bulwark.

Sauntering from his place near the companion
way, Miles halted beside the speaker; not that he
had a great liking for Francis Billington, but he
was a sociable lad, who must talk to some one, and,
as the bleak air had driven the women and children
into the great cabin, while the men were absent, —
the leaders conferring in the roundhouse and the
lesser men seeking firewood on shore, — he could
for the moment find no comrade save young Billington.

The latter was an unprepossessing lad, stunted
and small for his fourteen years, with elfish eyes
which he now turned sharply on Miles. "I take
it, Jack Cooke is ill, and Giles Hopkins has packed
you about your business, that you've come to spend
the time with me," he suggested disagreeably.

"I take it, maybe you've spoke the truth," Miles
answered unruffled, as he propped his chin on his
fists and braced his elbows against the bulwark.

Gazing thus northward, he could see all about him green hills, wooded to the water's edge, now higher, now lower, as the ship mounted upon the waves, and the strip of sand beach, off which rode the bobbing longboat. "I wish my father had taken me with him when they went to fetch the wood," Miles broke out at that sight; "it's weeks and weeks since I set foot on land."

"Pooh! I've been ashore thrice already," bragged Francis, setting one arm akimbo, though he took good care to grip the shrouds tightly with the other hand, for the bulwark was not the safest of perches.

Miles tried to swallow down his envy, but he could not help saying, with a touch of triumph: "Anyhow, you saw no savages, and my father saw 'em when he went exploring with Captain Standish, —six Indians and a dog, he saw."

"So did my father," Francis sought to crush him; but Miles, declaring sudden truce, was asking, with civil interest: "You did not see any lions when you went ashore, did you, Francis?"

"N—no, but Ned Dotey thought he heard one roar the other night."

"Father would not take our mastiff Trug on land lest they kill him. Trug would give 'em a fight for it, though. But he couldn't fight the serpents; nobody could. Did you know, Francie, there's a serpent here in America,—they call it the rattlesnake, — and if it but breathe on you, you die presently."

" How do you know ? " asked Francis, awed, but incredulous.

" My father read it in a book about plantations in Virginia. Maybe the serpents lie close in cold weather, though, so you did not see them." Miles was silent a long instant, while he gazed fixedly at the mysterious shore yonder, where all these rarities were to be met with. " The trees do not look like our English trees," he said, half to himself, "but I'd fain go in among them. Perhaps you found conies there, Francis ? There were a plenty of them on the common at home ; Trug and I used to chase them, and 'twas brave sport."

" Mayhap if you had Trug with you, you could start some here," suggested Francis. " Tell you, Miles, you beg your father let you go ashore to-morrow, and I'll go too, and we'll seek for conies together. Will you ? "

" 'Tis no use," Miles answered, scowling straight ahead.

" Why not ? "

" Father says I cannot go," the boy blurted out. " I answered him saucily this morning, and he said for that I should not stir foot off the ship for a week. I think — I think he might let me go ashore. Along the first I was coughing, so my mother said I must not venture in the boat; and then my sister Dolly was ailing, and I must stay to bear her company; and then it stormed; and now he will not let me go. And I am so weary of this ship!"

"I'd not bear such usage from any man," Francis boasted grandly. "If 'twere my daddy treated me so harshly, I'd tell him to his face 'a' was a sour old curmudgeon, and —"

"You need not talk so of my father," Miles interrupted sullenly, though he held his eyes fixed upon the shore line, not on the speaker. It was hard, while he looked toward the land of wonders, still unknown to him, to think quite kindly of the father who had arbitrarily shut him out from the enjoyment of it. "If you miscall him so again, Francis, I'll fight you," he added, conscience-stricken, in the hope of making amends for the disloyalty of his thoughts.

Francis bent his sharp eyes on his companion, but did not take up the challenge; indeed, a less discreet lad than he might have considered an instant before coming to fisticuffs with Miles Rigdale. The boy, for his scant eleven years, was of a proper height, with straight back and sturdy limbs, a stocky, yet not clumsy, little figure, that promised a vigorous stature when he came to man's age. His deeply tanned face, that was lightly sprinkled with brown freckles, was square and resolute; his blue eyes were very level and honest; and his tousled brown hair tumbled about his forehead in a way to make more women than his mother think him a bonny boy. For the rest, he was clad humbly enough in doublet and breeches of dark gray frieze, with long gray stockings and stout shoes; he wore neither cloak nor hat, and his clenched fists, that now rested firmly on the bulwark, were bare and chapped red by the wind.

It was the sight of the aggressive fists that made Francis use a different tone: "You're a pretty comrade, Miles, to fly out at me so."

"You may leave my father in peace, then."

"Perhaps you'd wish me to leave you in peace too. I know Goodman Rigdale has forbid his little son speak to me."

"I'm still speaking to you, am I not?" answered Miles, and bent to adjust one of his shoes, so Francis could not see his face; those last words had hit dangerously near.

"But you'll show me a clean pair of heels very speedily," sneered his companion, "for yonder the boat with your good father is putting off from shore, and when he comes — "

"That's how the wind blows, is it?" struck in a new voice close at hand. Looking over his shoulder, Miles saw, lounging on a coil of rope by the foremast, a certain Edward Lister, one of the servants of Master Stephen Hopkins. He was a slim, dark fellow of some twenty years, whom Miles admired for a tall swaggerer, because he always wore his red cap rakishly on one side, and, since the rules about lighting tobacco aboard ship were strict, was ever chewing at a long pine splinter instead of a pipe. "So if your father catch you with Master Billington here, he'll swinge you soundly, eh, Miles Rigdale?" he asked, with his mouth quite grave, but a glancing mockery in his black eyes. "Better show us how briskly you can run into the cabin."

Miles ostentatiously leaned his shoulders against the bulwark and crossed one leg over the other, as if he thought to finish the afternoon in that position. Shifting round thus, his gaze travelled beyond his companions to the high quarter-deck, where he spied several men trudging forth from the round-house. "Has the conference broken off?" he asked, forgetting in his curiosity that he was angry with both Francis and Ned Lister.

"How else?" the latter answered dryly, and, rising to his feet, sauntered over to the two boys. "D'ye think they would confer without the great Master Hopkins? And he quit the roundhouse long since. Wearied out, doubtless, with such vigorous labor. It has taken them an hour to deter-

mine no more than to send forth a gang to-morrow
and try a third time for a place where we may
settle."

"Another exploration ? Is my father to go on
it, do you know ? " Miles questioned.

" They won't let any but the great folk have a
hand therein ; daddy said 'twould be so," commented Francis.

" True enough," scoffed Lister ; "the Governor,
and Captain Standish, Master Bradford, Master
Winslow, Master Hopkins, and — the worshipful
Master Edward Dotey."

" Aha ! " jeered Francis. " They're taking old
Hopkins's other man Dotey along, and Ned Lister
is jealous of him."

" Hold your tongue ! " cried Lister, catching the
lad by the scruff of the neck, " else I'll heave you
over the bulwark."

Francis twisted up his face and opened his mouth
in a prodigious, dry-eyed howl, which would have
set Miles laughing, had he not been intent just
then upon the approaching boat. He could see her
visibly growing larger, as she bounded nearer and
nearer over the swell of the water, and each moment
he recalled more distinctly in what terms his father
had forbidden him have to do with " that Satan-
ish brood of the Billingtons." Miles shuffled one
foot uneasily ; perhaps he really ought to go into

the cabin now and see how his sick friend, Jack Cooke, was faring.

He turned away and had idled a few paces along the deck, when Francis, who had been suffered wrest out of Lister's hold, called after him: "Ah, Miles daren't let his father find him with me.   I knew so."

"It's not so, neither," Miles flung back, and made a great show of stopping by the mainmast, where he stood gazing down the open hatchway which led to those cabins that were in the depth of the hold.   "Aren't you coming with me, Francis?" he asked presently.

The other, quite undeceived, came snickering up to him: "Have no fear; I'll take myself off ere your father come.   Sure, you're a stout-hearted one, Miles."

"You're a pretty fellow to talk of courage," Miles was goaded into replying, "after the way you howled out but now.   You might have known Ned Lister'd do you no hurt."

"No doubt you'd not have been afraid," his tormentor scoffed.   "You're not afraid of anybody save your father."

"So are you, if you told the truth of it," Miles took him up.   "You'd not have Goodman Billington hear you vaporing so for all the silver crowns in England, and if Goodwife Billington came by and heard you, she'd cuff your ears smartly."

Francis's sallow face reddened.   " Much she
would !" he said angrily.   " I'll show you I be no
milksop to stand in fear of my father and mother.
Maybe now you think I'd not dare to — " he
paused, his eyes half-closed, while he tried to con-
coct some peculiarly wicked sounding project —
" to take some of my father's gunpowder and make
squibs ? " he concluded, with a triumphant look at
his companion.

" No, I don't think you dare," Miles answered
stolidly.

" Come, then, I'll show you," the other cried,
and headed for the companion way that descended
beneath the quarter-deck.

Four steps down, and, passing through a narrow
door, they entered into the stifle and stir of
the " great" or main cabin.   On every hand murmured the ceaseless confusion that always filled the
straitened space : underfoot, sometimes with fretful
wrangling, children were at play ; women were passing to and from their cabins, or dressing their meat
for the evening meal at the long table; upon the
benches several sick men, whose heavy voices were
audible through the shriller tones of those about
them, sat together in talk.   Over all, the brightness
from the narrow skylights fell wanly, so the corners
of the low apartment were dusky with thick shadows,
and the dim outline of the great timbers overhead,

and the slits of doors into the double tier of little cabins adjoining, could only just be made out.

Miles was glad of the half light, for he knew well that if his mother should chance to be there and see him with Francis, she would make a pretext of some task to call him to her. He caught sight of her now, as she stood by the table in speech with Constance Hopkins, and, almost treading on Francis's heels in his hurry, he slipped into the Billingtons' cabin.

It was the veriest closet of a room in which he found himself, black, save for a glint of sickly light that crept through an opening in the door, by which Miles contrived presently to discern the unmade bunk along the wall, the mattress, still spread out upon the floor, and the iron kettle and other vague household stuff that littered untidily the narrow space. Comparing it with his father's ordered cabin, he recalled his mother's indignant comment to Mistress Hopkins, that Ellen Billington was a poor, thriftless body, who would better be tidying her quarters than gossiping with her neighbors.

"Now you'll see what I dare, Master Miles," Francis broke in, as, with much panting, he dragged from beneath the bunk a small keg. "This is gunpowder, if you be not afraid of the sight of it."

"It does not take much courage to touch gunpowder," said Miles, bending forward from the bunk, where he had seated himself, and plunging his fist into the keg. "Let's see your squibs, Francis."

Young Billington stretched himself on his stomach and, grubbing once more beneath the bunk, drew out a fistful of rustling papers. "These are leaves I tore from a jest book of daddy's," he bragged. "No doubt you won't believe I durst."

Miles made no reply; after all, he scarcely cared to prolong his differences with a boy who had such a delightful plaything as a keg of powder. "Let me make a squib too, Francie," he begged, squatting down on the mattress beside his host.

For a space there was silence, while, with some hard breathing, the two, guided more by touch than by any sight they had in the dark cabin, labored industriously. Blacker and blacker it grew all round them, till they struck their hands together as they groped in the keg, when a ray of faint yellow light, that must fall from a lantern in the great cabin, stole through the door.

Now they could see how they were faring at their work, and Francis, who had laid his handfuls of powder on the papers and folded them quite dexterously, laughed in provoking fashion at Miles, who, new to this game, had spilt the powder and failed to make his papers stay folded. "It's all! very well," the boy retorted irritably, as one of his painfully

made squibs, bursting open, scattered powder between his knees, "but after you've made these
mighty squibs what else do you do?"

"Why, I'll light a bit of match," said Francis,
scrambling to his feet, "and then we'll touch 'em off."

Miles jumped up delightedly, and, reasoning that
a really satisfactory squib should be set off in darkness, took from the bunk a blanket which he fastened by two nails across the opening in the door.

Meantime Francis had struck his father's flint
and steel together, till at length he succeeded in
catching a spark upon the piece of "match" or
twisted tow steeped in saltpetre. Miles could see
the little red point shimmering in the dark and,
picking up the squibs, he moved warily toward it.
"Gi' me a squib," came Francis's voice, close at his
feet. More accustomed to the dimness now, Miles
could make out the boy's crouching figure and saw
him lean far forward with one arm outstretched to
touch off the powder.

Then he felt Francis crowd up against his knees,
and instinctively he drew back so his own body was
pressed against the wall. Out of the dark on the
floor, right at his feet, started a little flicker of
flame which, with a sudden whishing sound, leaped
up, a broad, bluish puff of fire, almost in his eyes;
then, before the exclamation had left his lips, died
sizzling away.

"That was brave, wasn't it?" spoke Francis, in a rather quavering voice. "You can touch off one now."

Miles eagerly seized the match and, setting it to a squib, flung the twisted paper a pace from him. The same whiz, burst, sizzle, but this time he lost the keen pleasure in a sudden hideous thought that, even as the squib left his hand, came over him. "Francis," he cried, before the flame died down, "is this safe, think you? Say the powder in the keg took fire?"

"Pshaw! You're afraid; I knew you'd be," replied Francis, his own courage quite restored.

Thereupon Miles lit a third squib to show his fearlessness, and then together they set off the remaining two. "That's the last, and I've no more paper," sighed Francis, and Miles echoed the sigh.

They were sitting now on the edge of the bunk; the cabin seemed very black to their eyes, still dazzled with the last flash, and the air was hot and heavy with the pungent odor of burnt powder. Miles sniffed it contentedly. "This is what 'twould be like in a great battle," he began. "Sometime I mean to be a soldier and have a musket. Did you ever shoot with a musket, Francis?"

"No, but I've shot off a fowling piece," answered the other. He clambered upon the bunk, groping audibly in the dark, and presently dropped down

"With his arm up to shut out the glare of the lanterns."

again beside his companion with something long and slender and heavy in his arms. "Look you, Miles, here's daddy's fowling piece now," he said exultantly. "What say if I shoot her off?"

"'Twould make a mighty big noise in so small a room," Miles answered longingly.

"Give me the match, then."

Later Miles remembered clearly how Francis had sprung to his feet at the word, but after that all was a confusion of dire noises, — a rending crash, then a sound of women screaming, of children crying, and of men running with clattering footsteps across the great cabin. Through it all he felt the weight of Francis Billington, who had pitched back against him, and he saw a little spurt of yellow fire that licked along the boards. Though he did not remember snatching a blanket from the bunk, one was in his hand, and he was down upon the floor, smothering the flames that would press out beyond the edges. A powder keg was somewhere near, he recollected, and he beat out one little jet of flame with his hand, that smarted fiercely.

It all must have taken a long, long time, but still the women screamed, and the heavy footsteps had only just reached the door. The latch rattled beneath a rough hand, the light streamed into the cabin, and Miles dropped back against the bunk, with his arm up to shut out the glare of the lanterns,

and the sight, too, of the angry faces in the doorway.
" Francis, Francis," he found himself saying, in a
poor whisper that he realized was not meant for
Francis Billington's ears, "we must 'a' killed some
one."

CHAPTER II

IN the great cabin two huge, smoky lanterns, that swayed from the beams overhead, cast blending white circles in the middle space, while the corners still remained dusky. Somewhere, there in the dark, a woman was crying hysterically, and others, calmer, but with startled, white faces, were standing beyond the group of men, who were gathered round the door of the Billingtons' cabin. Miles saw about him all the faces, terrified or menacing, but it was blurrily, as in a dream. He kept telling himself it was all a dream, an ugly dream, and presently he would awake to find he had never gone with Francis Billington, and very glad he would be to awake so.

But the grasp on his neck — it was big John Alden, the cooper from Southampton, who had dragged him out into the great cabin — was real, and so, he now found, were the faces of the men who confronted him. The Elder, William Brewster, with his gray hair, and grave Governor Carver, he noted among them, with a hopeless feeling that all the majesty of the company was come thither to judge him. Close by, he heard Francis Billington crying, with tearful sobs, not dry howls alone, but Miles dropped his shamed eyes to the floor of the cabin and did not look at his companion. He heard Goodman Billington's rough voice, thick with abuse and threats against his son, and then he heard the Elder cut him short: " Peace now, friend. Maybe the lad is hurt."

Just then, from within the Billingtons' cabin, whence a light smoke still drifted, spoke a quick, deep voice: " Come you in and lend a hand, Alden. There is work for two needs despatch. The floor here is over shoe thick with powder."

"Ay, Captain Standish," the young man answered promptly, and loosed his hold on Miles's collar.

There was a little movement in the group of men, and Master Stephen Hopkins, stepping closer to the cabin door, peered in and spoke solemnly : "A full keg of powder broke open ! 'Tis by the mercy of Heaven alone the ship was not blown into atoms."

" I did not have it in mind to blow up the ship," Miles faltered, raising his eyes. " I did but touch off a squib — because it would burn bravely." There the words choked in his throat, for, a little back from the other men, he caught sight of his father, and Goodman Rigdale's arms were folded, his heavy brows drawn close together, and his lips, beneath his beard, set in a way Miles knew of old. "I did not mean it," he repeated huskily, and, gazing at the floor again, began crushing a fold of his doublet in his hand.

About him there was questioning and answering, he knew, and he heard Francis whimper: "'Twas Miles. He touched off squibs, he did."

"Squibs do not make such a noise as that we heard," Governor Carver interrupted sternly.

"'Twas daddy's fowling piece. Miles Rigdale and I shot her off, and he —"

"Let Miles Rigdale rest," the Elder admonished. "Do you tell us of Francis Billington."

Bit by bit a fairly accurate story was drawn from the two boys, though by such slow and woful stages that before it was ended Captain Miles Standish and John Alden, with their hands all grimed with powder, came out from the cabin. Miles stole a fearful side-glance at the Low Country soldier, who, being trained in the brutal discipline of the camps, was likely to prove a harsher judge than the Elder or the Governor, but, to his relief, he saw the Captain halt beside Goodman Billington, to whom he growled out some pithy advice as to the expediency of keeping his powder covered up and out of reach of mischievous hands.

Miles took heart a little then, as much as he could take heart while he knew Goodman Rigdale was frowning in the background, and even ventured to look up when he heard Elder Brewster say, in a tone which a trace of amusement and much relief made almost kindly: " Well, well, 'twas no Guy Fawkes conspiracy, it seems, only the folly of two scatter-brained lads. Your Excellency scarce will set them in the bilboes ? "

" Nay, I leave it to their fathers to teach them not to meddle with such tools in future," Governor Carver answered gravely; and thereupon, with a surly mutter or so from other fathers in the company as to what the two culprits deserved to get, the men scattered to weightier affairs.

As the group thinned, Miles was left face to face with his father, who, making a curt sign for him to come after, led the way to the door of the cabin. Miles felt queer and empty at the pit of his stomach, and his fingers trembled as he began unhooking his doublet, but he followed along bravely. His eyes were still downcast, and, as he stepped, he counted the planks in the flooring and tried to think of nothing but their number.

Out in the darkness of the forward deck his father gave him such punishment as he looked for,— a beating with a rope's end, so hard that Miles had to set his teeth tight and clench his hands to keep from crying.   Once, in the midst, Goodman Rigdale stayed his arm, and in the instant's cessation Miles, standing in his shirt-sleeves, felt the wind from across the harbor strike cold on his hot flesh, that was quivering with the blows.   " That is for that you near destroyed the ship," his father spoke, gravely and without anger.   " Now I must flog you for that you disobeyed me, and had to do with one of those Billington imps."

The second whipping ended, Miles huddled on his doublet, stiffly and awkwardly, glad of the darkness that hid his face.   Goodman Rigdale was speaking again : " And ere you lie down to-night, my son, remember to give thanks unto God that by His mercy He has preserved you from being cast into His presence with the deaths of all that are within this ship upon your soul."

Miles did not quite follow the words, but, with a sense that he was the chiefest of sinners, and with a keen realization that his back and sides were smarting, he gulped out an unsteady " Yes, sir," and blindly fled away.

Aft of the foremast, as he stumbled uncertainly, he ran against a woman, and at once he knew it was his mother.   In an unformed way he was aware that she had been waiting to comfort him, and at each blow had suffered more than he.   Her voice was quavering now, though she tried hard to keep her everyday tone: "Come, come down to the cabin now. Father has shot a bird, and I've made a broth to our supper. Come, deary, it is turning chill here."

Shaking off the hand she laid on his arm, Miles broke away and ran to the mainmast, where the hatchway yawned. Slipping and swinging on the steep ladder, he descended headlong; he was not going to his father's cabin, nor did he know whither he was going, only that he wanted to be by himself. On the orlop deck he halted an instant before passing down into the hold; below, there would be many people, while here, for the moment, he was alone. He stood blinking at the dim lantern that hung by the ladder, till slowly it grew blurry to his eyes, and, raising his bent arm, he hid his face.

It seemed only a moment before he heard someone come tramping up from the hold, and felt a hand on his shoulder. He was turned round; he had to look up; and he saw, standing over him, Master Hopkins, very grim and stern, as was his wont. "I am glad to see these tears of repentance, Miles Rigdale," he spoke severely.

Miles wriggled out of his hold. "I am not repentant," he cried. "I wish I *had* blown *you* up. Now you can go bid my father flog me again." With that he dodged the hand Hopkins put out to detain him, and, jumping over some coils of rope, scrambled away out of reach.

Clambering over the chests and kegs that were placed upon the orlop, he paused only when he reached the next cleared space, by the forward hatchway that led to the gunroom. There it was all dark, a comfortable, thick blackness, and, to make it safer and lonelier, he crept under a table that was stored among other household stuff.

For a moment he sat panting, and listened to the lap, lap of the waves upon the side of the ship and to his own heavy breathing, but he heard no sound of any one's pursuing him. Doubtless Master Hopkins had gone away to tell every one that he was crying and repentant, Miles tormented himself; no matter, he was never coming out to be jeered at and preached to; he would stay under the table forever, and he would not shed another tear to please them.

So he sat, rigid and still, and each moment grew more keenly aware that he was sore from his beating, that his head ached, and his burnt hand throbbed, and his heart was big with a great burden of shame. Of a sudden, in the stillness and dark, he heard a sob. Then he found it was himself, lying with his head buried in his arms against the crosspiece that braced the legs of the table, and crying helplessly.

He had lost track of the minutes, but he had lain there a long time, he knew, for his arms were numb with the pressure of the crosspiece against them, and his throat ached with much sobbing, when he caught the sound of a footstep on the planking of the orlop. At the same moment, light beat against his smarting eyelids, and, opening his eyes, he raised his head to look.

The edges of the table under which he crouched were silhouetted blackly against the yellow lantern-glow, which crept midway into his shelter. Following with his eyes along the light, he could see beyond the table the joinings of the planks of the floor, a bit of the ladder that led to the main deck, and by the ladder, in shadow as the lantern was raised, the lower part of a man's body.

Miles stared breathlessly at the commonplace leather shoes and kersey breeches, — all the rest the table hid from his view, — while he strove to hold back a sob that was halfway up his throat. It would out, but he tried to turn it into a sneeze, which ended in a mournful, indefinable gurgle.

Instantly the light of the lantern, swinging round, swept almost into his face, and a deep voice commanded: " Come out hither."

Miles sat up, tense and braced. " Is it you, Captain Standish ? " he asked, in a small voice. Not that, to his knowledge, Miles Standish had ever hurt any one, but he was a brusque, peremptory man, reputed of a fiery temper; it was for this, probably, that Master Hopkins had sent him hither, as one fitted to deal out further punishment to such a criminal as Miles Rigdale.

"Come out, and you'll speedily find if 'tis I," Standish's voice rejoined grimly.

Miles rubbed his sleeve across his eyes, the rough frieze hurting them rarely, then dubiously crept from his shelter. The straight course was to crawl toward the light, but to go that way would land him squarely at the Captain's feet, — a last touch of ignominy that he could not endure. So he scrambled painfully over the crosspieces and round the table-legs, till he came out upon the open floor the width of the table-top from the enemy.

"It's naught but you, is it?" the Captain greeted him, and turned the lantern so the light fell full upon him.

The boy struggled hastily to his feet. "Ay, sir," he nodded, without speaking or looking up.

The other drew a step nearer. "You're one of the knaves who tried to blow up the *Mayflower*, are you not?" he questioned sternly. "Did you steal down here to fire the magazine and finish the work?"

"I—I did not go for to blow up the ship, sir," Miles pleaded, raising his eyes. With amazed relief, he saw that, for all his gruff tone, the Captain looked more amused than angry.

Standish must have taken closer note of him, too,

for he asked abruptly: "You're John Rigdale's lad, are you not?"

"I am Miles Rigdale."

The lantern was lowered suddenly. "My namesake, are you? Do you not think, sirrah, you bear too good a name to drag it into a powder-burning matter such as this?"

"I do not hold it a good name," Miles burst out. "I would they had called me plain Jack."

"Wherefore, pray you?"

"Miles is no name at all," the boy hesitated, between shyness and the desire to vent a long-standing resentment. "It makes me think of the stone in our village that said: 'Thirteen miles to London.'"

"Tut, tut, lad! Have you no Latin?"

Miles slipped one hand under the edge of the table against which he leaned, and picked at a splinter he found there, while he stammered: "N—no, sir. There was no school in our village, and, had there been, my father could not spare me from the farm. I must help him, for I'm mighty strong for my years," he added gravely. "And I never want to go sit in a school, either. I am glad there will be no schools here in the plantation, not till I'm a man and can do as I will. I hold that is the best part of all in planting a colony, except the lions and the savages."

"And what do you think to do with the lions and savages, Miles Rigdale?"

"Fight 'em, sir."

Captain Standish chuckled softly in his beard. "You'll fight 'em, eh? 'Tis a great pity, in truth, no one has told you what name you bear. You should know that Miles in the Latin tongue signifies 'a soldier.'"

Miles forgot that his cheeks were tear-stained and his eyes swollen, and looked up happily into the speaker's face. "I am right glad of that," he announced. "'Tis a good enough name, after all." He was sorely tempted to ask the Captain if he had been named that after he proved himself a soldier in the wars, or if they named him first and he grew to it afterward, but he concluded that would be over-bold.

Though, after all, he began to doubt if Captain Standish were such a terrible body. He looked pleasant enough now, as he stood in the lantern light, —a stocky, square-shouldered man of some six and thirty years, with yellow-brown hair and beard, and eyes so deep set under his brows Miles could not tell their color. The linen bands at his neck and wrists were small and plain, and along the sides of his doublet of dark maroon kersey the rubbing of armor had worn down the cloth. He was not so fine a gentleman, doubtless, as young Master Edward Winslow, but he looked the man of war, through and through, and, moreover, he neither scolded nor

preached at a small sinner; Miles began to be glad
in his heart that he bore the same name as the
Captain.

"So, after all, you're content to be named 'Soldier' Rigdale?" Standish suddenly read the expression of his face.

"'Tis a soldier that I mean to be," Miles confessed. "I like the smell of powder."

"So it seems," the Captain answered, in the dry-
est possible tone, and then, as Miles's cheeks began
to burn, went on hastily: "Which was it, you or
the Billington lad, put out the fire? We found
the blanket on the floor of the cabin."

"Mayhap 'twas I. I do not recall it clearly."

The Captain reached out his hand, and, taking
Miles by a fold of the doublet-sleeve, lifted his arm.
"No doubt 'twas you," he said; "you've blistered
your hand here."

"I know. It aches," Miles whispered, with a
sudden husky dropping of his voice.

"You'd better go to your mother straightway
and ask her to put oil on it; that will soon draw
out the fire."

"I can't," Miles gulped. "I can never go out
among the people again. When they all think I
tried to blow them up, — and when every one will
know I have been newly whipped. I shall stay
here forever." His voice died down as he spoke

the last: it did not sound manly, but uncommon silly.

"You'd get mighty hungry if you did," the soldier answered him coolly. "You're going to your mother now, my man. Run along with you. I've to go on down into the gunroom, but I'll light you up the ladder."

Miles gave a tremulous gasp of resignation, and scuffed slowly to the foot of the ladder, where he paused and smeared the back of his hand across his cheeks; then turned to his companion. "Captain Standish," he hesitated; then, as it was the only possible way of learning what he wished to know before he showed himself among the company, he blurted out desperately, "Will you tell me, is my face clean?"

Captain Standish looked down at him with a funny expression in his eyes. "I think 'twill serve in a half light, if you slip directly into your father's cabin."

"Thank you, sir," Miles answered; then added hastily, "You see, there was something flew into my eye, and one that did not know might think —I had been crying."

CHAPTER III

THIEVISH HARBOR

ONE sharp December afternoon, a week and a day after the Pilgrim leaders went forth the third time to seek a place for settlement, Love Brewster and his little brother Wrestling climbed down to the cabins beneath the main deck to visit their playmate, Dolly Rigdale. The cubby where Dolly and Miles and their father and mother had lived during the two months of the voyage over the sea and the five weeks of exploration that followed, was a dim box of a place, but the little boys liked to visit it, not only to talk with Dolly, who was nearer their age than most of the children in the company, but to see Trug and Solomon.

Trug was the big, grizzled mastiff, who had guarded the house and the cattle faithfully for so many years that even stern John Rigdale had not the heart to leave him to strangers; and Solomon, with the wise eyes of royal yellow, was the fat house-cat, whom Dolly had insisted on bringing with her to the new home.

"If it had been my pet, 'twould 'a' had to bide in England," Miles had told himself, in one bitter, jealous moment, of which he was justly ashamed. For, without question, Goodman Rigdale cared equally for his two children, only he held Miles, being a stubborn chip of manhood, needed frequent beatings, such as the Scriptures enjoined on good fathers to give their sons, whereas Dolly was just a little wench, with gray eyes like her mother, so she received very gentle whippings and triumphantly lugged Solomon on shipboard.

The sleek, striped creature lay beside her now, for Dolly, still ailing with her cough, was resting on the bunk beneath the blankets. Wrestling Brewster, a big-eyed, silent child, sat by her, and, sorry to tell, joined forces with the little girl in rumpling poor Solomon's fur. "You are the best pussy," Dolly purred meantime, and, either because of her flattery or because the warm blankets were comfortable, the cat made no movement to leave her.

Ordinarily Miles sniffed at the conversation of eight-year-olds, such as his sister, but this afternoon he gladly lingered in the cabin, for the accomplishments of the Brewster lads were amazing enough to lift them to the rank of companions. Both could jabber Dutch quite as fast as Miles could speak English, and Love, the talkative one, could tell wonderful stories of the queer Low Country city

of Leyden, where all his short life had been spent.
It was of Leyden he spoke now, sitting beside
Miles on the turned-up mattress, where at night
Goodman Rigdale and his son slept, and Miles,
with a question here and there to draw out what he
sought, listened again to the story of the Pilgrims.

Love had good reason to know it well, for his
father, Elder Brewster, had been from the first one
of the leaders of the little company. He had given
all his substance to help the cause of that faith
which the bishops of the great Established Church
of England held it right to crush out; he had suffered imprisonment for the sake of that faith; and
finally, that he and his friends might worship God
as they thought best, had gone into exile in Hol-
land.

There for twelve years the Pilgrim church held
its own, though its members, for all their efforts
to support themselves in that strange country, fared
hardly and poorly. Good Deacon Fuller, the phy-
sician, had been glad to earn his living as a say or
serge maker; Master William Bradford had been
a maker of fustian; and the Elder had maintained
his family and aided his poorer companions by
teaching English to Danish and German gentlemen,
and later by printing English books.

Love told also of Master Carver, the recently
elected governor of the company, who had given

his whole fortune to the Pilgrim cause; and he spoke of gallant Master Edward Winslow, who, travelling in the Low Countries with his newly married wife, had come to know and to respect the Pilgrim folk and finally to cast in his lot with theirs. And, best of all, Love could tell of Captain Standish.

There the boy turned to what Miles had been waiting to hear, and be sure that now he eagerly drank in each word: how the Captain came of a great family in Lancashire, where he had a vast estate which his kinsfolk had taken from him, — so Love had once heard him say to the Elder; how he had fought bravely against the wicked Spaniards, as far back as the time of Queen Bess, when Miles Standish was a very young man indeed; and how, of a sudden, he had come with his young wife and joined himself to the Pilgrims, why, none could say, for he was "not of our faith," Love gravely quoted the older people.

That last did not greatly displease Miles, perhaps because his own father was rather a Puritan than an ardent Separatist, as those were called who, like the Pilgrims of Leyden, broke off all communion with the Established Church. Goodman John Rigdale grumbled about the bishops and the vestments of the clergymen and other matters which Miles neither heeded nor comprehended, but, for all his grumbling, as often as the law insisted, he

D

and his household went to church.   One of the first
and liveliest recollections of childhood which Miles
kept, was of how the red light from the painted
windows that his father hated used to shift along
the dark oak of the old pews.

Lately, though, John Rigdale had spoken out
too openly against the service book, and there had
been a citation before the ecclesiastical court.   Miles
scarcely understood the matter, but he knew that
Dun-face, the pet heifer, had been sold to pay a
fine, and that their landlord, swearing that he was
too good a Church of England man to suffer a
pestilent Separatist hold a farm of him, had refused
to renew the lease, bought long ago by Miles's
grandfather, which now ran out.

Then had come Master Stephen Hopkins, the
London tanner, whose first wife had been a distant
cousin of John Rigdale's, and he had talked of the
new country over seas, where a man might have
land and a farm of his own for the asking and worship to please his conscience, not the king's bishops.
Master Hopkins had already made up his mind to
embark with the people from Leyden ; he had met
their agent, Master Cushman, and he was acquainted
with some of the London merchants who had
formed a partnership with the Leyden people, the
Londoners to furnish money to pay the expenses
of the long voyage, the Separatists to give them-

selves and their families to defend and till the plantation thus gained.

In the end, Master Hopkins's statements were so weighty that Goodman Rigdale followed his example. The stout farm horse and the cows and the pigs were all led away to market, and Dolly cried over each one; and Goodwife Rigdale, too, wept a little when most of the bits of furniture were sold. But Miles thought it all very merry and stirring,— the breaking up of the home he had known, the journey to Southampton, all amidst new sights and sounds, and the ship, and the long voyage over the sea, till the *Mayflower* dropped anchor off Cape Cod.

He was more than a bit weary of the voyage and the ship now, however, as he sat on the turned-up mattress in his father's stuffy little cabin. The dead air was cold without being bracing, and Miles broke short Love's discourse on the journey of the Leyden Pilgrims into England, by springing up and stamping his chilled feet.

"It *is* a shrewd cold day," said his companion. "See!" He puffed at the air, and his breath made a little white cloud. "Maybe we'd best go up on deck and run."

At that word the two older boys turned to the door, but Wrestling shook his head and, pressing closer to Dolly, whispered: "Before I go, I want that you show me the Indian basket."

Miles overheard, and delayed to draw from beneath the bunk the deal box in which the treasure was kept. Wrestling was so young that he seemed hardly more than a baby, and as a baby Miles had a kindly, protecting feeling for him ; when he rose with the box he opened it so the little boy might have the first sight. Within lay a tiny basket all of silk grass, pictured on which in black and white were birds and flowers of a curious pattern.

" Did your father truly bring it from the Indians ? " Love asked.

" He brought it home to me," Dolly explained proudly. " It was in an Indian house, and my father found it when he went ashore with Captain Standish. And so he brought it to me."

Wrestling touched the fragile thing gingerly. " I wish our father fought the Indians once," he murmured.

" It is better to be an Elder," Love rebuked him sternly ; then added, lest Dolly's feelings be hurt, " though, to be sure, there can be but one Elder in a company. The rest must be fighting men, must they not, Miles ? "

But Miles gave no heed ; for just then the sound of soft footsteps made him glance to the open door, at which the light drifted in, and there, standing on the threshold, he saw his mother.

Years afterward, when he looked back, Miles

realized Goodwife Rigdale had been a young woman then, not above thirty, but in those days it seemed to him she must be old, because she was his mother; he even wondered that she had not hair streaked with gray, like Mistress Brewster. Mothers were always old, he generalized rashly, just as they were always gentle-spoken and full of kindness; only that last judgment he revoked, after he came aboard the *Mayflower* and heard Goodwife Billington, a true London virago, rail at her sons and saw her cuff them.

But his own mother was not to be belittled by naming her with Ellen Billington; she was everything that was good and to be loved, even if she did not wear such a brave gown as Mistress Winslow, nor have such pink cheeks as Mistress Standish. Miles drew away from the bunk, against which he had been leaning, to make room for her to sit, though he did it awkwardly, because Love and Wrestling were looking.

"I'll bide a bit now with my little maid," she said, as she drew the blankets more closely about Dolly. "You'll want to be running up on deck now, I can guess, deary, and Love and Wrestling too, if Mistress Brewster will suffer it."

"Mother, is the shallop in sight?" Miles cried eagerly. For, since the exploring party sailed forth a week before, there had come so great a storm that

hearts aboard the *Mayflower* were not a little anxious
for their welfare.

"'They've made out a sail to the southward, I
heard the talk run. Go you and learn further,
Miles. Your father will be on deck too."

Miles reddened a little; why would she speak as
if he were a young boy, to need his father? "Come,
lads," he said, in a very old tone, to hide his morti-
fication, and led the way from the cabin. As he
passed out at the door, he heard a sorrowful wail
from Dolly: "O me! Mammy, can I not run
about with them soon?"

But Miles forgot Dolly's woes and all, when he
clambered into the bracing air of the deck, whither
the most of the hale ones of the company had, like
himself, bustled to watch the approaching shallop.
Shreds of dappled cloud half obscured the east, but
low in the west the sun was cold and yellow, and its
light flecked the water and made the sail of the distant craft gleam like gold.

Miles stared till for very dazzle he could see no
longer, then turned his gaze inboard, where it rested
on the slender figure of a woman, who leaned against
the mainmast. When the light got out of his eyes,
he perceived it was Mistress Rose Standish, who,
while he was still gazing on her, came to the bulwark beside him, but, without seeming to see him,
stood looking toward the shallop.

Once and again Miles glanced up at her, thinking how bonny she was with the flush on her cheeks and her brown hair straying from beneath her hood across her forehead; and then he grew suddenly hot, for she chanced to look down, and their eyes met. He drew away bashfully and stared again at the shallop; the sun had now dropped lower, so the waves around it were sombre, but within the boat sparkled a gleam of light on metal armor. Miles almost thought to be able to distinguish the forms of the men, and presently their faces. "Yon is the Captain," he broke out, half aloud.

"Do you see him, too?" Mistress Standish spoke, as if he had addressed her.

"That's he, by the mast, with the steel corselet."

She looked down again, and the boy noted her eyes were moist, though she smiled as she said: "You seem to know the Captain very well, sir."

"I'd know him anywhere," Miles answered earnestly. "You understand, he was right kind to me."

Then he broke off speech, for the shallop was now fairly alongside, and the men in her were calling to those on shipboard greetings and questions and answers. Mistress Standish moved quickly toward the gangway, and Miles saw her meet the Captain, when he clambered up the ladder.

Next after him came Master William Bradford, and suddenly it struck with a shock on Miles's remembrance that Mistress Bradford was dead, drowned alongside the *Mayflower* on the very day after the shallop sailed, and her body carried away among the waves. Master Bradford, for all the weariness in his movements, looked cheerful and hopeful as he gained the deck, and his eyes went glancing over the women gathered there with such a certainty of meeting one that, child though he was, Miles realized something of the pity of it.

But after Elder Brewster had led Master Bradford away, the horror and the pity slipped quickly from Miles. Drawing over closer to the gangway ladder, he stood watching the rest of the shallop's company scramble to the deck, and, listening to every scrap of speech, was soon eager as any of the other boys in questioning the sailors and Hopkins's man, Dotey.

The minutes ran on till dim twilight had darkened upon the water, when at last, bursting with news, Miles clambered down again to Goodwife Rigdale in the cabin. "They've found a place for us to settle, mother," he announced, barely within the door.

Goodwife Rigdale hushed him with a finger on her lips; Dolly was asleep, so he must speak softly.

Miles curled himself up on the floor at his mother's feet, with his elbow on her knee, and whispered: "'Tis at a place called Thievish Harbor —"

"Nay, that's an ill name," commented the Goodwife.

"'Tis because a savage stole a harpoon from a ship's boat that once put in there to truck, so says Robert Coppin, the pilot. It lies across a great bay here, and there are fair green islands and many brooks and cleared land and tall trees. We are going thither, all of us, mother. The ship is to sail so soon as the wind favors. And if they like of it on further look, we'll go ashore and stay. I want to go ashore again," he ended wistfully; "the week's out that father said I must stay on the ship. Won't you beg him take me ashore first thing when we come thither, mother?"

The flickering light that reached them from the lantern hung outside the cabin door was blotted out then, as Goodman Rigdale himself came in. Miles dared ask no favors of him directly, however, but, scrambling to his feet, stood silent and unobtrusive, though he listened eagerly to all his father had to say of Thievish Harbor, which he called Plymouth. "So it is named on the maps that were drawn by Captain Smith," he said, to which Goodwife Rigdale answered quickly: "I am glad for the name. Do you not have in mind, John, how kindly the people at our English Plymouth dealt by us when we had to put in at their harbor?"

But this new Plymouth in America bore little resemblance to Plymouth in Devonshire, as Miles found, to his surprise, when he had his first sight of the place where the company was to settle. It was on the afternoon of the day succeeding the return of the shallop that, the wind at last favoring, the *Mayflower* steered her course for the bay of Plymouth. The sunshine was strong and clear, and the air mild, so Goodwife Rigdale suffered Dolly come up on deck, where, well wrapped in a cloak, she stood between her mother and Miles.

Others in plenty, all the passengers who could walk about, were watching for a glimpse of the new home, but Miles, in his eagerness, scarcely heeded his companions. He strained his eyes to see the headlands, brave with evergreen, loom higher and higher, and ran to question his friend, Giles Hopkins, who had been talking with the sailors, as to what they were. Giles explained that the one on the left was not the mainland, but a well-wooded point, and on the right yonder the farther of the two islands, with the trees, was where the exploring party had spent their Sabbath.

By the time Miles returned to his mother with the news, they were running in between the point and the islands, and presently, well within the har-

bor, they dropped anchor in a safe mooring ground.
All about them were headlands and islands; far to
the right, across the bay, rose a great hill; and
just over opposite where the ship lay a broad
space of open land, with high hills behind, could
be made out.

"Yonder's where we'll settle," Miles assured his
mother.

"I see no houses," protested Dolly. "I thought
there would be cottages, maybe. Must we lie in
the woods, mammy?"

"Nonsense! We'll build houses," scoffed Miles;
he would have blushed to own that, half uncon-
sciously, he, too, had cherished the fancy of seeing
on the New England shore straggling streets and
tiny cottages, as in old Plymouth.

"You'll build houses, Miles?" teased his sister.

"Father and I and all the men," the boy bragged.
"Build them of great logs. Then in the spring will
come a ship with horses and cows and sheep, and
we'll have farms, just as we had at home."

"With a hedge round the dooryard?" Dolly
questioned.

"Yes, and meadow-land and ploughed fields.
We'll have all in order when the frost leaves the
ground," Miles answered confidently.

Then he looked up at his mother, and was
astonished to see that for once her eyes were not

on her children, but on the empty shore over opposite. Her face was wistful, and it came on Miles
that perhaps she was not as interested in the farm
concerns as he, who was a man, so he said quickly:
"And you can have a garden here, mother, full
of rosemary and daffadowndillies, just as at home.
Maybe you'll not have to labor so hard here," he
added more vaguely, not quite understanding her
silence.

She smiled a little then. "That's a good lad,
Miles," she said, putting her arm about his shoulders; then she bade him go to his mates if he would,
and she led Dolly back to the cabin.

Miles stood alone, gazing at the home-shore and
wondering where his father's farm would lie. Still
thinking on it, he was turning toward the hatchway,
when he almost ran into Goodman Rigdale. "O
father," Miles broke out before he thought, "may
I not go with you when we begin our farm? I'll
conduct me well and be obedient."

He stopped, surprised at his own forwardness,
and he was more surprised when his father, looking
down at him gravely, said without chiding: "Our
farm? Ay, Miles, so soon as there is work to do
on shore you shall come with me and bear a hand."

CHAPTER IV

HEWERS OF WOOD AND DRAWERS OF WATER

"TO-MORROW I am going ashore." Thus Miles Rigdale proclaimed, from his perch on the bunk in his father's cabin, to all who might choose to hear.

"'Tis the forty and third time you've said that in the last sennight," Ned Lister answered dryly. He was lounging in the cabin door, shirt-sleeved and shivering, while Goodwife Rigdale repaired his doublet; Mistress Hopkins, to whom the task ordinarily fell, lay ill, and her stepdaughter, Constance, was so busied that, to relieve her, Alice Rigdale had taken the young man and his mending off her hands.

"Why do you not put on your cloak, if you be cold, Ned Lister?" Dolly spoke up.

"Because 'tis too much labor to fetch it, Puss," Ned answered, whereat Miles laughed, and the Goodwife's brows puckered; another might have said it was because the sewing gave her trouble, but Miles, who felt uncomfortably that his mother disapproved of Ned as a scatter-brained, reckless fellow, guessed that she had not liked that last speech.

He was sure of his guess when she hastened to change the subject: " Does it still rain upon deck, Edward ? "

" Rain and naught else ; the third day of it now, yet by the look it might pour on for a week."

" And my daddy's yonder in the wet on shore," murmured Dolly, pressing close against her mother's knee, and the Goodwife sewed more slowly, with her eyes downcast.

But Miles burst into lamentation : " I think they might 'a' taken me ashore. Since we came into Plymouth Harbor they've explored and explored, and never suffered me to come, but they took Giles Hopkins with them.   And now the randevous is built on shore, and some of the men are staying there, it has rained and rained so I cannot go to them.   But I'm going to-morrow, the very next time the shallop sails."

" To be sure you shall," Lister answered, as he scrambled into his mended doublet. " I'll take you along with me."

Then he swaggered away jauntily, as if he had promised ample service in return for his mending, and Goodwife Rigdale, with a bit of a sigh, said softly to Miles : " 'Tis well meant of Edward Lister to see you safe ashore, but when you are there, re-member, you are to stay with your father, not go roving with him."

Miles's satisfaction at Ned's offer was a bit tempered by her words, but he lost the remembrance of them next morning, when he saw the sun was rising clear and the shallop would go shoreward. At once he clattered down to the cabin to get his cap and mittens, and Trug, who must go with him; then ran up on deck again, where, in the chill sunlight, the men were laboring briskly to load the shallop. Miles watched them while they put in the felling-axes and handsaws and hammers, all the tools that were to build the new town of Plymouth, and the biscuit and salt beef and pease that were to form the workers' rations.

About the time the labor was ended, Ned sauntered up to the gangway, and, seeing Miles, very speedily helped him clamber down the ladder, and made Trug leap after him. Master Isaac Allerton, who was settled comfortably in the stern, grumbled at burdening the shallop with children and curs, so Miles put his arms about Trug, and, cuddling down in the bottom of the boat, made himself as still and small as possible lest, after all, the company, thinking better of it, bid him scramble up the gangway ladder again.

But the time for that was past, for the shallop, with her sail hanging sluggish, had crept surely out from the lee of the *Mayflower*, and now, catching the light breeze, actually stood in to the shore. Miles forgot the discomfort of his seat among the tools while he gazed toward the approaching coast line, where was to be his home. Behind him the sun was up, and the hills that rose away inland from the harbor were bright in the cold, yellow radiance, and the water and the sky that spread about him were both very blue. He glanced back over his shoulder at the dreary old *Mayflower*, and was surprised to find that, as the sun struck athwart her patched sails, even she was beautiful.

Then the movement of those about him, and the sound of waves crunching on the shingle, made him look forward again. Under the shelter of a high bluff, where a great boulder ran out into the water, he saw those standing who had kept the randevous, and the randevous itself, a rude hut of boughs. In his eagerness Miles jumped up, and Trug, springing up too, began to bark, but no one took note or scolded, for the men were busied in running the shallop in alongside the rock, and some, leaping over the gunwale, were already splashing through the shallow water to the beach.

Ned and Giles Hopkins made the shore thus, so Miles must do the like, and came to land all drenched and dripping. But it was land, — good, stable, brown earth, not the hateful, rolling ship, — he had beneath his feet, and, in the delight of the long unused sensation, he forgot he was wet and chilled, forgot his father awaited him, and there was work to do. He knew only that far and near the shore stretched widely, where a boy could run, so, for choice, he set his face to the bluff that towered above the landing.

Up and up, through the keen, dry bushes, that whipped his hands and face so he laughed in the mere delight of struggling with them, he fought his way till he came breathless to the bare summit. All about him dazzled the blue of the harbor and of the unclouded sky, and yonder on his right, through its fringe of bushes, shone the blue of what seemed a cove. Down the hill rushed Miles, with Trug leaping and barking at his heels, and paused only on the shore of a great brook, that, flowing out between steep bluffs, widened into the sea.

Another was before him there, his distant kinsman, Giles Hopkins, who, for all he was a sober lad of six-teen, was a good comrade to the younger boy. He now bade Miles come upstream to the spring the men had found on their last exploration, and Miles very readily followed him through the scrubby under-growth, where the cove narrowed on the left hand, and on the right a high bluff kept pace with the boys. "It's on that bluff they mean to set the houses," Giles explained, over his shoulder.

"Then we'll have this big stream in our door-yards," cried Miles. "Won't that be brave? I

E

shall build me a raft, and sail to those wooded hills on the other side whenever I choose. Though, maybe, Indians dwell there," he added, with a dubious glance at Giles; he did not wish to seem afraid, but, though he intended to be a soldier, he did not purpose to fight without a musket and a long sword, and he wondered how much farther from the shore his leader would venture.

But speedily his wonder had an end, for, breaking through a thicket of leafless alders, Giles halted at a little cavity within the sand of the riverbank, where the spring of sweet water bubbled up. Down lay Miles on the turf, and, using his hand for a cup, swallowed his first draught of New England water. "'Tis better than the brackish stuff we have on shipboard," he said, as he wiped his wet hands on his wet doublet.

"The savages must have known the spot," answered the experienced Giles. "We found this path worn down hither from the bluff, and see, here is a line of stepping-stones across the brook."

Miles glanced about him, half nervously, lest along the path or across the stones he see one of their former savage passengers approaching. He was at heart relieved when, as Giles led the way up the bluff, he heard in the distance the sound of an axe crashing on a tree trunk. Giles did not turn toward the sound, however, but went plodding on uphill, for above the bluff a second summit reared itself steeply. Miles panted in his trail, endlessly upward, it seemed, till at last he stood exhausted on a lofty hilltop, whence, far as the sea spread out before him, he beheld the wooded uplands roll away to westward.

Giles was explaining wisely what a proper place this hill was for a fort, and how Captain Standish had advised the company mount upon it guns, which should command to southward the spring, and toward the harbor the landing place and the houses, which were to be built along the river bluff, when Master Hopkins and John Rigdale, tramping thither, ended their sons' holiday.

"Is this the way you would work, Miles?" Goodman Rigdale asked sternly, and, fearing lest the next word sentence him to return at once to the *Mayflower*, Miles ran eagerly about the task they set him.

All day he tugged chips and branches for the fire at the randevous, but it was work on land, in the free air, where a boy could shout as much as he wished, so he never realized he was weary till night came. He had to pack off to the ship with the other boys and near half the men, but he had no chance to grumble at this, as did some of his mates, for, once aboard the shallop, he leaned against Ned Lister and fell half asleep. Only when the shallop scraped the ship's side did he awake to stagger up the gangway ladder and stumble away to tell Dolly and his mother of the wonders he had seen ashore.

Next day, being Sunday, no work was done, and the next day, being Christmas, Miles, who remembered what a time of merrymaking that was at home, thought he must idle again. But here on Christmas, from sunrise to sunset, it was all stern work. "We stain this virgin soil with no Popish holydays," Master Hopkins said grimly, and, though the rest did not exult in words, they labored with double fervor to show they did no honor to the day.

Miles had his part to do on shore that Christmas and in the days that followed, though it was a different part from that he had hoped to have. When he talked to his mother and Dolly of building cottages, he had fancied that perhaps he would be allowed to sit high up on a ridgepole and drive nails. He knew he would enjoy doing that, but in practice he was set less pleasant tasks: he ran errands, not only for his father, but for every man who chose to send him; he fetched water up the steep bluff from the spring to the workers; and he carried firewood from where the choppers labored upon the bluff to where the first house was building.

On occasion he even tended the fire and saw that the porridge did not burn, and more than once was sent to carry a portion of the food to the men who, unable to rise and get their rations, lay ill in the half-built log cabins. The numbers of these sick ever multiplied, for the close quarters and bad food aboard the *Mayflower* had caused a fever to break out among her passengers, and the exposure to which the men and boys often recklessly subjected themselves increased the roll of the ailing, and, at last, of the dying.

Miles was sorry, of course, for the men and women who sickened and died, but it was a sorrow that did not go deep enough to prevent his enjoying the open-air life, and the moments of play that he snatched from his work. For death had not come near any that he loved; Dolly and Jack Cooke had been ill, but they were getting better, and none of his other near acquaintances had been touched. To be sure, he himself went sneezing with a great cold, but it meant nothing, any more than did his father's cough; he did not worry for it the half as much as he fretted at the dull routine labors to which he was set.

One day in January he had a hand in more exciting work, for Ned Lister and Giles Hopkins, who were going to cut swamp grass for thatch, invited him to come with them, and Ned even let him carry his sharp sickle. Ned himself turned all his effort to bearing a fowling piece, with the use of which, after the grass was cut, he had been bribed to the afternoon's labor, for he was afflicted with a hard cough that racked him most piteously when he was set to any work but hunting.

So soon as they reached the piece of marshy ground in the deep hollow behind the first range of hills, where grew the grass they sought, one of those coughing fits laid hold on Ned. He really wasn't fit to work, he said, but, when Miles volunteered to do the task for him, he found energy to direct the boy's clumsy attempts with the sickle.

Two bundles of grass the workers were expected to bring home, and Giles cut his, slowly and soberly, while Ned dallied with Miles, till he saw his companion had nearly gathered his share. Then Lister snatched the sickle from Miles, and, finishing the work in a surprisingly short time for a sick man, caught up his piece with the exclamation, " *Now* we'll go fowling."

Leaving the sickles and the bundles of grass where they lay, the three picked a path round the verge of the marsh and climbed westward over the hills. Last of all Miles trotted along bravely, very proud that he was one of the company, and full of interest at passing so far inland. But on the top of the second long hill, Giles suddenly cried out: " Look yonder. Is not that smoke ? "

Against the dull sky to the west Miles saw a

little fine curl of gray, and the question was on his tongue's end, when Ned Lister anticipated it: "No, it can be none of our people so far from the shore. Savages, maybe. Say we go down and see."

Shouldering his fowling piece, he set out jauntily, and the two boys came stoutly after. They scrambled down a rough hillslope and through another level piece, all open and stubbly, westward still, where the smoke rose. "This land has been cleared; 'tis true Indian ground here," Ned spoke suddenly, and halted.

Miles stopped short five paces behind his comrades. He looked to the hills ahead, where the bare branches of oak trees stood out clearly against the afternoon sky. It was a lowering sky, and night was coming. He glanced behind him, and saw only the barren wall of hills, no sign of the harbor or of the *Mayflower*. Ned and Giles were looking at each other with a something so dubious in their faces that Miles felt a griping sensation in his throat. He wondered if he could find his way back as he had come, and, doubting it, drew close to Ned, who had the fowling piece.

Ned was fiddling with the lock of the piece and he spoke rather sheepishly: "I'm not afraid. But I'm not going to run into Heaven knows what with two younkers like you on my shoulders."

"Say we march home, then?" Giles suggested,

and straightway, facing round, they retraced their steps pretty smartly.

Miles was still in the rear, and, as he went, he studied the long legs of his companions and thought how much more swiftly they could run for it, if anything came up behind them. Thinking so, he forgot to look to his feet, and, as they descended a gully, fell headlong with a great clattering of stones. "Wait for me!" he cried, in a sharp, high voice that did not sound natural.

Ned glanced back, with his face tenser than its wont. "Here, take the fowling piece, Giles," he said curtly; then, returning to Miles, he lifted him to his feet, and, keeping one hand beneath his arm, helped him to hurry along.

Thus they scurried down the hillside to the swamp, and, catching up their sickles and the thatch, pressed on toward the settlement. Not till they were panting up the landward side of the great hill and caught the faint sound of hammers in the street of the half-built town, did Ned suffer the speed to slacken. "You'll make a gallant soldier one day, Miley," he said then, and began laughing. "Though I take it no one of us was afraid; eh, boys?"

They all agreed they were not in the least frightened, and some such version Ned must have reported to Captain Standish, when he told how they had seen

Indian fires. For next day Miles found himself quite a hero in the sight of the other lads, because he had gone far into the woods and walked boldly right into an encampment of the savages. But Goodman Rigdale chided his son sternly for such a harebrained prank, and after that made the boy stay within his sight while he was on shore.

Miles did not greatly mind, for his father and Francis Cooke, the father of his playmate Jack, were now engaged in a delightful work in which he liked to help. Lately the whole company of the *Mayflower* had been divided into nineteen families, and these two men, who had been placed in one household, were building together a cottage, high up on the hillside. His father's house, Miles insisted upon calling it, though Goodman Rigdale was at pains to explain to him that the cottage belonged not to any one man, but to the whole company ; the Pilgrims at Plymouth and the merchants at London, who had advanced the money for the voyage, were to hold everything in common till seven years were up and then divide all equally, and till then no man could call a house his own.

Still, Miles knew that by and by his mother and Dolly and Jack Cooke would come ashore, as other families were coming, and they would live together in that house, so it seemed the same as if it belonged to his father. He looked forward to the time when they would all be under one roof, and he would be suffered to sleep ashore, for, though his father passed his nights at the Common House, there was no room for Miles, who at twilight had to journey off to the ship. But that arrangement drew speedily to an end, for the walls of the house, built of squared logs, soon rose to a good height; the chimney of sticks and clay was finished; and at last it was but a question of thatching the roof.

Of a dull afternoon in mid-January Goodman Rigdale set out to cut swamp grass for the thatch, and took with him Miles, who had not been so far afield since his exploit with Ned Lister. They went steadily up the slope on the shoulder of the great hill, and there Miles, who had run a little ahead with Trug, paused to look back proudly at the stanch, new cottage below. "Those are brave big logs in our house, are they not, sir?" he broke out. "'Twill last us a many years."

"That, or whatever house shall fall to us at the division, will last you all your lifetime," Goodman Rigdale answered shortly. "And you will lease it of no man. You'll hold a house and a farm of your own here one day, Miles."

They tramped on a time in silence, and Miles was making himself sport by crushing in the scum of ice on the pools along their path, when his father spoke suddenly: "You're in a fair way to lead an

easier life than your father or your grandfather before you, Miles.   And if you be the happier, you
should be so much the better man."

" Ay, sir," Miles answered vaguely, and tipped
back his head to watch a great bird that went flapping across the sky ; he wished his father had
brought along a fowling piece.

When they came to the swamp, Goodman Rigdale cut down the grass swiftly, and Miles bundled
it, though he found it hard to keep pace with his
father.   Goodman Rigdale, being in haste, must at
the last do the work himself, and, while he bundled
the grass, Miles, remembering the stolen pleasures
of his last thatching trip, picked up the sickle and
tried a slash or two on his own account.   He man-
aged to cut his hand, and, though he scarcely felt
the pain, because the hand was cold, he stared in
some fright when he saw the blood come streaking
out.

Goodman Rigdale gave him a rag to tie up the
hurt hand, and also gave him some good advice on the
need of care with edged tools, which Miles did not
think quite called for just then.   He tried, however,
not to show any sign of pain, because that always
displeased his father ; and, as he thought he had
borne himself quite bravely, he was much hurt, when
Goodman Rigdale, on coming down into the settlement, said : " Get you to the shallop now, Miles,

and bide on board the *Mayflower* till I send for you. You'll be of no service with your hand cut. Mayhap you'll be better off with your mother, too. After all, you are but a young lad."

" As you bid, sir," Miles said, respectfully, but very stiffly, and walked away down the path to the landing.

Once he stopped to kick a stone out of his way, and once, before he rounded the base of the bluff, something made him face about and look back to the Common House. His father was standing by the door, watching him, and Miles, feeling much rebuked, walked on rapidly. But the image of his father remained in his mind very clear.

CHAPTER V

BECAUSE Miles's hand was hurt, Goodwife Rigdale made much of him, till he fairly resented it, for he had grown into the age where he was sheepish and awkward under open petting. He soon slipped away from his mother and the sympathetic Dolly, and went to spend his time with Jack Cooke, who, during the day, while his father worked on shore, was glad of company. The boys had now almost room enough on shipboard to play satisfactorily, for many of the passengers had gone ashore; but it must be quiet playing, for, of those who still remained in their cabins not a few were ill.

Goodwife Rigdale was busied to and fro in caring for the sick ones, and, at her bidding, Miles ran many an errand, to fetch water from the casks on deck or heat a pot of broth in the ship's galley. But their joint labor soon ended, for, a few days after the boy's return to the ship, came a message from Goodman Rigdale: he was just touched with the fever, he said, though nothing serious, but a many lay sick ashore, and the Goodwife could aid them as well as himself; Mistress Brewster, who, with her family, had gone to the settlement, had offered to shelter her, and he prayed her come.

Next morning Goodwife Rigdale bundled her cloak about her, and set out in the shallop. Miles, standing by the bulwark, watched her go, but only for a time; it had snowed the night before, so the railings were white and smooth to the touch, and he found it of more absorbing interest to poke off strips of the frozen snow, and send them splashing into the cold-looking water beneath the ship's side. By the time he looked again to the shallop, it was so near shore he could no longer make out his m' ther's figure, and his feet were chilled too, so he went back to Dolly in the cabin.

At first he found it manly and grown up to be left in charge, for so he esteemed his position. The cut in his hand was healing well, and he felt he would have been working ashore, if it were not that some one must mind his father's quarters on ship-board and care for Dolly and Solomon. He ordered his sister about in a paternal manner; he rebuked her severely if she so much as showed her small, snub nose on the frosty deck without wrapping herself up well; and he even insisted on her going to bed punctually at sundown, while he, in the glory of manhood, waited in the great cabin to hear what news those who came from the shore would bring.

But Dolly took her turn when it came to their daily meals, for she had certain deft, housewifely ways, which Miles could not hope to imitate, and he was ashamed even of trying to better himself, after he heard the little woman speak like her mother of " men and boys that set a body's kitchen in a mash." Miles might tug out the pot of broth, —'twas all he was fit for; Goodwife Dolly would herself do the stirring and tasting; and though, among so many cooks, the broth sometimes burned, yet they always contrived to eat it.

The four of them — Miles, Dolly, Jack, and Solomon — ate their food together in the Rigdales' cabin: most times it was only broth, or perhaps salted meat and biscuit, which Goodwife Rigdale, before she went away, had laid out for them ; but once Goodman Cooke brought them from the shore a large piece of a cold roast goose. There was but one drumstick, and each felt he should have it, — Jack because he had been ill, and Dolly because she was a girl, and Miles because he was the eldest. Solomon said nothing, but he purred his loudest and rubbed his head against Dolly's knee. They ended by eating the drumstick together, each a bite, turn and turn about, and what they could not get from the bone was left to Solomon, who dragged his ration beneath the bunk, and, with eyes big and fiery, growled at them.

The children remembered that supper, not only because of the cold goose, but because it was the last they ate together, for next morning Goodman Cooke took Jack to the shore. Miles watched his friend's small preparations enviously, and Dolly, who had come also to stand in the doorway of the Cookes' cabin, voiced a sorrowful wish : "I think I'd best go too, and see father and mother."

"They've no place to put you, lass," Goodman Cooke explained. "So soon as there is place, they'll send for you both, be sure. For Doctor Fuller says your father grows heartier, Miles," he went on ; "you've no need to worry yourself."

"Indeed, I have not worried," Miles answered, in some surprise.

After Jack went, life on shipboard was not so pleasant. Dolly began to fret for her mother and scoff at Miles's authority ; Miles grew cross ; and the broth burned oftener than ever, and finally, giving out altogether, left them with nothing to eat but dry biscuit. With this woful tale of starvation, Dolly betook herself at last to Constance Hopkins in the great cabin, and Miles, glad that some one should make known their unhappy state, yet ashamed to do so himself, lagged on behind.

Constance Hopkins was Giles's sister, a slip of a

lass, not three years older than Miles, but to him she seemed quite grown up. Certainly she bore the responsibilities of age in those days, for not only must she nurse her stepmother, Mistress Elizabeth Hopkins, who lay helpless in her cabin, but she must care for the baby, Oceanus, born on the voyage across the sea, and the little half-sister, Damaris, a baby also, not two years old. Yet somehow motherly little Constance found time to comfort Dolly, and cook a bit of meat for hungry Miles, and assure them both that their father and mother surely would come soon to look to them.

Dolly hugged the "big girl," but Miles could scarcely do that, and he knew no civil speech to tell his gratitude, so he was glad when, his eyes falling on Damaris, he thought to pick her up. "I'll mind her for you a bit, Constance," he offered.

Damaris was pleased with Miles's tousled hair and sturdy arms, that held her more firmly than her half-sister could; and Miles, never guessing what a source of misfortune her liking would prove to him hereafter, was much elated at his success with her. He tugged baby out on deck to show her the gulls looking for food in the water, and the bright crusted snow that sparkled in the sunshine on the wooded point. Damaris gurgled appreciatively and pulled Miles's hair; then, when he carried her back into the cabin, slept like a kitten,

F

whereat Constance was so relieved and pleased that Miles gladly cared for the baby, *his* baby, the next day, and the next.

But the third day, a Friday, a pelting fine rain set in that made an airing on the deck out of the question, not for the baby alone, but for a well-grown boy and girl. Miles and Dolly went up to spend the afternoon in the great cabin, because in their own quarters there was no one to talk to, and, moreover, it was cold. In the main cabin they would find some one to keep them company, and they could, at least, warm their hands at the little fire burning in a tubful of sand, which Constance often used in heating food for Mistress Hopkins.

But this afternoon the fire was out and Constance busied with her mother, so the two children, disappointed, sat down together on a rude bench, at the angle in the stern where two rows of little cabins joined. "I wish I were with my mother," sniffed Dolly ; and " 'Twill do you no good to cry," Miles checked her sternly.

"I was not crying, Miles Rigdale," the damsel answered hotly.

It was on Miles's lips to reply, when close at hand a voice spoke his name, " Miles Rigdale!"

Readily enough he jumped up and went to the half-opened door of the adjoining cabin. It was Captain Standish's cabin, he remembered now, and,

"Dolly plaited a fold of her apron between her fingers."

as he halted in the doorway, he perceived Mistress Rose Standish lying in the bunk. A little of the afternoon light sifted in through the tiny port-hole, and by it he noted how her hair fell loosely about her face, unlike the way she wore it when on deck; but her cheeks were rosy as ever, and her voice quite steady as she spoke: "It's you, the lad my husband told me of? I thought I heard one call you by name. Will you not do somewhat for me, Miles? Fetch me my jug here full of water again. Goodwife Tinker was to look to me to-day; I felt very well this morning. But she's ill now herself, and when I tried to rise,—" she laughed, with a nervous catch in her laughter, — "why, then things went whisking round me very strangely. But you look as you still could stand stoutly, sir."

"I'll fetch you the water, and gladly, mistress," Miles answered, so eagerly that he stammered. He stepped into the cabin to take the jug from where it rested on a chest beneath the port-hole, and Dolly, following shyly after, hesitated on the threshold.

"Is this little maid your sister?" Mistress Standish roused up to ask. "Won't you come in and bear me company, sweetheart, while Miles fetches the water?"

Dolly plaited a fold of her apron between her fingers and nodded dumbly.

"That's well," said Mistress Standish. "Sit you

down here on the chest by me. And I've some raisins of the sun you shall have if you'll stay."

"Dolly must not eat your raisins if you be sick." Miles formulated the relentless principle which had been enforced as regards himself when Dolly lay ill. "And I'll fetch the water speedily." He stood a moment on the threshold, balancing the jug in one hand. "Mistress Standish," he blurted out, with sudden resolution, "would you not rather have beer than water?"

"Than the water from the ship's casks, yes," she answered; "but 'twill relish well enough, Miles. At even, when Captain Standish comes, mayhap he'll get me a draught of beer."

"I'll get it for you now," Miles said cheerily, and walked away, with his head up and the jug swinging.

Outside the door of the great cabin the chilly rain, that stung finely on his cheeks, pricked him alive to realization of what he had undertaken. Since Christmas, when the supply of the Pilgrim emigrants had given out, beer could be obtained on board the *Mayflower* only from the ship's stores, through the courtesy of Master Jones, the captain; and he was a terrible person. Most times he ranged about the high quarter-deck, where only the chiefs of the Pilgrims dared go; once Francis Billington, to show his daring, had clambered thither, and Master Jones, without parley, had bidden his quartermaster, " Kick that young imp down into Limbo, where he belongs." From that experience Francis had been black and blue, and subdued in manner for a week.

So it was no wonder now that, for long minutes, Miles stood shivering in the rain at the foot of the companion ladder, while he tried to summon courage to venture up. He might never have arrived at such hardihood, had not Jones himself, strolling forth upon the quarter-deck to study the weather, observed him, and presently bellowed lustily : " What beest thou staring up hither for, hey ? "

" I — I want to come up, if it like you, sir," Miles piped quaveringly.

" Then come up. Beelzebub fetch thee ! What's hindering thee ? "

Miles could have answered truly that it was a loud-voiced, broad-shouldered man, with a bushy gray beard, whose name was Jones, that hindered him ; but he thought best, even on so poor an invitation, to scramble in silence up the steep ladder to the quarter-deck. The wind there was high, so he gripped the bulwark to keep erect.

" Well, now thou art up, what is it thou wouldst have ? " roared Jones.

" Beer, sir. For Captain Standish's wife. She is ill."

Master Jones hesitated a little minute, then caught Miles by the collar of his doublet, and only let go when he landed him within the roundhouse. Miles said nothing to this, but his heart thumped alarmingly at finding himself thus tumbled head-long into the very lair of the Master. Yet the roundhouse proved a harmless place, with its ship-shape bunks and table and stools; and one of the mates, who lay upon a bunk, rose up at Jones's bidding, to do nothing more formidable than fill Miles's jug from a keg that stood in one corner.

"Now see to it thou dost not filch the beer by the way," grumbled Master Jones. "I be ready to give to your Captain's wife, but not to fill the stomach of every knavish lad on shipboard; dost thou hear?"

"I wouldn't take the beer that was meant for Mistress Standish," Miles said indignantly.

"Nay, but boys be a slippery race," growled the Master. "The saints be blest I never had none!"

Miles privately was glad of that, for he could not help thinking how unhappy a boy would be, with such an alarming father as Master Jones. Very prudently, he did not say so, but, seizing his jug, backed out of the roundhouse, almost too hastily to say "Thank you."

He had come back to a good conceit of himself, however, by the time he had manœuvred safely down the ticklish ladder, and he walked in on Mistress Standish and Dolly quite proudly. Mistress Standish thanked him mightily, enough to make Miles redden and shuffle his foot on the floor. "But I liked to do it for you," he muttered.

After that he was persuaded to sit down on the chest beside Dolly, and tell Mistress Standish all about how they were building houses on the shore, and how he had gone to the Indian fields, and what a wonderful dog Trug was. Dolly chimed in there to tell what a rare pussy Solomon was, and how he would leap over your hands. Then Mistress Standish, who lay listening, and seemed to like their talk, though she said little, bade Miles bring her a box from a shelf against the wall, and in it, sure enough, were a few big raisins and a small handful of currants.

The sight was too much for Miles's scruples, and when she urged the children eat of them, he yielded, weakly as eager little Dolly. "We'll take two raisins each," he said, with an effort at firmness, "and three currants." Then, with a sigh, he shut the box up tight, and ate his own share very slowly.

Dolly finished more speedily, and straightway Mistress Standish urged her sing to them. "Dolly told me while you were gone that she is wont to sing to mother," she explained to Miles. "Now

I want her to sing to me. You shall have more raisins if you will, Dolly, in spite of Brother Miles."

Dolly was bashful, and, for all it was now murky twilight, so faces were not plain to see, insisted on sitting on the other side of Miles, where she could hide behind him. Then, at last, she sang. " Though it is a worldly song," she protested.

" No matter. I am what your people call a worldly woman," Mistress Standish answered.

So Dolly cuddled up to Miles and sang : —

> " Skip and trip it,
>   Hey non nonny !
>   For the lark is in the clover,
>   And the fields are green and bonny,
>   And a dappled sky shows over.
>   Sing hey nonny nonny !
>   'Tis blithe world and gay,
>   When spring comes bonny
>   And the winter packs away."

There Dolly broke off, short and sudden, and Miles, looking to the dusky doorway, saw a man's sturdy figure blocking it.

" 'Tis you come back, Miles ? " Mistress Standish spoke quickly. " Come you in and sit down. Your namesake and his sister have been caring for me bravely — "

" I'm sorry," came the Captain's voice out of the dark. " That is — You must be wearied now, sweetheart. Come, Miles, my soldier, I want to speak with you."

Miles wondered why, as he stepped out from the cabin, the Captain troubled to put one arm about his shoulders; he was pleased at the caress, yet awkward in receiving it. " I want you to go in here," said Captain Standish, leading him to the cabin that the Brewsters had occupied. " Constance Hopkins is waiting within to tell you somewhat. And you must remember, Miles, that you are to bear you like a man."

Miles wrested round suddenly and faced the Captain. There was a little dim lantern light in this part of the great cabin, not enough for him to read the other's face, but he could guess and feel what was coming. " Has anything gone wrong with my mother? Tell me; tell me, quick!" he cried.

" Not your mother, Miles. Your father."

CHAPTER VI

GOODMAN RIGDALE had died that day at noon; he had seemed sure of recovery, but there came a sudden change, and, with the ebbing of the tide, his life went out. So much they made Miles understand, gently as they could. Dolly cried with choked sobbings, and Constance Hopkins, who had come out and taken the little girl in her arms, cried too. But Miles, who sat apart from the others, astride one of the benches, did not cry,—just scowled before him in stupid fashion, and half snarled, "Don't touch me," at Goodwife Tinker and the other women who had hastened up to sympathize.

He was aware of the people about him and the lantern light; that was all. Something inside him seemed benumbed, and he did not care to talk, or cry, or do aught but sit still. He listened to Dolly; she was wailing now, "I want my mother. Oh, take me to my mother!" He wished she would hush; it worried him.

Then he heard some one else speak: "Look you, Captain; Will Trevor and I are fresh enough to do 't, and there's the small boat belongs to the shallop. And Rigdale's goodwife will be wanting her bairns to-night. If you give the word, Will and I, we'll row them ashore."

Miles looked up and saw Ned Lister, his cap on straight and his face earnest, speaking with the Captain. He rose, and, a little unsteadily, pushed the women aside, so he could clutch Ned's arm. "I want to go ashore," he whispered chokedly. "Take me now."

"You shall go," said Captain Standish. "I'll bid them make ready the boat."

"You and the little wench get on your cloaks briskly," Ned admonished, as he turned to follow the Captain. "We'll be ready ere you be."

Constance came down with the two children to the cabin beneath the main deck. It seemed darker and colder than ever before, and Dolly's cloak strings were tied in a hard knot, and Miles could not find his mittens. At the very last, as, in stupid fashion, he searched for them a third time in a bag that held some odds and ends of his mother's, he heard Dolly cry, "Oh, Solomon, poor Solomon! Don't leave him behind, Miles. I know they'll not tend him. And daddy was fond of him."

The cat was dozing among the blankets, but when Miles, slow and uncomprehending, tried to seize him, he took fright and ran beneath the bunk.

"We've the boat ready. Quickly, Miles!" called
Ned Lister in the passageway.

Miles saw Solomon's eyes shining yellow in the
dark beneath the bunk, and, making a grab, he
clutched the cat. The creature spit and clawed, but
Miles, with his hands bleeding, still clung to him,
and, headlong, thrust him into the bag that had held
their biscuit. One white paw came struggling out,
but the boy shoved it in roughly, and drew the
strings tight.

"Wait, wait! Your cloak, Miles." Constance
detained him, and fastened his cloak about his neck.
Miles suffered her, like a very little boy, and then,
slinging Solomon's bag over one shoulder, he followed Dolly up on deck.

The rain, pelting on his cheeks and forehead,
half blinded him, and the faces of the men, seen fit-
fully beneath the flaring light of the lantern at the
gangway, looked strange to him. Their voices had
no meaning, and they must repeat the question
when one asked: "What have you there, Miles ?
Give me the bag; I'll hand it you."

Miles shook his head and pressed the bag tighter
beneath his arm ; he could feel the cat's soft body
writhing and struggling within. They brought him
over to the gangway ladder, and, holding by one
hand, he scrambled down it. How black the line
of bulwarks looked against the lantern light, as the

ship heaved upward ! There he half slipped, when he felt some one catch him round the body, and he was dropped down on the stern seat of the little boat. Dolly pressed close to him, and, putting his arm round her, he held tight to her and to Solomon. They had turned the lantern now so the light flashed into the boat, and he realized it was Lister who sat upon the forward thwart, and the other man, who was standing up to push them off from the ship's side, was the sailor, Will Trevor.

At last they were clear, out on the wide, rough water, and, with a motion of spitting on his hands, Trevor dropped into his seat and gripped his oar. As the boat swung round, Miles had sight of the black bulk of the *Mayflower*, with a lantern gleaming on her high quarter-deck and another just receding from her gangway. Then, as the boat headed for the shore, he could see the ship only by turning his head, and that was too great an effort to make.

The thole-pins creaked, and the water slapped against the prow. The waves were running high, and, as the little boat leaped them, she seemed to throb through her frame. The oars and the sea that wrestled together made the only sound, for the rain that dropped steadily was a quiet rain, and the men who rowed for the most part kept silent. Once, to be sure, Trevor growled: " How're we heading, Ned ? "

Miles noted dully how Lister rested on his oar and turned his face landward. " I can just make out a light," he answered. " Pest on this rain ! More to larboard we must run."

For another space they tugged at the oars in silence, while Miles stared unheedingly into the dark, till suddenly Trevor called, " Hey, lad, what's wrong wi' thy bag ? "

Solomon's struggles had loosed the fastenings, Miles found ; he thrust the animal back and tied the strings again, slowly and stiffly, for his hands were cold and sore too, where they had been scratched.

" What sort o' luggage be ye travelling with ? " Trevor asked, between strokes, in a tone that was so amused that Miles felt an angry shock : what right had the sailor to find any merriment in life, while Dolly was sobbing so ? Next moment the anger passed, and instead, Miles wondered that Dolly should cry, for it was not true, whatever they had said ; his father would surely come forth from the Common House to meet them, and he would look just as Miles had seen him on that last day.

Yonder beneath the black bluff shone a light. Miles could see it now, and he stared unthinkingly, till it grew larger and brighter, and then a sudden jar almost threw him from his seat. " I'll hold her steady," spoke Trevor. " Do thou get out the younkers, Ned."

"Come, come, Miley, are you asleep?" said Lister. Miles saw him kneeling on the rock close beside him, holding the boat's gunwale with one hand, and with the other outstretched. "Give me the bag. Now then, steady. Ah! You did yourself hurt?"

Miles picked himself up from the rock where he had fallen; his knees were aching, and he suddenly felt he should like to cry. "Yes, I hurt me," he said dazedly. "Give me Solomon."

He made his way, groping through the dark, to the path beneath the bluff that led up to the settlement. The ground had thawed, so broad puddles had formed; he must have splashed into one, for, as he stepped, his shoes squeaked with water. Ned Lister strode up alongside him, with Dolly gathered in his arms. "You come with me up to the Elder's house, Miley," he said breathlessly, for Ned was wiry, rather than robust, and Dolly was a heavy little maid.

All the way up the hill Miles had a sickening sense of awaking to something full of dread. The ground and the sky and the dimly seen houses were now all real; he felt the rain and the cold and the weight of the bag on his arm, and he began to realize that what had happened also was no dream.

"Oh!" he cried, with a sudden hard gasp, and, dropping the bag, broke into a run. He stumbled and slipped, but pantingly he held on till he reached the Brewsters' cottage. From one of the tiny windows a light shone forth, but it blinded without aiding him. He fumbled a moment at the heavy door, then, grasping the rude latch at last, thrust it open with his shoulder, and plunged headlong into the common room.

On the hearth, opposite the door, a fire blazed, and on the table flickered a candle. Spite of the dazzle of sudden light, Miles made out a woman, just turning from the fire, and, knowing her for the Elder's wife, ran to her. "Where's my mother, my mother?" he cried.

"Hush, hush, Miles! You must quiet yourself ere you see her," Mistress Brewster urged, never so gently.

But there came from an adjoining room his mother's voice: "Miles, I am here. Come to me."

The narrow chamber was dark, but, seated in the far corner, he could distinguish a woman's bowed figure, and, stumbling heavily across the floor, he flung himself on his knees beside her. "Mother! Oh, mother!" he choked, and, burying his face in her lap, burst out crying.

CHAPTER VII

AT first Miles found a jarring unfitness in everyday life. Only eight and forty hours before, they had buried his father on the bluff overlooking the harbor; they had read no prayers over the dead, as the ministers did in England, and, lest the savages should spy and note how few the colonists were becoming, they had levelled the grave, like the many round about it. A raw wind had blown from off the sea, so Goodwife Rigdale shivered as she stood by the grave, and Miles's hands were senseless with the cold.

Now it was over, and Goodman Rigdale dead and buried, but life went on, just as usual. Goodwife Rigdale helped Mistress Brewster prepare food, and ate of it herself; and Love and Wrestling, sorry though they had been for their playmates' sorrow, frolicked gayly with Solomon, whom Ned Lister had brought to the cottage, bag and all. By the second day, though her eyes were still heavy with crying, and her mouth tremulous, Dolly plucked up spirit to join the boys. Even earlier, Miles had begun to fetch wood and water for Mistress Brewster, lay the fire, and help where he could; if only everything had stopped for a time, till he could realize what had happened and master himself, he felt he could bear it; but the petty acts of living would go on.

In such a mood of wretchedness he trudged forth on the third morning, up the path beyond the spring, to fetch sticks from the edge of the wood where the trees had been felled. He gathered the fagots, and was trying to tie them strongly, as his father tied the swamp grass that last day they worked together, when he saw Francis Billington, also in search of wood, drawing near.

"Why, Miles!" the newcomer greeted him, in some surprise, for in these days Miles avoided his old comrades. But now there was no avoiding till the wood was tied up, so Francis came to him and, a bit awed, tried clumsily to be sympathetic. "I'll help you tie that wood, Miles."

"I c'n do 't alone."

"Look you, my daddy's going fowling to-day. Mayhap he'll take us."

"I don't want to go," snapped Miles, with a sick sort of anger that other boys still could talk of their fathers.

"You might at least be civil to a body," Francis said rather huffily. "What need to carry such a face for it, Miles? You were mortal afeard of your father while he lived. And now he can never flog you no more."

Without warning, other than a small catching of the breath, Miles sprang to his feet and struck the speaker in the face. Francis, thoroughly surprised, hit back, and, clenching, they pitched over among the crackling sticks. Miles fell uppermost, and, hardly realizing how or why, he was pommelling Francis lustily, when a mighty hand heaved him up by the scruff of the neck. "You must not strike a man when he is already worsted," spoke the voice of long-legged John Alden.

Miles stood biting his lips that twitched. "' A ' shall not say —" he began, and there his voice broke. " Oh, I wish he could flog me again ! "

Alden stared a moment, then, with sudden understanding, swung round upon the whimpering Francis and rated him mightily, while Miles, glad not to be noticed, caught up his bundle of wood and stumbled away toward the settlement.

Yet this was the last outward showing of the boy's grief. Little by little, as the busy days came, he found himself fitting into his new life, and at length even taking a certain zest in it. For he was now man of the family, and the cares he felt called on to shoulder did not a little to distract him from any sorry broodings. He must work with

his full strength, wherever they sent him and who-
ever bade him ; he must keep flibbertigibbet Dolly
out of mischief; above all, he must run after his
mother, as she went about to nurse the many sick
of the settlement, and see to it that she did not catch
cold or come to any harm.

The greatest and most important labor, however,
he did in the earlier days of his loss, when he went
to fetch his father's goods from the *Mayflower*.
Others might have said the work was done by Ned
Lister, for Master Hopkins, who had promised
Goodman Rigdale to look to his family, so far as
he was able, sent him about this task ; but Miles,
who was sure he was the leader and Ned only the
assistant, felt the whole expedition a tribute to his
own new-come manliness.

They went out in the shallop to the *Mayflower*
on a morning so bright and open that it scarcely
recalled to Miles his coming from the ship. Once
aboard, to be sure, the half-homesick pang laid
hold on him, when he scrambled down to the little
cabin that had sheltered him so long ; but there
was so much to do he soon cast it off. The
bedding must be tied up securely, and the pots
and platters loaded into the biggest kettle ; and
Ned, who had a coughing fit and said he didn't
feel very well, let Miles do it all. He recovered,
however, in time to help drag the stuff to the deck,

and to get up from the orlop a small chest of Goodman Rigdale's; and he was also selfish enough to take charge himself of the loud, manly labor of transferring the goods to the shallop.

Somewhat disappointed, Miles clambered down again to the cabin to fetch the box with Dolly's Indian basket, and, when he came back, the shallop was so near ready to push off that he had only time to drop into the bow beside Lister. Glancing round the great sail toward the stern, where such other passengers as were going from the ship were placed, he caught sight of Captain Standish, who sat stiffly, with one arm about the muffled figure of a woman. "Yon is Mistress Standish, is it not?" Miles questioned Lister, very softly.

His companion nodded. "Set to come ashore, poor lass!" he answered, in the same low tone. "'Tis the last trip she'll ever make in the shallop." This Ned spoke sympathetically; then had no further leisure to talk for settling himself comfortably with his back against Goodman Rigdale's bedding.

Miles moved a little to give Ned room, but, without heeding him, continued to gaze at Captain Standish and Mistress Rose. He could not see her face for the hood about her head and the cloak drawn up above her chin, but he marked the listless droop of her whole body; and he noted, too, how

the Captain sat with his eyes looking straight out
and his mouth hard.   Miles wondered if what
Lister said of Mistress Standish were true, and,
what with wondering and watching, was taken by
surprise and nearly overset when the shallop bumped
up to the landing place.

For a moment he lingered by the boat, feigning
to busy himself with unlading the kettle, while he
watched Mistress Standish.   The Captain and
Alden, who was waiting at the landing, helped her
from the boat, and half carried her away between
them up the hill.   The Captain's face was still so
grave and stern, that Miles was a trifle frightened,
and very sorry; he wished he were a man like
John Alden, so he could have spoken to the Captain and helped Mistress Standish.

Then he had to think of other matters, for Ned,
with an access of energy, was tumbling the goods
ashore, and they must together drag them up to
the Elder's house.   Just at present that was home
to Miles, because his mother and Dolly lived there,
and he sometimes ate with them, though, as an
additional mark of manhood, — so he esteemed it,
— he spent his nights at the Common House.

It really came about because his friends could not
shelter him.   Goodwife Rigdale and Dolly had the
last spare bed at the Elder's house; the cottage
higher up the hill, on which Goodman Rigdale had

labored, and where Goodman Cooke and Jack had now one bunk, was filled with men whose houses were building; while Master Hopkins, however well he might mean by his friend's son, had not a roof to cover his own family. So Miles slept with Giles Hopkins at the Common House, where at night the beds were placed so thick one need not step on the floor in passing from the fire to his sleeping place.

On Sunday all was changed, however, for then the Common House became a meeting-house. They tucked the beds up in corners, and swept the floor, as Miles knew to his cost, for on this, his second Saturday on the mainland, they pressed him into the service. Twice on the Sabbath the Elder taught his little company, and prayed with them there, — a sorry little company indeed, of whom fair half lay sick within the cheerless cabins, or dead beneath the level ground of the harbor bluff.

The thought of his own dead father made Miles listen attentively that day; and, when he walked staidly up to the Elder's house before twilight, he took Dolly apart into his mother's cold little chamber, where he read to her from Goodman Rigdale's black-letter Bible. He was a painful reader, but he felt it was the fit thing for him to do in filling his father's place, so, with the great book on his knees, he sat on the floor, beneath the little window that

let in the light sparsely through its oiled paper, and
Dolly sat by him, with her head on his shoulder.
He was much elated at finding her so quiet and attentive, but, when he paused to recover breath at the
end of a very tough sentence about the Perizzites,
he perceived the little girl was fast asleep.

Miles did not wake her; just sat with the Bible
in his lap and his stiffening arm round his sister
till, when it had grown darker, his mother came to
seek them.   He had nothing to say to his mother
that night, but afterward it was something to remember keenly, though with an under-pang of
sorrow, how he had sat close by her in the dark
and had felt her hand rest on his head.

Next day was dreary with rain and sleet, and a
dull twilight that, closing in early, drove Miles into
the house, where he played at Even-and-Odd with
the little Brewsters and Dolly, very quietly, because the Elder was writing at the table.   Elder
Brewster was always kindly-spoken, but the fact
that he knew such a deal about the next world, and
what would befall you if you were not good, put
Miles in great awe of him.

When he went forth at length, Miles, feeling
more like himself, raised his voice, and even let the
trenchers clatter while he and Dolly laid the table.
But he had no desire to be noisy, when, late in the
evening, the Elder returned from the house where

the sick lay. A word or two passed between the older folk that sent Miles with a whispered question to his mother, who told him simply that Mistress Rose Standish had died that evening.

Dolly cried, because she was a foolish girl, but it did not stir Miles so deeply. Indeed, he did not come to feel a hearty grief till next morning, when, as he climbed the hill to Elder Brewster's cottage, he saw Captain Standish, grim and set-faced, trudging up to the woods through the sleet and rain. The weather was too bitter for work, and the axe which the Captain carried was, Miles guessed, a mere pretext. All through the day it made him shiver to think of the solitary man, lingering in the cold among the pines; he wondered if even to himself the Captain would make pretense of working, or if he would sit idle among the wet logs.

But forty-eight hours later the Captain was going and coming and working among the rest, just as before, though maybe a bit more silent. For the hale ones who could labor were few; the work must be done; and, where so many were falling, there was small space to grieve for a single life.

Miles had even grown somewhat blunted to the sight of the sorry little companies that twice and even thrice a week trudged with the body of a friend or kinsman to the bluff above the harbor. His own life went on methodically; he worked, and even played with Jack Cooke and Trug, and some days, when he was allowed to go fowling with Ned Lister and Giles Hopkins, fairly enjoyed himself.

But Ned began presently to have coughing fits even when he was bidden to go hunting, though Miles, who had grown distrustful of his convenient illness, urged him to "have done with fooling and come along." One morning in February, when Lister, instead of going about his work, was wasting his time thus with Miles and Jack and Giles by the fire in Goodman Cooke's cottage, came another to urge him, no less a one than Master Hopkins. Miles remembered a long time the terrible rating he gave Ned for his laziness and trickery, and he wondered that the young man sat with his head leaning on his fist, and flung back but a single protest: "I can judge better than you, sir, whether I be ill or not. 'Tis my head that's aching, not yours."

To which Master Hopkins retorted grimly that, if there were a whipping post in the colony, something besides Ned's head would ache.

Then, for that there was no help for it, Lister took his fowling piece and slouched away from the fire. "I'm going, since you drive me," he said sulkily, "but these youngsters need not follow at my heels. 'Twill be all I can do to fetch myself home again, let alone three brats."

Much disappointed, Miles spent the day in the

less joyous labor of fetching and carrying on the great hill, where they were putting the last touches to the platform on which the guns were to be mounted. He came to be interested, none the less, when Goodman Cooke told him how, in a few days, they would drag the guns up the hill and put them in place. That would be a brave thing to see, Miles thought, for the sailors from the *Mayflower* were to come ashore and help, and the street from the hill to the landing place would be noisy and busy. Not so busy, though, as the crew of the *Mayflower* would have made it a month before, for the sickness now had settled on the ship, where it was raging unchecked.

At dusk, as Miles came down from the hill, he chanced on Master Hopkins, still grumbling at Lister, who bade him go see if that malingerer were loitering anywhere in the settlement. It seemed a spying errand, but, not thinking of disobedience, Miles started down the street. Nearest the shore stood the Common House, the house for the sick, and the storehouse, all three of which, to make the search complete, he visited.

In the big main room of the sick-house lay the men who were ill, and, as Miles stepped in, on tiptoe because of his heavy shoes, the first thing he saw beneath the candlelight was Ned Lister's black head, half hidden under the coverlets of one of the

bunks.   Miles stole up to him.   "Why, Ned, ha'
you cheated the Doctor himself?" he whispered
cheerfully.

Lister raised his head and looked at him, with
his eyes very bright.   "I'm cheating you all; yes,"
he said, with a laugh.   "Go tell Hopkins be more
cautious next time how he wastes so good a property
as a serving man.   A pity!   If I die he'll be out
my passage-money.   Well, I always owed him a
grudge for bringing me to this forsaken country,
and I'll even scores now."

The thought seemed to please Ned mightily, for
he laughed, till Doctor Fuller, stepping from the
inner room, sharply bade him hush.   "Get you to
Master Hopkins and tell him the man is ill," he
ordered Miles; and, as he let the boy out at the
door, added, for his ear alone, "very ill."

Somehow Ned's overthrow frightened Miles more
than any other illness.   Lister had always seemed
so tough and wiry that his succumbing at last set the
boy to asking himself, in some fright, if he, too,
might not fall ill.   A soreness in his throat or an
ache in his head made him nervous.   He questioned Jack minutely as to how he felt before he
was taken sick, and then he began at once to feel
as Jack had felt.   He started to tell his mother and
get her to comfort him, but then he was ashamed;
she was busy and anxious all the time for the

people she was called on to nurse, and he was a great, strong boy, who, of course, would not be sick.

But one day his head ached in good earnest — no imagination; and next morning the ache was worse, so he was too stupid even to go out. Wrestling Brewster was ailing too, so Dolly and Love stayed by his bed to amuse him, and Miles was left quite alone. All day he sat toasting himself by the fire, till he was too warm and was sure his head ached because of the heat, so out he went, and tramped up and down the street till his teeth chattered with cold. He wanted no supper, but he went back to the house to bid his mother good night and get to bed early.

"Mother came home very weary and has lain down within," Dolly said, so he went into the bedroom. A cold light streamed in at the little window, but the corners of the low room were dark and the pallet was in shadow. His mother was stretched upon it, with the cloak that had been his father's wrapped round her, but at his step she raised her head. "It's you, my lad?" she asked, and reached out her hand.

"I came in to give you good night, mother," he said, in his manliest tone, because it made him proud to think he was hiding his illness from her. "I'll mess at the Common House to-night."

She put up her hand, and, drawing his head down to her, kissed him. Her cheek felt hot as it pressed against his, and even in the dim light he noted that her face was flushed, but his head ached so lamentably that he made nothing of it. "Why, deary, you're not ill?" he heard her say.

"Indeed, no, mother. No more ill than you," he answered bravely, and, bidding her good night, went softly out of the room.

The west was all a chill yellow, and a northerly breeze was astir that set Miles shivering long before he reached the Common House. There a fire was alight that looked comforting, and, going up to it, he snuggled down in a corner of the hearth. At the table of boards laid on trestles some of the men were eating their supper, but Miles was sick at the mere thought of food. He sat staring and staring into the heart of the flames, where he could see the outlines of the farmhouse at home, and then he saw nothing, but he faintly heard steps upon the floor, and somebody caught him up.

"What are you falling on the fire in that fashion for, eh?" one asked, and the man who held him — he had a vague notion it was Alden — questioned, "What's wrong, lad?"

"Oh — h!" wailed Miles, "I think I'm dying."

CHAPTER VIII

TO be sure, Miles did not die, but for some days he lay in the sick-house, too ill to give much heed to what went on about him, or take thought for anything save his own misery. From a mass of hazy recollections one or two moments of that time afterward came back clearly.

One such memory was of a dim morning within the cheerless room, when, through the familiar patter, patter of rain on the oiled paper at the windows, he heard a latch creak somewhere and men tread cautiously. Turning weakly on his pillow, Miles looked to the door that led to the inner room, where the sick women lay, and he saw Goodman Cooke and Edward Dotey come forth, stepping carefully, and carrying on a stretcher between them something that was muffled up and motionless. He turned his face again to the wall, and neither thought nor reasoned of what it meant, —just listened to the lulling patter of the rain.

The other time of which he kept remembrance was a crisp night, when the whiff of wind that blew

in at the outer door, as it was opened, smelt fresh
and good, and Cooke, who came to tend the fire,
piled the logs high. Dozing and waking, Miles
watched through half-closed eyelids the crowded
pallets about him, and the shadows that flickered
up and down the rough walls.   He must have slept
a moment, but he roused up suddenly to see in the
waning firelight Elder Brewster, who bent over him
with a cup of drink.   Leaning against the arm that
supported him, Miles swallowed the draught obediently, and then the Elder, with more care than he
usually had time to bestow on a single patient,
laid him down and drew the coverings round him.
" Poor little lad ! " Miles heard him say, under his
breath.   " God comfort you ! "

Miles wondered a little, but, too stupid greatly
to heed what was said, soon dropped to sleep once
more.

The crisis of his sickness must have passed
on that night, for a day or two later he felt enough
like himself to swallow with some relish a dish
of broth.   Ned Lister, packed out from the sick-
house while still convalescent, to make room for
others, fetched him the broth, and helped him eat,
with a choking great spoon that made the process
slow.   Miles wondered whether Ned had grown
thin or his clothes had grown baggy ; perhaps 'twas
a little of both.

Then, on the idle wonderment, followed more serious thought, and, speaking slowly and weakly, he asked, as Lister settled him in his pallet again: "Tell me, Ned, why has not my mother been here to nurse me, as she did you and the others?"

"Haven't you been well enough looked to, Miley?" questioned Ned, bending down to tie his shoestrings.

"'Tis just the men have cared for me."

"Well, you're a man yourself, and want only men to look to you, eh?"

"No, I'm not a man," said Miles, the ready tears of sickness welling into his eyes, "and I want my mother."

"I heard she had a touch of the fever herself," answered Ned, still busy with his shoes. "We're all helpless with it, Miles. There's only seven of us now that can crawl about to do aught. And the Captain and the Elder are working each like three. By the Lord, those be two good fellows!" This earnestly, for Ned; and then, gathering up his bowl and spoon, he walked away to minister to the next sick man.

Every one ill, and the care of the whole colony on the shoulders of seven men, some half sick themselves! Miles realized vaguely that he ought to be patient and not fret at anything, but still the next two days of his slow convalescence were long and hard to bear.

H

He was glad enough, one dim morning that seemed like all the others, when the Elder came into the sick-room with Dolly at his side. "The little wench begged to come to you, Miles," he said, as he seated her on the edge of the boy's pallet. "But she is to talk only few words, and softly, because there are others lying here very ill."

So soon as he had turned and left the children to themselves, Dolly bent and dabbed a kiss upon her brother's chin. "Though you make me shy, near as if you were a stranger, Miles," she explained, in a subdued whisper, "you are grown so peaked, and your eyes are so very round."

Miles smiled weakly, but happily; it was so good to see the face of one of his own people. "I'm glad you came, Dolly," he said, drawing her hand tremulously into his. "Mother will soon come too, will she not? Why did she not come with you?"

A choke made Dolly's whisper broken: "She — could not."

"Is she ill?"

Dolly nodded, with a piteous face.

Miles's thin fingers gripped her hand fast. "Dolly, she isn't — dead?" His voice rose high and frightened.

"Oh, you mustn't, Miles," Dolly gasped. "And I can't tell you. They said I must not speak of her to you.   Oh, Miles, Miles, she has been dead these four days!"

They carried Dolly away, the mischief done, and Miles, hiding his head beneath the bedclothes, cried so long as strength was in him.   Then he lay watching the red and orange streaks that flashed before his tight-closed eyes, and, thinking how stuffy it was beneath the coverlets, wondered if perhaps he would not smother.   He hoped he would, so he had a first sensation of fretful disappointment, when some one uncovered his head; and then, as he caught the clearer air on his face and looked up at Captain Standish, felt vaguely comforted.

" Drink you this, lad," spoke the Captain, gruffly, yet, Miles realized, with vast pity in his tone. " Then sleep."

" I'll — try," swallowed Miles.

" That's well.   Bear it soldierly, as we all must."

" Like a soldier," Miles repeated over and over to himself, and, shutting his lips, pressed his head into the bolster, till, worn-out, he slept.

When he awoke, the realization of his loss returned, keen almost as ever; but he was a healthy lad, so inevitably strength came back to him, and with it, little by little, as he mastered it in silence, his grief abated.   Those about him were kind, too, and did what they could to comfort him.   Captain Standish himself cared for him; Ned Lister and

Giles visited him often; and once they even let poor, guilty Dolly come to see him. She fetched in her arms fat Solomon, who yowled so piteously that, just inside the door, Doctor Fuller, who was up and able to tend his sick again, made her put him down, whereupon the cat fled home, fast as four legs could bear him.

"'Twas such a pity when I fetched him so far to see you," Dolly lamented to Miles, as she exhibited the scratches on her hands, "but he will go home safe to Mistress Brewster's house. He likes it there, and so do I. I am going to live there always with Love and Wrestling and Priscilla Mullins. She made me a poppet of a piece of scarlet cloth, and I called it after her. I shall bring it to show you next time, though you'll laugh at it, because you are a boy. Indeed, I do like it at Mistress Brewster's. If only mammy and daddy were there too!" she added, in a lower tone.

Elder Brewster himself had, at the very first, paused by Miles's bed, and spoken gravely to him of how his mother was now in a more blessed place, and he must try always to be a good boy, so some day he might join her. Though he listened dutifully, Miles did not care for the Elder's admonitions as much as he cared for Mistress Brewster's words. Newly risen from her sick-bed, she came to him, and, sitting by his pallet, whispered him of his mother, and how, before she died, she had left her love for him, and bidden him always be a good lad and a good brother to the little wench. "Though my lad will be that without my bidding," Alice Rigdale had added. "He has always been a good little son to me."

Miles listened, with his face held stolid; it was only when Mistress Brewster bent and kissed him, like his mother, that he blinked fast and turned away his head.

Day by day he grew stronger, till he sat up in bed, and then, by slow stages, was suffered to put on his clothes and walk staggeringly across the room. The next advance was his going out into the air, which would doubtless have been longer deferred if any one had had time to give close heed to the sick boy. But Doctor Fuller was busied elsewhere, and the Elder was looking to others of the sick folk, so, one morning when Lister had helped Miles into his clothes, the boy took matters into his own hands by slipping out at the door.

It was a rare, mild March day, with a tender wind of the spring that came from the western woods. The earth was soft beneath the foot; the few bushes that clambered up the bluff across the way were bursting with brown buds; and the blue harbor dazzled under the vivid sunlight. Leaning against the doorpost, Miles joyfully drank in the freshness of the morning, though his eyes grew wistful as he looked again to the bluff yonder where were the levelled graves.

Presently he summoned up his strength, and, stepping cautiously off the doorstone, picked his way round to the east side of the house, where the sun was warmest. Here the ground was trodden and bare, save for the chips scattered about the logs, of which there was a great heap stacked against the house-wall. At the other side of the pile, a tub of water rested on a great block, and, most marvellous of all, over the tub, busily washing a mass of bed-linen, bent Captain Standish.

Miles caught his breath in a gasp of surprise that made the Captain look up. "So you're well recovered, Miles?" he asked cheerily.

The boy nodded, and set himself down on the woodpile.

"Cast on my doublet, there beside you, if you will be sitting here," said Standish, and, shaking the water off his hands, came and wrapped the garment about Miles.

Snuggling down against the sunny logs, Miles gravely watched the Captain. He washed the clothes deliberately, with a good deal of sober splashing and a lavish use of soap; and then he wrung them so vigorously that the muscles of his bared arms stood out. So earnest and busy did he

"'Do you like to do it, Captain Standish?'"

seem about the undignified task that, before he thought, Miles blurted out: "Do you like to do it, Captain Standish?"

"Not in the least," the Captain answered cheerfully, as he twisted a sheet so hard that a jet of water spurted over the front of his shirt, "not in the least, Miles. But there's no one else to do it, and it must needs be done."

Miles pondered a moment. "I take it, that's how it is with living; somebody has to," he said at length.

"And somebody is right glad to," Captain Standish answered, with a quick glance at Miles. "You must get well and run about and do a man's share of the work that's before us, and you'll soon be rid of any heavy thoughts."

Miles sat still in the sunlight, and, reflecting vaguely, called to mind that, if his father and mother both were dead, Mistress Rose Standish, who was all the Captain had, likewise rested yonder on the bluff. Out of the fullness of knowledge the Captain was trying once more to teach him how to bear all bravely, he guessed, so he began stoutly: "Yes, I'm going to be a man, sir. Because now I'll have to take care of Trug and Dolly and Solomon."

Captain Standish smiled a little, as he gathered the wet clothes into his arms. "You're a true man already, Miles," he said. "At least, you're a man in the way you group your women-folk with your cattle."

After the Captain had gone behind the house to hang out his wash, Miles rested a time very thoughtful. The sunlight was warm and pleasant, and southward across the harbor the great bluff was dense with evergreen. A brave world, and he was going to do a brave part in it, as his mother had looked for him to do.

A step upon the chips made him rouse up just as Master Hopkins came leisurely round the woodpile. His face was pale, for he, too, had been touched with the sickness, and his manner was kinder than Miles had ever known in him. " So you're hale again, Miles Rigdale ? Do you think you could make shift to walk up the hill to my house ? "

" Yes, sir," Miles replied promptly. The house that Master Hopkins was building when Miles fell sick stood just across the street from the Elder's, and the boy had made up his mind to drag himself to the latter's cottage that day. It made his heart quicken to think of seeing again the rooms where his mother had lived that last month, and of talking with Dolly and Mistress Brewster. He hoped, too, that if he got up to the house they would keep him there to supper, perhaps all night. So he answered Master Hopkins's question confidently and happily: "Yes, sir. I can surely walk that far up the hill."

"That's well," said Master Hopkins; "you shall eat dinner with us this noontime."

"Thank you, sir," Miles answered, not overjoyed, but civilly.

"I'll take you to the house with me when I go back thither," the other pursued. "You understand, you are to dwell with me hereafter."

When Captain Standish returned from his drying ground, Stephen Hopkins had gone on down to the landing, and against the logs huddled a piteous-faced small boy, who at sight of him cried: "Captain Standish, Master Hopkins says I must live with him."

"Do you not wish to?" asked Standish, nonchalantly, and, tipping the water out of his tub, set himself down on the block where it had rested.

"I'd rather go anywhere else in Plymouth, unless 'twas to Goodwife Billington. Must I go to him, Captain Standish?" Forgetting his usual respectful demeanor, Miles rose, and, stumbling the few steps to the Captain, leaned against his knee. "I thought — maybe I should go with Dolly to Mistress Brewster," he said in a low voice.

Standish suddenly put one arm about him. "A pity it couldn't be so, Miles! But the Elder's house is full, and at Master Hopkins's there's half a bed; you can sleep with Giles. In any case, Master Hopkins was your father's kinsman."

"I could go to Goodman Cooke," pleaded Miles. "Or — or — I wish I could live with you."

Standish laughed outright, though when he spoke his voice was gentle: " I would take you, laddie, and be glad to, if things were — as I thought they would be. Rose had a liking for you." He stopped short, and Miles, looking up in some awe, noted that his eyes were fixed on the blue harbor, yet he seemed to see nothing of it. When he spoke again, his tone was quick and altered: "But as things have fallen out, John Alden and I are sleeping in an unfinished cabin and eating where we can find a bite. And a little young fellow like you would be better off in a household where there are women than with two clumsy men. So they have arranged it all for your best good."

Miles nodded, not trusting his voice to speak. He was thinking of what the Captain had said about being a man and things that had to be done, and he meant to make a good showing before him. " I like Giles," he began slowly, "and I like Constance, and Ned Lister will be there too; I'll try to like Master Hopkins — if he'll let me bring Trug."

So he had put on quite a brave face by the time Master Hopkins came to fetch him to his new home.   To him it was all so much a matter of course that he offered no explanations or commonplace cheering words to Miles; just bade him come, and soberly led the way up the hill.   Miles, with his feet like lead and his brave resolution flagging, loitered half-heartedly behind him, till Master Hopkins turned.   "You're not yet as strong as you thought, Miles Rigdale?" he said gravely, but kindly enough, and, lifting the boy in his arms, carried him up the hill.

Miles rested passive, one arm thrown perfunctorily about Master Hopkins's neck, and wished he were anywhere else.

CHAPTER IX

MASTER HOPKINS'S GUEST

> " ' In Wakefield there lives a jolly pinder,
> In Wakefield all on a green,
> In Wakefield all on a green, — '

There, there, Damaris! Hushaby, hushaby! Go to sleep, like a good lass."

Damaris gurgled at Miles with a provokingly wide-awake crow. "I never saw such a bad baby," sighed the little boy. "Do go to sleep, honey.

> ' In Wakefield there lives a jolly pinder, — ' "

"Oh, Miles," laughed Constance Hopkins, who, standing at the rude table, was scouring the biggest kettle, "you have sung that half a score of times. Is there no other song you know?"

"It is no time for the child to sleep now," interrupted Mistress Hopkins. "I'll wrap her up, and, since 'tis so mild a morning, you may take her forth into the air."

"O dear!" thought Miles, "I'm a man, not a nurse." He never considered that it was any kindness on his new guardians' part when, instead of putting him to heavy outdoor tasks, they set him to minding the baby and helping about the house. " Like a girl," Miles told himself, with an indignant sniff. It was not two weeks since he left the sick-house, and his legs were still a little uncertain, but he was sure he was fit to work again, or, at any rate, fit to run away and play with the other boys.

But he took the baby now and walked forth meekly, because he lived in some dread of Mistress Elizabeth Hopkins. She was a thin-lipped, energetic young woman, who mended Miles's clothes scrupulously, and, with equal conscientiousness, boxed his ears whenever he tracked dirt on her clean floors. Her sharp tongue, though, he feared more than her hands, for Mistress Hopkins scolded at everything and everybody; indeed, the only members of the household whom her words never troubled were Oceanus, who was so young he just blinked his eyes when she talked, and Master Hopkins, on whom people's fretting had as much effect as it would have had upon the great rock at the landing place.

After all, Miles was rather glad to get out into the air, away from the living room, where Mistress Hopkins was already chiding Constance. The morning was fair and warm, with no wind stirring, and the harbor sparkled invitingly, so, shouldering the unwelcome Damaris, he started happily to the shore.

But his contentment speedily had an end, for, not halfway to the landing, he was overtaken by Francis Billington, Jack Cooke, and Joe Rogers, who at once addressed him in disrespectful wise. "Ho, Miles, that's brave work, tending a baby," jeered Francis.

"You meddle with your own matters," Miles replied sulkily.

"Come with us, Miles," Jack put in pacifically. "We're going along shore to the first brook —"

"We do not want a baby with us," Joe interrupted.

"*You* might stay with me, Jack," Miles pleaded, as the others turned away.

Jack, a freckled little fellow with merry eyes, dug the heel of his shoe into the dirt. "The other lads will be having sport," he said half-heartedly.

"Then go with them," cried Miles. "Only you were very fain to play with me on shipboard."

Even this last thrust failed; Jack ran after the others down the hill, and Miles, feeling cross and ill-treated, was left to himself.

'Twould look too much as if he were following his ungracious friends if he went on to the landing, so he turned back to Elder Brewster's house. There Priscilla Mullins, a girl orphaned by the winter's sickness, who, because she was eighteen, was classed by Miles as a woman, was sweeping the doorstone with a broom of birch twigs. She paused in the labor teasingly to throw him a kiss, and tell him his busy sister and the lads were cooking by the brookside.

Sure enough, in the level space between the base of the bluff on which the cottage stood and the cove, Miles found Dolly, and Dolly's poppet Priscilla, and Love, and Wrestling, and Solomon, and Trug, who was not admitted to Mistress Hopkins's house because his great paws dirtied her floor, — all busied in making delectable pies of mud.

But when Miles joined them, Love withdrew from the mud-pie game, and wished to play at holding a council, such as his father and all the men were holding that morning in the Common House to regulate the military affairs of the colony. Dolly insisted that she should be allowed to come to the council too, for all Love urged that women never were invited thither, and the argument was growing bitter, when an unwonted tumult in the village street drew Miles's attention. A confused sort of calling and shrill shouting it seemed, that made his heart quicken between curiosity and alarm; so, snatching up Damaris, he scaled the bluff, while the rest of the children scrambled close behind him.

On the doorstone Mistress Brewster and Priscilla were gazing in silent wonder toward the street, and, looking thither too, Miles saw a man stalk past to the landing, very deliberately, as if he knew the place and held he had the right to come there. It was no one of the settlers, though, but a great, half-naked fellow with a coppery face — an Indian.

Dolly and Wrestling clutched Mistress Brewster's skirts, the little boy fairly crying, and Miles himself, it must be owned, held Damaris fast and drew a step nearer the doorstone. But next moment he noted the Indian carried for weapons only a bow and two arrows, with which he could not kill all the settlement, and, moreover, at his heels tagged venturously Giles Hopkins and several of the other boys, and even Goodwife Billington, very clamorous, and the Governor's serving maid.

So Miles, not to be outdone by a petticoat, swaggered into the roadway and joined himself to the little group of curious folk, who, always ready to flee if he should turn on them, followed close at the savage's heels, down the steep hill, past Peter Browne's cottage, even to the door of the Common House.

The noise in the street had already disturbed the men at their conference, and they came flocking forth at the door, the Governor, the Elder, and the Captain, with a score of other stout fighters crowding behind them. But the Indian, never a whit abashed, strode boldly up to them, would even have pressed into the house, had not their ranks barred his passage. Nothing chilled, he halted, and, stretching forth his hands, spoke in a guttural tone: "Welcome."

"Do Indians talk English?" Miles whispered to Giles, who stood beside him. "Hush, hush, Damaris! The black man won't hurt you."

But Damaris, quite unconvinced, clutched Miles tightly round the neck and went on crying lustily, till at last Goodwife Billington seized him by the collar. "Thou good-for-naught lad!" she scolded. "Wilt thou kill the poor babe? Take her back to the house, thou runagate! Ay, ay, let her scream herself ill, so thou mayest gape and gaze. I would I had the up-bringing of thee!"

Some people besides himself liked to gape and gaze, Miles thought, but, without reply, he gathered the wailing Damaris into his arms and trudged slowly up the hill. There, by the Governor's house, it chanced he met with Francis and Jack and Joe, who, scenting something unusual in the village, had hastened back through the fields. "What is it has happened, Miles?" cried Joe.

Miles, glancing over his shoulder, saw with unkind satisfaction that the men had taken the savage into the Common House, out of sight. "'Twas naught," he said airily. "Just a great Indian came into town."

"Did you see him?" urged Francis. "Tell us about it."

I

"Humph! You've no wish to talk to me when I'm tending a baby," sniffed Miles, and trudged on to Master Hopkins's house, so elate at his triumph that he forgot to be angry with Damaris for dragging him away from the sport.

At the noon meal, indeed, he heard all and more than he could have learned, had he lingered about the door of the Common House, for Ned Lister was bubbling over with talk of the Indian. As Master Hopkins had stayed at the Common House and Dotey had none of his fellow-servant's faculty for gathering news, he proved the only tale-monger of the household ; so the whole family harked to him respectfully, and even Mistress Hopkins forgot her usual sarcasms on his galloping tongue.

"This is not a savage from these parts," Ned explained ; " he comes from the eastward, from Monhegan, whither the ships out of England go to fish. He has been on shipboard there and so has got a smattering of the English tongue. One Captain Dermer brought him to Cape Cod, and he has been in these parts now some eight months. And he told us a deal of the nations hereabout. This open place where we have settled is called Patuxet. It was a village of the savages once, but three or four years back came a great plague, and all the people died, so now we are undisputed masters of the soil. Next unto us dwell the Massasoits, a tribe of some sixty fighting men; and to the southeast, those savages whom our men gave a brush to on their explorations in December, are the Nausets, near a hundred strong."

Ned paused to secure himself another slice of cold mallard; then started on a new train: "You should 'a' seen the Indian fellow eat. He asked for beer, but we gave him strong water, and biscuit and butter and cheese and pudding, and a piece of mallard thereto, and he liked all very well, and ate right heartily."

"He is not the only idler who looks for a full meal," said Mistress Hopkins scathingly. "Where have they put the vile creature now?"

"Vile creature, mistress?" Ned repeated. "Sure, he says that in his own country he is a great lord of land, a Sagamore—"

"I would he were back in his own country," Mistress Hopkins answered sharply. "The murderous wretch! I shall not draw a breath in peace till he be hence. Here, Ned, 'tis little enough work you'll do if you go forth, do you stay this afternoon in the house to protect us."

There was an instant of disappointed silence on Lister's part, then, "'Tis you she means, Ned Dotey," he cried, and, without staying to take his cap, bolted out at the door.

Nor was this the only desertion which Mistress

Hopkins suffered; for, at their first opportunity, Dotey and Giles also slipped away, and Miles stayed behind only because he was so little that the mistress shook him when he attempted to follow. But speedily he had a bright thought, and asked Mistress Hopkins if perhaps, since she was afraid of the Indian, she would not like him to fetch Trug to the house to guard them.

Thus Miles was allowed, at last, to bring his dog home, and so grateful was he, that he remained patiently tending Damaris all the long afternoon. He found a certain enjoyment in his position, however; he was sole man in the cottage, and he wondered, should other Indians follow this first one, if Mistress Hopkins wouldn't let him take one of the muskets and fight for her. When it came dark at last, he knowingly inspected the fastenings of the door, and told Constance not to be afraid; he and Trug could defend them.

Poor Constance needed more comfort than that, for she was in a sorry fright. Her hands shook as she laid the table, and, when a step sounded crisply in the dooryard, she gave a nervous cry and dropped the pile of trenchers. It was only Ned Lister, however, who stamped in, bareheaded and whistling cheerfully.

"You have come back, then, since 'tis suppertime?" Mistress Hopkins greeted him sarcastically.

"Nay, I'm not hungry," Ned answered, as he sauntered over to the fire where Miles sat with Damaris, "'tis that the master sent me ahead to bid you make ready the guest chamber and the bed of state. Our Indian lord there, the Sagamore Samoset, is to lodge here to-night."

For a moment Mistress Hopkins looked at the speaker in dumb amazement. "If Master Hopkins does not punish you roundly for such a lie, Edward Lister," she said at last, deliberately, "it will not be for want of my urging him."

"It's the truth, though," Ned answered indifferently.

"O me!" Constance cried, with a sudden nervous wail, "I know we'll all be slain ere daybreak. O dear!" She turned to run into the bedroom, when Lister caught her by the arm. "Don't cry, Constance," he urged; "there's no need to fear. Captain Standish and some of the others are coming hither to spend the night and keep watch. You'll be safe enough."

But the girl, breaking from him, vanished into the chamber, whither Mistress Hopkins, snatching up Damaris, followed her; so, for some moments, Miles was free to ask questions and Ned to answer, as it liked them best. But, so soon as Master Hopkins's deliberate step sounded on the door-stone, Mistress Hopkins came forth and, as he entered the living room, confronted him : " Is that savage to be lodged here to-night, Stephen?   Among us, where my children are ? "

" He must go somewhere, Elizabeth," the master of the house replied unruffled. " He is set to stay among us for the night, and the tide is out so we may not convey him on shipboard. We can lodge him in the little closet next our chamber."

" He shall not come into the house ! " said Mistress Hopkins, with her thin lips set.

" Edward Lister, do you spread out the bed within the closet," Master Hopkins went on unheedingly.

With a wink at Miles, Ned crossed the room in unusual haste, and Miles, taking a candle, followed after into the closet, a tiny room with one black window, where stood an old chest and a hogshead and a rolled-up mattress, which Ned began leisurely to spread out. " What think you, Miles ? " he whispered, as the boy closed the door behind him. " It's good there is one person in the house whom the dame cannot rattle off as she list, eh ? "

Miles nodded vaguely, his attention all fixed on the least details of the commonplace room which now had a fearful interest from the guest it was to shelter. The thought of the savage stranger filled the place with such awesome fancies that he could not help going out from it very hastily ahead of

Lister, who grumbled a little that Miles was so speedy to be off with the candle.

Once in the bright living room, however, he became very brave indeed, and wondered to Giles Hopkins when the Sagamore Samoset would come. His mood grew the bolder when the elder lad showed him a dirk knife he had placed under his doublet. "For there's no being sure with these treacherous savages," Giles said seriously.

But when the Sagamore came at last, the boys found that the Hopkins household would be well guarded, for with him were not only Master Hopkins and Dotey, but big John Alden and Captain Standish. The very sight of the latter reassured Miles, so down he sat on the floor by the hearth, with his arm round Trug, who, as soon as he spied the Indian, bristled the hair on his back and uttered a throaty growl.

Mistress Hopkins and Constance and the two babies kept within the south chamber; but the men by themselves were enough to fill the living room. There were but two stools, besides the form on the hearth and a chest against the wall, so long-legged Giles must curl himself up on the floor by Miles, while Ned Lister set himself upon the table. They bade the Indian be seated on the form by the fire, right over against Miles, who, be sure, stared at him with eyes wide open.

The Sagamore Samoset, he saw, was a tall, straight man, of complexion like an English gypsy, smooth-faced, with coarse black hair that fell to his shoulders behind, but was cut before. Since his coming into the settlement, his English hosts had put upon him a horseman's coat, which he wore with much pride and dignity ; indeed, all his gestures and carriage were not only decent, but of a certain stateliness. " Why, he is somewhat like other men," Miles whispered softly to Giles, but Trug grumbled in his throat.

Only one candle was burning in the room, but the firelight cast a flickering brightness on the faces of the men. Captain Standish and Lister and the Indian had lighted pipes of tobacco, and the air was so heavy with the smell of the smoke that Miles half drowsed, but through his drooping eye-lids he watched his English comrades, and watched the Indian. Captain Standish was sitting adventurously right on the form beside the Sagamore, and now and again they spoke together. Miles noted that in the Indian's speech came strange words, which the Captain seemed to try to understand, and once or twice the Captain even sought to make use of them himself.

Miles wondered at this, and then his only wonderment was as to whether he had been asleep. The logs on the hearth had broken into red embers ;

the men had risen up; and, rubbing the heaviness from his eyes, Miles saw Master Hopkins and the Captain usher their Indian guest into the little closet room.

Straightway a certain tension in the company seemed to slacken; Giles rose stiffly from the floor, and Trug put down his head upon his paws, though he still kept one bright, half-opened eye fixed on the door through which the Indian had gone. With a great creaking of the trestles, Ned Lister dismounted from the table. "If he come to kill us," he said in a low tone to Alden, "do you run in and call me so I can have a share in the scuffle." Then, stretching himself mightily, he disappeared into the north bedroom, where the serving men and the boys of the household slept.

"Since you have two others to keep watch with you, Master Hopkins," spoke the Captain, as he took down his hat from the wall, "I'll go walk a turn about the hill. I'll be back ere the half-hour is up."

He had put his hand to the latch, when Miles, on the impulse, sprang to his feet and ran to him. "May I come too, sir?" he whispered.

"You, Miles? Why, you were better in bed. Nay, come if you like."

Out of doors the air was crispy and silent, and pleasant smelling after the smoky atmosphere of the crowded room. Overhead the stars were dense and bright, but below, the lonely little settlement lay in darkness, with never a spark of a candle showing. "How late is it, Captain Standish?" Miles asked, in a hushed voice.

"I should say it was near on to midnight," the other replied, stepping along so briskly that Miles's breath for talking was lost in the effort to keep pace with him.

Up and up they toiled; past Goodman Billington's cottage; past the black cabin where Alden and the Captain lived; and then by the well-trodden path up the sheer hillside, till the planking of the broad platform sounded hollow beneath their feet, and they stood among the guns. The spark in the Captain's pipe gleamed red in the darkness, but Miles could not see the Captain's features; he perceived only that he turned his face from quarter to quarter, and remained longest gazing into the black west, where the ridge of hills ran jagged against the starry sky.

He watched the Captain's movements, but he did not venture to speak till Standish himself broke out: "Well, there'll come no bands to frighten us this night, I take it. We can march home, Miles. We've a fair starlight to make the march under," he added, and, as they stepped from the platform to the yielding turf, lingered an instant to gaze skyward.

"Which is it that is the North Star, sir ? " Miles hesitated.

"Why, that one yonder, lad. You know it well."

"I knew 'twas the North Star in England. I knew not if 'twere the same here. It is such a long ways from home."

"It's the same sky, Miles, and the same Heaven, I take it, that we had over us in England."

Miles threw back his head and once more stared up into the sky, that was so vast it made him shrink and feel smaller even than before. He sighed a little, he scarcely knew why, and put his hand on the Captain's sleeve. Standish took Miles's hand in his, and so kept hold on him as they came down from the hill, and in that pressure was something so comforting that Miles was sorry when they reached the door of Master Hopkins's house.

Within was heavy air, and a dull fire, and sleepy faces ; Giles had gone to lie down on his bed, and it did not need the Captain's bidding to send Miles blinking after. Once, in the darkness, he was wakened by hearing Lister protest inarticulately that he would rather have his throat cut in his sleep ten times over than rise and watch ; and once Miles guessed hazily that some one was shaking him, and he tried to say he was getting up, and in the midst dropped back on his pillow.

At the last the dazzle of warm sunlight on his face, and the rattle, rattle of trenchers, brought him staggering and blinking to his feet. Oh, yes, he remembered; the Sagamore Samoset had been there last night; but he was not afraid of him, especially since 'twas daylight; indeed, he wanted to see him again, so out he rushed into the living room.

"Well, sleepyhead!" Constance laughed at him, and Mistress Hopkins was beginning to scold him because he had not awakened, for all her efforts, till mid-morning, when Ned Lister sauntered in. "His Lordship the Indian is safe departed, Constance," he said consolingly, as he made a slow business of getting an axe from the chimney corner. "They gave him a knife and a bracelet and a ring, and he is gone away content."

"A good riddance, too!" snapped Mistress Hopkins. "And now do you, Edward Lister, fetch two buckets of water and wash out the place where the creature lodged. To bring such heathen under a Christian roof! I hope I never set eyes on another of the coppery wretches again."

Ned shrugged his shoulders and said nothing till his mistress was quite done; then he added meekly: "I misremembered; he said he was coming back again in a night or two, and next time he is going to bring with him a goodly number from the tribe of the Massasoits."

CHAPTER X

SAMOSET proved as good as his word. The very next morning, for all it was Sunday, back he came, and with him five other tall Indians, who were even more wonderful fellows than he, for they were clad in skins of deer or of wild-cat, and had dressed their hair with feathers, and painted their faces in black streaks. To divert their English hosts, they sang and danced, which Master Hopkins called a violation of the sanctity of the day, but Miles privately thought most edifying.

He was even better pleased when that night, at the departure of his comrades, Samoset was ill or feigned to be, so, spite of Mistress Hopkins, he must be sheltered in her husband's house. Thus for three days Miles dwelt under the same roof with a live Indian, and ate at the same board, till he came to have not the least tremor at sight of a copper-colored face. Indeed, he neglected every task he was set, to dog the Indian guest about the street and make shy efforts at talk with him, and he was heartily grieved when at last, on Wednesday, Samoset went away into the forest.

"No doubt he'll come again, the mistress always makes him so welcome," Ned Lister consoled Miles, "and each time he goes, for his further encouragement, they give him a present. This morning they gave him a hat and shoes and stockings, and a shirt and a loin cloth. I take it, 'tis because I am what Master Hopkins calls a son of Belial that it makes me to laugh, when I think of Sagamore Samoset in an English headpiece with a flapping brim."

"I'm mighty sorry he went," sighed Miles, uncomforted. "I was learning the Indian words, so I could talk to him presently, like Captain Standish. 'Cossaquot,' that means *bow*; and 'et chossucke' is *a knife*; and 'petuckquanocke' is *bread*; and —"

Ned yawned suggestively, and fell to work again. He and Miles that afternoon were busied in the spaded garden patch at the north end of the dooryard, where they were pressing the seeds into the soft earth. The sun was hot, and, as Miles worked, he smeared his warm face with his fingers, till Ned assured him he was all streaked brown, like an Indian.

But though it was hot and dirty labor, it was far manlier than to be ever dandling a baby; so Miles toiled on earnestly, spite of Ned's indolent example, and did not pause even to stretch his cramped legs or straighten his aching back till mid-afternoon. Then he started up at a noise of people hurrying through the street, the sound of a quick footstep, the rattle of the house-door.

" 'Tis Master Hopkins has taken his musket and gone forth," spoke Ned, who was lounging farther down the garden. " Somewhat's afoot." Away he went to look into the matter, and Miles ran stiffly after.

Out in the street the men and boys, and even one or two girls, were hastening toward the bluff above the spring. As they went, a confused talking spread among them, from which Miles learned that yonder, on the great wooded hill across the brook, Indians had been seen, — Indians who brandished their bows and whetted their arrows in defiance. Captain Standish and Master Hopkins and two men from the *Mayflower* had gone down to cross the brook and parley with them. Look, yonder they went now !

From where the company had halted, high up beyond Goodman Cooke's cottage, Miles could see the bright river and the hill opposite, thick with unleaved woods. Up its base wound slowly the little band of Englishmen, now half-screened, now wholly visible ; but Miles looked from them, higher up the slope, where the bare branches were agitated, as if something moved among them. " 'Tis the savages!" said one; but, strain his eyes as he would, Miles saw through the bushes only the sad-colored English doublets.

Yet, with an anxiety he scarcely comprehended, the men lingered on the bluff, watching and discussing in grave tones, till the Captain and his followers came toilsomely up the path from the spring. They had seen naught; the savages had not suffered them draw nigh them, Captain Standish explained, so briefly that he seemed curt, while his puckered brows still were bent on the slope whence the Indians had sent their defiance.

Slowly the little group of curious and troubled people scattered, some of the weightier ones to speak with the Governor and the Captain, others to simpler tasks. Miles went back to his garden, but the sunlight had now left that corner of the yard. The great hill, where stood the guns, looked black against the sky, and there seemed in all out-of-doors a menace that made him glad at dusk to get within the house. Throughout supper the men kept from speaking of the savages with an elaborateness that made their silence the more suspicious, and the unspoken anxiety wrought on Miles till at bedtime he smuggled Trug into the chamber and made the dog lie near him.

Next morning, in the clear sunlight, Miles's courage revived mightily, but his elders still looked sober. None the less, whether Indians threatened or no, the work of the colony must be done: all the morning men and boys trudged about their tasks, though none went far afield; and after the noon meal the men gathered once more at the Common House, to consider the public business which the first coming of Samoset had broken off.

Oceanus was ailing that afternoon and needed his mother, so Miles had to mind Damaris for a dreary hour. As he sat with her upon the doorstone, he spied a noiseless little group of some five Indians passing down the street, and, alert at once, he begged leave to run see what might happen; but Mistress Hopkins, all a-tremble herself, forbade him venture out while those bloodthirsty wretches were abroad, and even made him come in and shut the door fast.

But speedily there sounded a rattling knock to which the mistress must open, and in came the men of the household, so hurriedly that straight-way the living room was in confusion. For the great Sagamore Massasoit, with his brother Qua-dequina and sixty warriors, was at hand, just across the brook. One of the Indians, Squanto, who could speak English, had gone back to bid him enter the settlement, and the men of the colony must get under arms to receive him; perhaps even to defend themselves, Master Hopkins let a word fall.

K

There followed a great throwing-on of buff-jackets and buckling of sword-belts, while Giles, newly appointed drummer to the colony, rattled over the pots and kettles in a meaningless search for his drumsticks, which some one had surely moved from the place where he left them. Oceanus wailed, Damaris, indignant at being neglected, screamed aloud, Trug barked, and Mistress Hopkins scolded, but somehow, in the midst of the hurly-burly, the three men equipped themselves and tramped away; and right at their heels went Giles, with the drumsticks which Constance had found.

But the door closed behind them and shut Miles, a soldier in name only, in with the women and children for another tedious hour. Damaris found little rest in his arms those minutes, while he ran from the western window, whence he could see a bit of the street and the path to the spring, to the eastern window, whence, far down the street, he beheld the men gathered in martial line, all in armor, which glimmered bravely in the afternoon sun.

He was still gazing down the street when Constance, who had ventured to the other window, called to him in a terrified voice: "Miles! Oh, Miles! Come hither. 'Tis Indians indeed. Hundreds of them!"

With no wish to see further, the girl drew away

from the western window, and Miles thrust eagerly into her place. Yes, there were Indians indeed, swarms of them, it seemed at first sight, so he flinched back a little from the casement. For they were filing past the house, and that brought them so near that Miles could see even the grotesque figures in which their faces were painted. But soon he perceived English musketeers marshalling them, and he saw, too, that the savages were unarmed. Their mission must be peaceful, he judged; so, eager and unafraid, he stared at them, and was sorry when the last one disappeared down the street.

Just then, as he turned from the window, sounded the tap, tap of a drum. "It is the Governor and the rest of the men with drum and trumpet marching up the street," spoke Constance from the eastern casement. "They have led the savages into the unfinished cottage by the Common House, and now they are going in to them."

Miles, at her side, squirmed with impatience. "There's Jack yonder beneath the cottage window," he exclaimed, "and Francis and Joe. And there's such a deal to see. And I'm sure they are all good, harmless Indians." He gave a glance toward the bedroom, where he could hear Mistress Hopkins lulling Oceanus, then whispered Constance: "Won't you mind Damaris? I'll tell you all about it when I come back."

"I see not why you wish to go forth at such a time, but I'll do 't for you. Run quick, ere stepmother stop you," answered kind-hearted Constance; and away sped Miles.

Still, he was too late to share in the main excitement, for when he came into the yard of the unfinished house, he found the door fast shut and all the great folk, white or copper-colored, gone within. Only two musketeers remained outside to keep watch, and Edward Dotey, who was one of them, proved so unsympathetic as to cuff Francis Billington when he tried to get a peep in at the window. Much discouraged, for where saucy Francis failed to go there was no hope for the others, the small boys of the colony gathered in a patient little group in the dooryard to talk of these great happenings.

"Master Winslow has gone out amongst the Indians," said Jack, "and they're holding him as hostage for their old King. 'Twas right valiant of him —"

"Pooh! The Captain would 'a' gone just as quick," Miles retorted jealously. "There's naught to be afraid of, anyway. I would I were Giles Hopkins, and stood there in the house with the savages."

"My father is in there too," spoke little Love Brewster, who had attached himself to Miles, "but he is so good I do not think even an Indian would hurt him. But there were very many of them, and if my mother had come close to see, I am sure she would have been afraid. Perhaps I were best go home and tell her there's no need to fear. You come with me, pray you, Miles."

Young Rigdale had no wish to take his eyes from the door of the house, but plainly the little boy was fearful enough to want his company up the street, so he went with him, and at the Elder's cottage stayed a moment to reassure the women grandly.

Dolly had no interest in Indians, since she found in the case of Samoset that they did not carry about with them a store of pretty baskets, such as the one her father had brought her; but Priscilla Mullins was eager to know everything, and questioned Miles and listened to him most flatteringly, till he offered: "If you wish to go forth and view the Indians, Priscilla, I'll go and take care of you."

Whereat young Mistress Mullins laughed, and, slipping her hand under his chin, kissed him for his courtesy, " like a baby."

Red and indignant, Miles flung out of the house; then forgot the insult, as he saw Giles, with a platter in his hand, hurrying up the street from Governor Carver's cottage. "What are you doing there?" he called, running to intercept the elder lad.

"Fresh meat," panted Giles. "The Governor

wished it for the King.   I had this bit of a goose from Mistress Carver, and now I've remembered a mallard I saw stepmother set to boil."

It took him very few minutes to hurry into his father's house, and out again with a second larger platter balanced in one hand, but, short as the space was, Miles had laid a plan.   Stepping up to Giles, he took from him Mistress Carver's dish of meat. "Let me aid you," he proffered innocently.

"So that's what you're scheming," laughed Giles ; but he let Miles, under that pretext, come at his side down the street, past the little group of envious boys, up the doorstone of the unfinished cottage, and so into the very council chamber.

The room was close and hazy with smoke from the pipes of tobacco that the King and the chief of the English puffed at, but, spite of the dimness, Miles speedily made out the shapes of the Indians. Black, red, yellow, and white, their faces were partly or wholly smeared with paint, and, through the wavering smoke-wreaths, their look was so grim that for an instant he hesitated on the threshold.

But Giles went on, so he followed, across the room, between what seemed endless rows of Indians in hairy skins who stood or squatted on the floor, up to the table, where sat a tall, stalwart savage. Imitating Giles, Miles set down his dish of meat before him, and, with an agitated bow, drew back to the wall, where he wedged himself in between Lister and young Hopkins. "That's the King, yonder at table," the latter whispered him softly.

He did not look at all as Miles thought a king should look, that savage at the table. He wore a scant covering of skins,—a dress like that of his followers, save that the King had also about his neck a great chain of white bone beads. His face was painted a dark red; and face and head alike were oiled so he looked greasy; he fed untidily with his fingers, and sometimes, when he would give a morsel to one of his followers, rent the meat with his hands.

But, for all he seemed so busy with feeding, his quick eyes were darting about the smoky room,— now resting on the Governor, who sat at table near him; now on the English musketeers who lined the walls,—and, to Miles's thinking, the King looked on them timorously; now on his own fol- lowers, who crowded silently about him. One of the Indians, squatting on the floor, held in his hands the English trumpet, on which he tried to blow, and, for a moment, the King paused to hark with a child's wonder to his efforts, then once more began tearing Mistress Hopkins's mallard.

When nothing but bones was left of the bird, Giles slipped the platters from the table, and now the serious work of the conference seemed to begin.

Up from the floor behind the table, where they had
sat, rose two savages, who should interpret between
Massasoit and the Governor; the one was a stranger, probably that Squanto whom Master Hopkins
had mentioned; the other, Miles's old acquaintance,
Samoset. A transformed Samoset, however, with
an English felt hat low on his brows and an English shirt worn over his meagre native garments
after the manner of a carter's frock. Ned Lister,
standing rigid and soldierly against the wall, took
Miles a sudden dig in the ribs, and winked at
him with a " Didn't I tell you as much " expression.

Miles, on his good behavior, neither looked at
him nor smiled, but fixed his gaze on the men
about the table. The sun had now shifted down
the sky, so a great bar of light thrust in at the
western window. The yellow brightness flecked
across Elder Brewster's grizzled head, made Governor Carver's stiff ruff even more dazzlingly white,
and gleamed back again from Captain Standish's
steel corselet. It rested, too, on the papers which
Master William Bradford had laid on the table
before him, but Master Bradford's grave face, as he
bent forward to write what the Governor bade, was
in shadow. The features of Massasoit, too, were
dark to see, but here and there, as the sunlight,
bursting through the smoke, wavered across the

room, the painted face or coppery bare shoulders of one of his followers stood out.

The two interpreters jerked out the gutturals of their outlandish tongue, to which the King grunted assent, or now and again the Governor spoke a measured word. But outside the window a bird was singing in a high, purling strain; and Miles wondered if it were a fat, red-breasted bird, and thought more on its song and on the motes that swam in the sunlight, than on what the Governor was saying.

After all, he was glad when the conference broke up. He was tired of standing stiffly, and the air of the room was heavy; and the Indians, when they neither ate nor played with trumpets, but just sat stolid, were a bit stupid. He scuffed softly but impatiently at the rear of the train, as the company filed forth; the Governor and the King, side by side, went first, and then, all in some semblance of order, the Indian warriors and the English leaders and soldiery.

Outside, a guard of honor formed about the Governor and his guest, and gave them fitting escort to the brook; but Miles remained behind and roused the envy of his mates, with an account of what he had seen, till, in fickle fashion, they forsook him at the coming of a second guest, Quadequina, the brother of Massasoit, who, in his turn, would have a taste of English hospitality. He could not, however, compare in dignity and importance with Massasoit; he was just a tall, comely young savage, who liked English biscuit and strong waters, but liked the English muskets so little that his hosts good-naturedly laid them aside. Massasoit was not cowardly like that, Miles assured his comrades; Massasoit was every inch a king, and it was a mighty honor to have been in the same room with him.

Quadequina had been but a short time gone, and the long shadows were filling the river valley with a grayness, when back across the brook, quite un-ruffled by his long detention, came Master Edward Winslow. His fellow-colonists might be glad to see him, and he to return unscathed to them, but he carried it laughingly. He was all sound, save that he was uncommon hungry, — Miles, following admiringly, caught a scrap of his speech to Captain Standish, — the Indians had tried to buy the armor off his back and the sword from his side, and he knew not but he might have sold them for a mess of pottage, only he saw no such savory viand among the savages, nor anything, indeed, but groundnuts.

Now that Master Winslow was returned, the colonists released the Indians whom they had held as hostages for him, and sent them away. Save only Samoset and Squanto, no Indians were suffered to remain in the settlement, but the rumor went that King Massasoit and all his people had encamped for the night on the wooded hill across the brook, so a strict watch was set.

"Do you think there will be fighting yet?" Miles questioned Giles, as they walked home to supper. "Quadequina was afeard of our muskets. I take it, we could beat those Indians."

"To be sure, there'll be no fighting," answered Giles, as he tucked his drum under one arm in a professional way. "We've struck a truce with the savages."

Later, at supper, Miles heard it all explained. This was a dolorous meal, for the meat had been devoured by his Majesty, Massasoit, and Mistress Hopkins was ill-tempered and rated Miles for running away that afternoon, and, to add to her discomfort, Samoset came blandly to sup with his old entertainers. "This has been an ill day such as I wish never to see the like of again," fretted the poor woman.

"It is a happy day for our colony," said Master Hopkins gravely. "Do you not realize, Elizabeth, that we have this afternoon made a peace with our heathen neighbors that, by the will of Heaven, shall prove lasting? King Massasoit has covenanted that none of his people shall do us harm as we go abroad; and, if he be attacked, we shall aid in his defense, or if other tribe of savages assail us, he shall do us the like service. Yea, the hand of Providence has been with us this day. Yesternight it was all menace; but to-night we can hope for peace."

Miles, in his place at table, looked at Samoset, very solemn in his funny shirt and hat, and, blinking sleepily at the candle, took little concern for the earnestness of Master Hopkins's words. He scarcely realized that this was almost the second founding day of New Plymouth; but he did know that he had stood within arm's reach of King Massasoit, an exploit of which no other boy in the colony could boast; and, when he went to bed, he dreamed all night of red and blue and green Indians.

CHAPTER XI

EVEN Mistress Hopkins must at last somewhat overcome her fear of the savages, else her life would have been miserable beyond endurance. For Massasoit having plainly made the treaty in good faith, his people were ready at all times to visit their English allies and eat of their food. Coppery faces grew so common a sight in the single street of New Plymouth that each boy in the colony had his own little tale of a friendly Indian encounter, and Miles Rigdale was no longer alone in his experiences.

Still further to rob Miles of his prestige among his fellows, his own particular Indian, the Sagamore Samoset, with his hat and his shirt, which he used in wet weather to remove carefully, lest they be damaged, took himself off to his own land to the eastward; and Miles found no one to fill his place.

To be sure, Plymouth had now a resident pensioner in the Indian Squanto, but he lived with Master Bradford, and so was accessible to other boys as well as to Miles. "I see not why he is let dwell among us," the latter said jealously, in the early days of Squanto's stay.

"Because, if he were any but a heathen, one might say this land where we have planted belongs to him," Master Hopkins made a brief explanation, which to Miles was no explanation at all.

But later, of a morning when Master Hopkins's force of laborers was busied in building a fence round the garden patch, Giles, who had listened to the talk of his elders, took the trouble to set forth the substance of it to Miles. "You'll understand, this Squanto truly belongs at Plymouth. Back in the time when an Indian village, Patuxet, stood where we have settled, he dwelt here. But there came an Englishman named Hunt —"

"Who was rather more of a knave than even a trader should be," parenthesized Ned Lister, who, seated comfortably on the ground near by, was hammering the palings together.

"He was a scoundrel," said Giles, warmly. "He toled Squanto and nineteen others from Patuxet, and some from among the Nausets, on board his ship, pretending he would truck with them ; and then he hoisted sail and steered away for Spain, where he sold them all for twenty pound apiece. But somehow this fellow Squanto made shift to reach England, where a good merchant of London cared for him. 'Twas there he came by the knowledge of our tongue that he has. And at last they sent him back hither to his own country ; but meantime the plague had been among them at Patuxet, and all were dead."

"The Lord removed the heathen to make way for a better growth," said Dotey, who had just come thither with an armful of fresh palings.

" Truly ? " muttered Ned Lister. " Then I'm thinking the Lord in His wisdom laid His hand pretty heavily on the poor silly savages just for our profit."

There was little enough love already between Lister and Dotey, so Giles headed off a possibly bitter argument by continuing hastily : " So, as my father says, Squanto is, in a way, the owner of the land here, and as such has a right to shelter and food amongst us."

Miles listened to this story with a grave, stolid face, such as the others kept, and made no word of comment. But afterward he thought much of what had been told him, and wondered if Squanto had had a wife and copper-colored babies, and had come home to find them dead. He felt sorry for the poor, lone Indian, and watched him with new sympathy ; but to all appearances Squanto was more occupied in consuming English biscuit and butter than in grieving for his lost friends.

Whether or no he had a claim upon the English, the Indian speedily showed himself able to repay them for any kindness.   He told the men how they must wait yet some days before they planted their corn, and how there would then be plenty of fish in the river, which they must set with the seed ; and much more that was useful.   But nothing of the Indian's arts impressed Miles so much as his prowess in eel-catching, for he would go often into the forest and return, after a few hours, with fat, sweet eels, as many as he could lift in one hand.

Of an afternoon in April, nearly a fortnight after the coming of Massasoit, Ned Lister and Giles Hopkins went to the southward with Squanto on such a fishing trip, and, as Miles was very eager to share in it, they let him come too.   Their course took them over steep, wooded hills, where always they had blue water close on the left hand, and, looking back over their shoulders, could see the bay of Plymouth, with its flanking headlands.   A tender leafage was upon the trees, and in the southern hollows, where the birds sang, the air was warm ; but on each hilltop a chillier blast stung in the faces of the fishermen and urged them to trudge more briskly.

At length they came to a gully, where two hills curved into each other, and descended it, half running, to the bank of a small river that flowed seaward through a level reach.   Here was where the eels dwelt, Squanto gave his companions to understand ; and then, without spear or any implement, he waded gently into the quiet water. The three English-born, from the bank, watched him intently, yet they scarcely realized how he did it, when he suddenly made a swift dart forward, and rose with a long, slimy thing writhing in his hands.

"Do you just tread 'em out with your feet, Squanto?" Ned queried after a time, as, keeping pace with the savage, they trailed along the bank.

When the Indian gave an "Um" that implied assent, Ned presently suggested: "Say we venture it, lads. It has a simple seeming. Tell us, Squanto, can a white man take eels that way?"

"White man try," advised Squanto, stolidly. He had caught enough for a mess, so he probably thought that the splashings of the English fellows would do no harm now.

Ned and Giles, stripping off shoes and stockings, waded in; and Miles, not to be outdone, followed after. The water felt stingingly cold against his bare legs, and set his teeth chattering so he could not talk. The very ooze of the river bed was clammy; and then he suddenly found his tongue and gave a frightened scream, as his toes touched something that rolled beneath them.

"Did you take one, Miles?" cried Giles Hopkins, splashing to the spot.

"I d-d-don't know," chattered Miles, from the shore where he had sought refuge.

Giles spattered to and fro a moment. "'Twas naught but an old branch," he announced contemptuously.

"It was an eel," retorted Miles, "but, to be sure, he will not stand there the day long till you choose to come seek him."

With that he forced himself to put his purpling feet into the water again, but, spite of this brave showing, Ned and Giles would chaff him on his flight, and even Squanto looked amused at the conduct of the youngest of his allies.

Yet, for all they were so ready to laugh at him, Miles noted his English comrades did not take a single eel, and that gave him a kind of comfort. But even then there was little pleasure in wading through the icy water, in the expectation of stepping on a soft, squirming thing; so he was not sorry when Ned gave the order to take up the homeward march.

The east wind, that had turned chillier as sunset drew on, smote bleakly on the hilltops, and in the hollows, where the shadows were creeping through the undergrowth, the warmth had died out of the air. The gathering darkness pressed ever closer upon the fishermen; the sea on their right turned gray and dim; the blue faded from the sky, and the green of the distant headlands of the bay changed to black. Just off the beach point they could dimly make out a dark bulk, where a single speck of light showed — the old ship *Mayflower*.

"They say she'll be hoisting sail for home soon," Giles spoke, as they trudged through the twilight, with a surety that his comrades knew to what he referred.

"So soon as the wind swings round into the west," answered Ned. "Then she'll up sail, and it's 'Eastward, ho!'"

Then presently, in the dusk, Ned began whistling a sorry little tune, unlike those he was wont to sing, very slow and monotonous, with a sudden rising to a high note and as sudden a sinking again, like the sharp indrawing of breath in a sob. "What song is that, Ned?" Miles asked, because he would rather hear Lister talk than whistle that pitiable strain.

"'Tis the Hanging-tune, Miley; the one to which they set the last confessions of men who are condemned to die." He fell to whistling once more and half humming the words: —

> "'Fortune, my foe,
> Why dost thou frown on me?'"

and Miles harked to the tune till it went crying itself through his head.

Next morning it still came back to him keenly, — the walk in the twilight, the look of the distant ship, the woful minor of the Hanging-tune. For the wind was hauling round to westward, and of a sudden Indians and gardening and house-building ceased to be matters that men talked of in the street; instead they spoke of the going of the ship that had borne them from England.

Already she had stayed longer on their shores than any had expected, because of the sickness that had been among her crew. But now, on shore and on ship, the sickness was stayed; just half the settlers lay buried on the bluff, and the crew of the *Mayflower* mustered in diminished numbers, yet enough survived and in recovered health to work the ship back to England. With the first favoring wind she would set forth upon her voyage; and with that bit of sure information went another, that Master Jones had offered to take home in her any one of the settlers who might wish to go.

"Right generous of him, is 't not?" Ned Lister spoke bitterly to Miles. "Who does he think is going with him? The Elder and the Governor and Master Bradford, all the chiefs, if they showed their faces in England, they'd be clapped up in prison. And the lesser men, or even our great Master Hopkins here, they've ventured all their substance in this plantation. If they go back, they must starve or beg in London streets, and 'tis as easy and pleasant to starve here. There's none in the settlement I know of has the wish to go home, save myself, and I cannot go, because I've sold my time to Hopkins, the more fool I!"

"Why did you ever come hither, if you hate it so?" Miles questioned.

"Because a penny fell wrong side up," Ned answered. "I woke up in London one fine morning, with no shirt to my back and but one penny in my pocket. 'It's either 'list for the wars, or get me into a new country and start afresh,' I said, so I tossed up the penny, — heads Bohemia, tails America. It fell tails; so I sold Stephen Hopkins my three years' time in return for my passage over. And a precious fool I was! Faith, I'd liefer dig ditches in England than play even at governor here. And so soon as my time's out!"

Miles listened soberly, but with no sympathy; he did not understand why a tall, grown fellow like Ned should think on home with such longing. He did not care himself; he had come to New Plymouth to live, and he looked forward to the departure of the *Mayflower* as a novel happening in the round of everyday occurrences.

Yet when it befell, it seemed quite a matter-of-fact event. A clear breezy morning it was, and, as the household sat at their early breakfast, Francis Cooke came leisurely to tell Master Hopkins that the wind was setting steady from the west, and Master Jones had rowed ashore to bid his former passengers good-by; so soon as the tide was at flood, the ship would put forth.

There was wood and water to fetch as every day; and Miles did the tasks hastily. As he came down the path by Cooke's house, he could feel the wind stirring his hair, and yonder in the harbor the waves were ruffling, and the dim old sails of the *Mayflower*, unfurled, bellied in the gusts.

When he had set the dripping bucket within the living room, he ran down toward the bluff, to see what more was to see, but, finding his playmates lingering by the door of the Common House, he joined them. Within the house, they told him, Master Jones was drinking a friendly draught with the colonists, and taking his leave. Presently, indeed, the Master, a low, broad-shouldered figure, in his wide breeches and loose jacket, came forth, attended by most of the men of the colony, and rolled off to the landing place.

Some of the boys straggled respectfully behind their elders, but Miles raced with those who ran to be first at the landing. There, alongside the rock, rode the ship's longboat, and Will Trevor and several of the lesser men stood talking with the sailors who sat in her. The youngsters, too, would gladly have borne a part, but the Master, coming right on their heels across the sand, broke up the little group; he was speaking boisterously with the

Governor, so his loud voice could be heard even above the confusion of the embarkation.

Indeed, it was all so noisy and hurried that nothing of those last moments remained clear in Miles's mind; he remembered only that men spoke of letters and packets, and the Master wished them many a "God be wi' you," and there was a bustling to and fro and a deal of hand-shaking. Then the Master, sitting in the stern seat, was cursing at his sailors; the width of blue water between the longboat and the landing rock was increasing; and for a moment Miles watched mechanically the sway and swing of the seamen's bodies, as, bending to their oars, they rowed the boat away.

When at length he turned slowly about, he was aware that, halfway up the rugged slope of the bluff, a little group of women, all that survived in the colony, were standing, and the children with them. He scrambled up to be with Dolly, why, he could not say, only somehow he wanted to be sure she was safe and near him then; and he noted Mistress Carver, who sat upon a stone with her hands clasped tensely in her lap, and Priscilla Mullins, whose hair blew unheeded about her face, while she gazed out to sea.

He almost stumbled over Wrestling Brewster and the little Samson boy, who had sat down on the turf and unconcernedly were playing with some bright pebbles; but he did not pause to speak to Wrestling, just clambered a few feet higher up the bluff, where Dolly, holding to Mistress Brewster's gown, stood with her wistful face turned seaward. "Look you closely, Dolly," he greeted her. "See, they're hoisting sail on board the *Mayflower*."

Dolly, pressing up to him, whispered for her only reply: "Do you mind, Miles, how we came in on the ship, and mammy and daddy with us? I wish we'd all stayed in England."

"Now hush, Dolly," Miles admonished in a gruff tone, and scowled vexedly as the little sister, hiding her face against his doublet, began to cry. Then, half pitying, he bent to speak to her, when a sudden gasp, as if the women about him all drew in their breath, made him look to the harbor. There he saw the *Mayflower*, with the western wind swelling her dingy sails, had heaved up anchor, and was heading out upon the ocean.

The sun was bright and made the dirty sails gleam like silver; the water was blue, and the wind was brisk; and the ship stood seaward swiftly, very swiftly. Miles thought on how she had set forth from Southampton; and he knew that on board men would be clattering across her deck, and hauling at ropes, and the Master would be bellowing orders.

But on shore a great silence had fallen. The

most careless of the men had no word to say, while of the graver sort some had bowed their heads, and some, coming higher up the bluff, had drawn close to their wives and children. For a moment there was no sound save the lap of waves about the great gray landing rock, and the swish of shingle as the swell receded; then suddenly one of the women — it was Mistress White, six weeks a widow, who stood with her baby in her arms and her other little child holding to her skirts — burst out sobbing.

Miles gazed about him in wonder. Why, men never cried; Captain Standish's face now was hard as a stone; and he himself had not the least inclination to shed a tear. But among the women round him was a stifled weeping, so anguishing for being half suppressed, that some pity mingled with his contempt, and, with a feeling that he was ashamed to listen, he slipped away from the bluff. He thought he were best run up on the great hill to watch the *Mayflower* depart; and he found that his friend Jack and several other boys had had the same thought.

All together they raced up the street to see who should gain the hilltop first, and by the time they came thither, with laughing and struggling, had clean forgot their elders, who, from the bluff below, watched the receding ship through a dazzle of tears. From the top of the hill the lads could see the white sail of the *Mayflower* in the offing, out beyond Sagaquab, speeding ever farther into the horizon; but Miles never saw it vanish, for Francis Billington had discovered a nest of snakes at the other side of the hill; so, in the midst of their watching, the boys must run thither and look upon the wriggling little creatures, then scrupulously stone them all to death.

When Miles clambered again to the hilltop, there was never a distant glimmer of a sail upon the sea; but he could not think of the ship's departure sadly, with the day so fair and his time at his disposal. He felt hungry, though, so he ran down to the house a moment to eat his dinner; and, for all it was long past the noon hour, he found no dinner ready.

Ned was out by the woodpile, nailing together a hand-barrow, with a sudden fierce spurt of energy, but he was in a sulky temper; and within the house Constance went about with her eyes red. She gave Miles a piece of bread in his hand, and bade him run away and eat it; stepmother had shut herself in her chamber, and father was with her, trying to comfort her. "I see not why you all make such a to-do because the old ship has sailed," Miles spoke, with his mouth full.

"Because we're left alone. Because no ship will come ere the autumn. Maybe it will never come,"

Constance burst out, with sudden passionateness. "And we are here, and home is there, and the ship has gone. You'd understand, if you were older."

No, Miles did not understand yet. What with the excitement and the change, in spite of the sad bearing of those about him, the meaning of it all did not come home to him till next morning. He had risen early with the others and run forth to fetch wood for the morning fire. The sun was just reddening the horizon line, but the rest of the world looked faint and gray. A white mist, rolling off the fields, was shrinking away inland from the sea whence it had come. But out to sea he could distinguish clearly the dusky beach point, and the islands and — There he rubbed his eyes. No, it was no trick of the mist. There was the old anchoring ground, but it was empty; the clumsy, old, dark hulk was gone.

Miles walked on to the woodpile, trying hard to whistle, but the only strain that came was a sorry snatch in a minor key, — the Hanging-tune. The chill of the dawning struck into his bones. Once more he looked to the anchoring ground that was vacant; then he sat down suddenly among the damp logs. He did not cry, — he was too big and old for that, — but he leaned his folded arms against a log, and hid his face between them.

CHAPTER XII

"TO be sure, though, I was not weeping," Miles declared to Constance, who came out from the house to see why he tarried so long at the woodpile, "for I never even thought on going back to England."

He little guessed that, at one time, the leaders of the colony had spoken seriously of returning Dolly and himself to the home-country. But Master Hopkins had urged that, in such case, the children might be drawn back into the faith of the Church of England, from which their father had sought to snatch them; and Elder Brewster had added that it was a weary journey for such little folk, and no prospect at the end save of hard fare among grudging kindred.

John Rigdale left no near relatives; and his distant cousins, to whom the children would have to go, were poor tenant-farmers, just as he had been, who would find it burdensome to feed two more mouths. For Miles and Dolly, not only would childhood prove hard and laborious, but there would be nothing better to look forward to; as the boy grew to manhood, he could hope only to toil for daily hire on some farmer's land. "Unless he fling away his soul's welfare by going as a mercenary in some iniquitous foreign war," said Master Isaac Allerton; whereat Captain Standish smiled a little behind his beard, but made no answer.

But here in New Plymouth, though Miles would have plenty of work to do, he would have, as his inheritance from his father, a claim to a share of land and of whatever cattle or other property the settlers should hereafter hold in common. By the time he was a man, there would be enough for him to have a small farm of his own, where he could live in more comfort than he would have known in England; and, till he was grown, Master Hopkins was willing to feed and shelter him, in return for what labor he could do.

As for Dolly, her case was simple enough, for if Miles stayed, she stayed; and Mistress Brewster was quite determined that the little girl should stay in no house but hers. So the *Mayflower* sailed away, and Miles Rigdale, with his little household, remained behind; and he never dreamed that people had thought of continuing the colony without his aid.

The boy had some cause to rate his services highly, for, in the weakened condition of the settle-

ment, every atom of strength had to be used, and
tasks were set for him as seriously as for burly
Edward Dotey. The full working-force of New
Plymouth mustered but twenty-two men, — count-
ing in the venerable Elder, the Governor, and the
Doctor, who all labored with their hands as readily
as the rest, — and nine boys — some half-grown
fellows, like Giles and Bart Allerton, who, at a
pinch, could bear a musket and do almost a man's
work, and some small rascals, like Miles himself,
who, with the best intentions, did not always, for
lack of strength or of wisdom, accomplish what was
bidden them.

But, old or young, laggard or brisk, every male
member of the colony was expected to turn out now
and bear a hand, for the mid-April season approached, and the precious corn, that was to feed
the settlement, must be planted. To the elders, it
looked like a stretch of hard work, but Miles hailed
it joyously, as a dignified, manly labor.

It began excitingly, with the coming of the alewives up the river, just as Squanto had foretold ;
and straightway some of the men set to taking them
with seines, while others with hoes scored up the
rough soil of the cleared fields to the north, that
once had been the planting land of the Indians of
Patuxet. Still others got out the corn, a precious
supply of seed which they had found buried in an

Indian basket under the sand of Cape Cod, and had made bold to take against this sowing time.

For the present, Miles's part was only to splash about at the river brink, where he fancied he was hauling at the seines, or to carry a bucket of water to the workers in the field, or bring a stouter hoe from the storehouse. Planting was no labor, just sport, he went to assure Dolly, at the end of the first twelve hours.

He tried to see his little sister once each day, but this time the work had been kept up so late that it was past twilight before he could run across the street to Elder Brewster's cottage. A lingering warmth was in the evening air, so Dolly and tall Priscilla Mullins, their faces dim in the candlelight that shone from within the living room behind them, were sitting on the doorstone. Some one else stood leaning against the doorpost, some one with a deep voice, who called Miles by name.

" Is it you, John Alden ? " the boy asked, and, because Alden was the Captain's friend, would have talked to him, had not Dolly, saying she had a great secret to tell him, dragged him away, round the corner of the cottage.

" Now guess what 'tis, Miles," she bade, as they halted in the ray of light that streamed from the house-window beside them.

" I cannot guess, Dolly. Be not so childish."

"I'd give you three guesses. 'Tis something Love and I found in the woods, up beyond the spring, on a southern hillside. 'Twas so far I was near afraid, but I am glad I went. We were playing in the dead leaves, and we found these. Look on them."

She drew her hand from her small bodice, with three wilted pink flowers clenched tightly in it. They were small flowers, of a star-shaped form and a rare, deep pink color, but Miles scarcely heeded color or size in his enjoyment of their sweet, spicy smell. They were unlike any blossom he had ever seen, so he was not ashamed to show his interest, even if a flower was a girlish trifle. "You and Love found them, Dolly? And no one else knows?"

" 'Tis a secret," Dolly nodded. "We told only Wrestling and Priscilla and Mistress Brewster. Ay, and the Elder too, because Mistress Brewster said perchance he might know what flower it was, he is so wise. And John Alden, Priscilla told him. And Love told Harry Samson and Milly Cooper—"

"It's a mighty great secret when all the colony knows it," Miles said sarcastically, and then, at Dolly's hurt look, was sorry; so he added, "but I'm glad to know 't, Dolly, and I'll go seek for some myself."

"There are buds yonder on the hillside, but no

blossoms.   Maybe, though, we could find some, if we went and searched.   Priscilla wishes to get some too.   Oh, Miles, could we not all three go to-morrow ? "

" I must work," Miles answered proudly.   " I'm not a child or a girl, so I cannot stop to play."

Yet he was child enough to think he should like to go get a handful of those rare, pretty flowers. After he got them, he would not greatly care for them, but there would be the zest of owning something that every boy in the colony did not own ; and if he gave the flowers to Dolly or to Constance, it would please them, since they were girls.   So, before dawn next morning, Miles tumbled out of bed, and, taking in his hand the hunch of bread that formed his breakfast, ran away up beyond the spring.   Perhaps before work-time he could find a blossom or two, he thought ; and so grubbed hopefully among the damp, dead leaves of the hillslope.

The mist that precedes the sunrise melted from the air ; a bird sang faintly in the distance ; and even amidst the undergrowth the light grew yellow and cheerful ; work-time was near, and Miles had found only a poor half-dozen blossoms.   He hated to give over, but there was no help for it ; so, getting slowly to his feet, he was starting down the path to the settlement, when a man crashed out through the bushes on his left.   It was John Alden, Miles

M

saw at once, and he carried a great handful of the pink flowers.

That was palpably an unfair arrangement, Miles held, so, as he fell into step at Alden's side, he queried : "You did not come hither and strip our place, did you ? "

" Whose place, lad ? "

" Why, mine and Dolly's and Priscilla s and — "

" Do you think I should dare plunder the holding of so many proprietors ?   I have been to northward."

Miles was silenced a moment, then insinuated, " John Alden, what do you want of posies ? You're a man."

" Well, what do *you* want of them, Miles ? " John smiled down at him.

" I'm going to give mine away ; I'm taking them to the Elder's cottage — "

" Give them away there, eh ? To Mistress Mullins, now, perhaps ? "

" No, to be sure," Miles said indignantly. " I do not like Priscilla Mullins."

" Then you are the only one of that mind in New Plymouth. Why do you not like her ? "

Miles went in silence a time, kicking at each hump and hummock in his path, but Alden was waiting for his answer, and he wished to please him. " Well, if you must know, John Alden," he broke out at last, " I do not like Priscilla Mullins because she kissed me."

Alden began to laugh, then, suddenly picking Miles up by the back of his doublet, shook him a little. " Miles Rigdale," he said solemnly, as he set the boy, rather breathless, on his feet again, " you are an ungrateful little cub."

Miles held that a most uncalled-for charge, but he had no time to defend himself, for just then they came over the brow of the hill by Cooke's cottage and saw men astir in the street, so the day's labor must be beginning. Miles ran to join Francis and Jack, and, in bragging to his comrades of his flowers, forgot to take them to Dolly. That night, when he stopped to have a word with her, he told her all about them, but he found that she was not interested in a story of six blossoms, seeing that Priscilla Mullins, since the morning, had had a fair large bunch of them, such as no one else in the settlement could show.

But in the days that followed Miles had little time to go seeking flowers on the hillslopes, or gossiping with his sister in the twilight. For, with never a minute of daylight to rest, the whole colony worked now in good earnest, — taking alewives in the brook, tugging them up into the fields, setting the little hills with corn seed and with fish to keep it moist. To crown all, the planting fell in a season .

of heat, and an intense heat, unlike the milder warmth of England, that sapped the heart of the stoutest worker.

The first day Miles was bidden to plant corn, putting two shiny alewives into each hole, and Jack Cooke was set to plant the row next him. But unhappily they chattered so much that Miles presently realized, in some horror, that he had supplied several hills with alewives, but no corn, and, while he was pulling up the ground to set the matter right, came Master Hopkins. He was angry; not that he blustered, but he cuffed Miles smartly, and, saying he could not be trusted at such important work, sent him down to the shore to labor hereafter.

From that time on, Miles tugged fish, — a dreary task, in which he was coupled with Francis Billington, another scatter-head. They had a great flat Indian basket, in which they heaped the alewives, taken all slippery from the big pile that lay upon the river brink; then they would lift the basket between them, to each a handle, and, panting and heaving, struggle up the steep bank from the river, and so through the settlement, out to the hot, open fields.

It was not a great load they could carry at one time, so their usefulness depended on the number of trips they made, but there they were sluggish. Often the basket upset, and they had to sit down to refill it; and again, more and more frequently as the hot days went on, they must halt to quarrel, when Francis vowed Miles was bearing down on his end of the basket, and Miles declared Francis was not doing his share.

One morning it came to such a pass that Miles took a basket by himself, but he found the journey single-handed so hard that he was in even less hurry than usual to return from the fields and get a second load. Loitering along, he was amusing himself by trying to carry on his head the empty fish-basket, which *would* fall off, when, as he paused to pick up the troublesome article for the fifth time, Captain Standish, coming shirt-sleeved and grimy from the fields, overtook him. Rather guiltily, Miles straightened up very erect, and said, "Good morrow, sir," as he always said it to the Captain.

"You're journeying back to the brook, Miles?" asked Standish. "At this speed you'll not come thither ere dinner-time."

"I'm hastening now, sir," Miles answered, accepting the words as an invitation to trot along at the other's side.

The Captain had his own concerns to look to, plainly, by the way he tramped along, but, right in the midst, he glanced down at his small companion and asked unexpectedly: "Where are your shoes, Miles?"

"I — I could not wear them," the boy explained, kicking his bare feet in the sand. "Down by the river 'tis very wet. And then 'tis hot, so I laid off my doublet and my shoes and stockings too. I like to go barefoot," he added defensively. "In England, they never suffered me; they said only beggar children went barefoot. But —" his voice grew suddenly anxious, "I am sure my mother would think it right now, do not you, sir?"

The Captain did not look convinced.

"It is a great saving to my shoes," murmured Miles.

"You were better save your feet," the Captain answered. "When your shoes wear out, there'll be new ones for you. Now do you go to the house and put them on, before you step on a thorn or do yourself some hurt." His tone was brusque, and he hurried at once about his business, as if he had no time to waste.

Obediently Miles went to the house to finish dressing; he was a little sorry, because he liked the fun of going barefoot in the soft dirt, yet, on the whole, it was pleasant to have Captain Standish speak to you and order you into your shoes, as if he had some concern for you. So flattered did he feel, indeed, that he only smiled in a superior way when Francis Billington, barelegged and unregenerate, sneered at him for putting on his shoes and stockings.

But that was the last happening of the week which Miles remembered with enjoyment, for the first excitement had now gone out of the labor, yet the work dragged heavily on. All through the weary day he felt the weight of the basket pulling at his arm and the heat of the steady sun scorching upon his bare head; and at night, when he lay on his pallet, with his feet throbbing and his back aching, he dreamed of tugging fish up the breathless pitch of a never-ending bluff.

A little respite came on the Sabbath, when, of course, no work could be done, but with Monday's light all were in the fields once more. It was a day of sweltering heat; the rays of the sun seemed beaten upward again by the steaming earth, and the languid air was heavy and sick. Toward the fiercest hour, about noon, as Miles was panting through the fields on a return trip to the brook, Master Carver called to him.

The Governor had knelt to set the corn at the head of one of the rows; his doublet was off and his hands were grimy, but, for all the heat, Miles saw that his high, bald forehead was quite dry of perspiration. "Here, lad," he said, as Miles ran to him, "can you fetch us a pail of water hither to drink?"

"Ay, Governor," Miles piped in a respectful treble, and, much impressed by the importance of his errand, trotted off briskly.   At the spring he longed to dally a moment, to drink of the water and to stir up the great green frog who lived in the cool sand of the bottom, but, so soon as his bucket was filled, he resolutely turned back through the glaring heat to the fields.

Short as the time had been, a change had taken place.   At first he thought it a mere trick of the dazzling light, but, as he looked again, he saw that indeed most of the men had risen from labor and, drawn together, were gazing in his direction. Nearer at hand, he beheld two coming toward the settlement; the one was John Howland, a member of the Governor's household, and the other, who leaned heavily upon his arm, was the Governor himself.   They passed within arm's length of the boy, and Miles took note how the Governor's down-bent face was now of a dull reddish hue, and he noted, also, how the grime of his homely toil still clung to his limp hands.

Surprised and a little awed, though he scarcely could tell why, Miles tugged on into the fields, and, finding Goodman Cooke among those who stood gazing after the Governor, asked him eagerly what was wrong.   "Why, naught," spoke Cooke, "only Master Carver complains of his head; 'tis along o' the heat, so the Doctor ordered him back to his house to rest.   He'll be well again by eventide."

But with eventide the word went among the colonists that Governor Carver lay unconscious, and at those tidings faces grew grave. Miles, in his youthfulness, gave little thought to it all; he was more concerned with his own half-flayed hands and aching legs than with Master Carver's illness, and each day these physical pangs grew keener.

The height of misery came on a sultry afternoon toward the close of the week, a breathless, stifling time, when, for sheer weariness and hopelessness, Miles sat down in the hot dirt in the middle of the field and thought he never could rise again. Yet he scrambled up briskly, when he saw his guardian approach, though Master Hopkins, whose face was very grave, did not scold the boy, but, after a first sharp look, bade him go rest in the shade till the day was out. "The hot sun is deadly," he said, as to himself; but Miles realized only that he was bidden to cease from labor.

He dragged himself back to the house, where he lay down upon his bed, and watched the little patch of sunlight clamber higher up the wall and harked to the drowsy sounds of out-of-doors; then heard nothing clearly till the men tramped in to supper. He sat up slowly, and listened to catch what gossip they might bring; their voices were subdued, and he half guessed what had befallen ere he heard

Master Hopkins say solemnly that the good Governor Carver was dead.

Miles thought on it the night long; this death, lonely by itself, was so much more awesome than the crowded sicknesses of the last winter. It seemed the order of life must show some change, but, with the heat of the next rising day, the colonists, as usual, only more silent, filed forth to their labor in the fields. For whether men were well or ill, or lived or died, the corn that was the hope of the settlement must be planted.

CHAPTER XIII

THE fields of New Plymouth at last were sown, — twenty acres of Indian corn and six of English seed, wheat, barley, and pease, — enough to yield an ample harvest. There was besides another field, where the corn, however tall it grew, would never be reaped, for, that the savages might not know the number of the dead, it was planted upon the graves of those who perished in the winter's sickness.

Among them lay John Carver, buried honorably with such poor military pomp as the colony could show its governor, and with a more precious tribute of grief for a good man lost. Near him lay now his wife Katharine, who at his death had grieved and pined, till within six weeks they had dug for her a grave in the new-sown corn-land.

Master Bradford was the new governor; a grave, wise-headed gentleman, with a gift of kindly speech and a shrewd sense of humor, but, to Miles, his greatest claim to respect was that the interpreter Squanto had chosen to dwell with him. For Miles

Rigdale, to use Mistress Hopkins's vexed phrase, was "ever beating the street after the heathen savage." It must be owned that to his guardians he was a troublesome boy; not a bad boy, but a careless fellow, who, though he might mean to do well, was likely, when sent to weed in the fields, to be found swimming in the river, or hunting strawberries on the hills, or fishing with Squanto.

Miles did not reason out his new dislike for responsible labor, did not take into account the influence of lazy Edward Lister, or the distractions of the spring and early summer in this new country; but he did feel there was a difference between working with his father, when he knew the harvest would be for his mother and Dolly, and grubbing in a corner of a great field that was the property of no man, but should feed the whole colony. He no longer took pride in his labor, and, if he had taken any, Mistress Hopkins's dissatisfied comments would have destroyed it. Yet, much though he disliked the bustling woman with the sharp tongue, he neither disliked nor feared her the half as much as he disliked and feared her husband.

Years later, when he had come to manhood, Miles was able to think on Master Hopkins with gratitude, for, in all honesty, this severe, undemonstrative man used him like a son, as kindly as he used his own boy, Giles. Except in the stress of planting-time, Miles was never set to tasks beyond his strength; he was well fed, — as the fare of the colony went, — well sheltered, decently clad, while the little store of his father's goods was scrupulously left untouched for his later use.

Master Hopkins tried also, conscientiously, to keep him to the path of strict virtue, with admonitions, and, if need were, with corrections. It was an age of whippings, and, on occasion, Miles was whipped painstakingly. Master Hopkins's floggings were, on the whole, not so severe as Goodman Rigdale used to give his son, but Miles resented them with an amazing outburst of anger. "You are not my father; you have no right to beat me," he cried, the first time Master Hopkins took a birch rod to him, and, swinging round in a fury, he lustily kicked his chastiser's shins.

After that one attempt and the sorry consequences which it entailed, he never again tried to defend himself, but, though he had to submit, the old feeling remained; to the pain and shame of a beating was now added a rankling sense of the injustice and, so to speak, of the illegality of it all.

Beatings, though, were something every boy in the colony, even the sober Giles, had a good share of, so Miles made shift to endure; but Master Hopkins presently devised a new-fangled means of persecution, for he insisted on teaching him to read.

The boy had clung to the black-letter Bible because it was his father's, and sometimes of a Sunday, between the morning and afternoon teachings at the Common House, when it grew irksome to sit quiet and do nothing, would take the book and spell out half a chapter, and amuse himself with looking at the funny black letters. But one Sunday, a warm May Sunday, when Miles was lying with his book in the young grass in the shadow of the house, Master Hopkins, noting his unusual employment, bade him read aloud to him, and, as he was a man of education, was honestly shocked that, as he put it, " the lad could scarce spell out his mother-tongue."

From that time dated Miles's tribulations. It was useless to protest that he could read well enough, he did not wish to read better; Master Hopkins's decree went forth that every night after supper the boy was to come to him with his Bible, and read aloud a chapter. Miles never reflected that, after a day of hard labor in the fields or woods, or of serious consultation with the other leaders of the colony, it could be neither restful nor pleasant to Master Hopkins to hear a stupid little boy stumble through a dreary waste of words. But he was quite aware of the unjust fact that the space of daylight, in the long summer evenings after supper, was the time when all the other lads were at liberty to play, while he must drone out the chronicles of dead and gone Hebrews with unpronounceable names.

The reading lesson always took place just without the house-door, where there was a bench on which Master Hopkins sat; Miles stood beside him, where he could see the harbor and the street, with the boys passing down it to the beach, perhaps; and where, too, it was convenient for Master Hopkins to cuff his ears when his attention strayed hopelessly from the book to the affairs of his playmates.

Sometimes, when he wished to get away and join them in carrying out a long-laid plan of sport, Miles would pore over his chapter twice or thrice in the day, and so, when evening came, be able to read it fairly. But on such occasions Master Hopkins always said there would be time to finish another chapter; and when it came to that, poor, disappointed Miles always stumbled, so that his lesson ended in disgrace and bitter rebuke.

Early in July, however, he had a blissful holiday, for Master Hopkins went with Master Winslow and Squanto far inland to visit King Massasoit, so for five days there was no one to bid Miles read a word. Neither did any one whip him, for all he shirked his weeding, and ran away to fish in the harbor with Ned Lister and the sailor, Trevor, and played by the brookside with the other boys till long after dark.

Dotey, to be sure, one morning when Miles forgot to fetch a supply of water, and he had to fetch it himself, threatened to "swinge" him ; he was a steady fellow, was Dotey, and, since Giles was but a lad, in his master's absence was tacitly admitted to the headship of the household.   But when he talked of beating Miles, up rose Ned, and called him, with an oath, a great bully, swaggering in his little ha'-penny borrowed authority, and threatened, if he laid hands on the little fellow, to break his head for him.

It was in the living room this happened, just before the noon meal ; Miles remembered afterward the good smell of the roast fish Mistress Hopkins was setting on the table, and what an overpowering heat came from the great fire on the hearth.   He was standing near the fireplace, backed up against the wall, a little conscience-stricken and fearful of a whipping, but still more frightened by the vehemence of the two men.   Lister had swaggered across the floor, and stood before him, and Miles was glad of his protection, though he half realized that it was not alone the desire to defend him, but the desire to defy Dotey, the trusted and sober, that spoke in Ned's tone.

Constance's quiet voice, as she stepped between the two young men, quelled the squabble : " Don't curse so, pray you, Ned.   And, Ed Dotey, do not you whip Miles ; he only forgot —"

" He does not merit whipping," spoke slow Giles, who held his own little resentment that his father's servant was set in authority over him.

Mistress Hopkins interrupted tartly that Miles needed a strong hand to correct him, and Dotey was quite in his right; her approval made it lawful enough for the young man to carry out his intention, but Dotey, like a discreet fellow, had no wish to bring about a scuffle with Lister and a hot family quarrel in his master's absence. So he said, as if it were a concession, that he would do as Constance asked, and let Miles off this time; and with that they all sat down peaceably to dinner. Miles ate his full share of the fish, and, believing this episode happily ended, put it quite out of his head.

He had good cause to remember it some ten days later. By then Master Hopkins had returned, so it was necessary for all to be busy, and Miles weeded in the corn-field till his back ached, and every evening read his chapter in the Bible. But one morning, a hot, dull morning with an overcast sky, Ned and Giles planned to go with Squanto to fish for perch in a pond far up in the woods, and Miles received a reward for his diligence of the last few days in a permission to go with them. Giles and the Indian started on ahead, to take the bait, while the two others stayed to make ready the extra tackle, which, being left to Ned's management, was always in a snarl.

N

Lister was sitting on the bench by the house-door, whistling a little, as he disentangled lines and adjusted hooks, and Miles, kneeling on the grass beside him, was giving what help he could, when Master Hopkins and Dotey came out of the cottage. Dotey, who had an axe on his shoulder, headed away through the garden to the hills whence firewood was fetched, but Master Hopkins came and stood over Ned.

How it went and exactly what was said, Miles scarcely comprehended, but he heard Master Hopkins's stern voice and Ned's sulky answering tones, and in the lulls the rattle of trenchers, as Constance, inside the house, cleared the breakfast table. The gist seemed to be that Master Hopkins had found out about Ned's threatening to break Edward Dotey's head, for he rated him soundly that he durst lift his voice against one set in authority over him, a sober man, who was his better —

"He is not my better," Ned retorted, flinging up his head, with his eyes sullen and angry.

"Do you grow saucy to contradict me?" Hopkins asked frowningly.

Too much had been said of Dotey for Ned to cast off rebuke with his usual shrug; flinging aside the tackle, he started to his feet, but, before he could walk away, Hopkins caught him by the shoulder. As they stood thus Miles noted, with sudden surprise, that alongside Master Hopkins Ned looked slight and almost boyish; somehow Miles had always thought of him as a man, because he was old enough to use a razor.

"You shall stay till I have done with speaking," said Master Hopkins; and then Ned made a sudden movement to free himself, flung up one arm, half involuntarily, — and Stephen Hopkins reached him a blow that, taking him beneath the chin, stretched him flat on the ground at his master's feet.

The women came to the house-door, and it surprised Miles that it was not Constance, but Mistress Hopkins, who cried, in a frightened voice: "Stephen, Stephen, I pray you — "

Ned rose to his feet with his face white, and stood brushing the dirt off the side on which he had fallen; there was a great brown streak of it along one sleeve and the shoulder of his shirt. "There's work you have made for the mistress, sir," he said, and began laughing in a high key.

"That's enough," Stephen Hopkins checked him. "Remember, I've never laid hands on you ere now, Edward Lister, but if you mend not your ways, this will not be the last time." He lingered yet a moment ere he turned away to the door, as if awaiting an answer, but Ned made no reply, just stood fumbling at the fishing tackle with one hand, while the other hung limp at his side.

Only when Master Hopkins had passed out of sight into the house did Lister raise his head, and then, squaring his shoulders, he led the way toward the street. "Will you not take the tackle, after all?" asked Miles, running at his side. Ned's only answer was a shake of the head, and to all Miles's further efforts at talk and one clumsy effort at sympathy he kept silent.

They left behind them the sandy street, and, skirting along the bluff, came to the path to the spring and the stepping-stones, beyond which lay the trail to the ponds. Ned did not turn off there, however, but trudged on till he reached the little stream that flowed from the pool where they had cut thatch. "Whither are you going?" panted Miles, for the third time.

"Where you were best not come," Ned answered, crashing into the bushes on the right hand. But Miles turned doggedly in his steps, through the first crisp thickets and then along the miry ground by the edge of the pool, where the air was so muggy that he wondered Ned cared to keep up his reckless pace.

Of necessity the speed slackened, as they clambered over the pebbles and pushed aside the crackling undergrowth of a dry gully in the northern hillside, but it was not till they were tramping through the hushed woods on the summit that Ned spoke: "Did

you know, Miley, my father was a gentleman? A
great family, the Listers, up Yorkshire way. But
he was a mere younger son, and he married a pretty
serving wench out of his father's hall, so they would
have no more of him. But he was a gentleman, and
he tried to give me a smattering of decent breed-
ing, — " there Ned began to laugh, with the corners
of his mouth drawn up, and his eyes mirthless, —
"and I am a brisk serving fellow, whom the master
pommels at will, eh, Miles? And they set a clod
like Edward Dotey over me."

There was going to be a fight, Miles guessed, but
though at another time he might have been secretly
glad at the prospect of such excitement, he had
seen one man knocked flat that day, and it had
not been amusing, so now he was not over-zealous
for the sport. "Come back and fish, Ned," he
coaxed, plucking at his companion's sleeve, when
that very moment, on the hillside below them, both
caught the sound of an axe falling on wood.

After that Miles scrambled down the slope, eager
as Ned himself, in his curiosity to see what would
follow. A little clearing it was they came out in,
where one tree had been newly felled, and its clean
stump showed yellow; by the tree trunk, leaning
on his axe and wiping his sweaty forehead with his
sleeve, stood Dotey.

"Well, Neddy, I've come to talk with you," Lister greeted him, in a fleering voice, and on the word set himself down on the stump, with his hands clasped about one knee.

At first it was a talking that lay all on Ned's side, while Dotey tried to keep up a pretense of work.   Ned spoke words, well-chosen and stinging, that should make even stolid Dotey wince, and spoke them in a jibing tone, with a hateful laugh that startled Miles, even more than the sight of the little pulsing motion of the blood in Ned's dark cheeks.

Dotey swung round impatiently at last.   "Hold your tongue, will you?" he cried.

"It is thou who wert better have held thy tongue, Neddy, before thou wentst blabbing to Hopkins of what passed between us."

"I did not," Dotey answered blankly.

"Thou art a liar," quoth Ned, quietly, and still hugging his knee.

Then Dotey strode over to him, and Ned, laughing up into his face, jeered at him, "threaten a man with his fists, would he, when he had just set Hopkins on to rebuke him for the like offense;" but at length he rose up and cast his mocking manner.   "We are agreed there is one Edward too many in the house," he said slowly.   "Now say we despatch one forth of it.   Will you fight me like a gentleman, rapier and dagger?"

In a daze Miles listened to Dotey's first protests,

Ned's taunts, till the final agreement was struck and the arrangements made. "I'll contrive to fetch rapier and dagger from the Captain's house," Ned concluded, "and do you, Miles, take those that hang in Hopkins's chamber, and bring them unto us behind the Fort Hill."

Unquestioningly, Miles sped upon the errand. The sun had burnt away the fog now; among the trees it was hot and breathless, and, when he ran through the fields, the drying earth crumbled under his feet. Yet he scarcely minded heat or dust, as he thought on what was now to come, and thrilled with anticipation; for, down in his heart, he told himself Dotey and Lister would never hurt each other, and he had never seen anything livelier than a bout at quarterstaff, and a real duel would be a wonderful thing to witness.

By the time he came to the house, he was all of an excited flutter, but happily Mistress Hopkins alone was within, and she was so busied in scouring her pewter platters that she only looked up to ask sharply what brought him back.

"Just to fetch somewhat for Ned," Miles answered guiltily; and then fortune favored him, for Damaris, within the bedroom, set up a wail, and Mistress Hopkins bade him run in and soothe her.

So Miles sang to baby, and, singing, took Master Hopkins's dagger from the shelf and hid it beneath his doublet; then slipped the rapier from the wall, and, after a hasty glance to see that none were looking, dropped it out at the open window. Still Damaris would not hush, and he had to pace the floor a time, singing always, though his voice shook with impatience, and his forehead was wet with perspiration.

At last the child was quieted. Placing her on the bed, he passed quickly out through the living room, and, running behind the house, snatched up the rapier from the grass. Still none saw or intercepted him; the men and boys were at work; the intense heat of the day kept the women within their cottages. But to Miles each doorway seemed full of faces, and, in a panic, he ran for the northern spur of the hill, at a pace that brought the heart strangling into his throat.

On the west side of Fort Hill was a little level space in the abrupt descent, where some pine trees stood wide apart, and the ground was brown and slippery with pine needles. There Lister and Dotey, both with their doublets and shoes cast off, were awaiting Miles; Dotey, with his stolid face grim, sat on the ground, turning a rapier in his hands, but Ned Lister was pacing slowly to and fro.

"I came — fast as I could run," panted Miles.

"You saw no one?" questioned Lister, as he

"Saw the two young men close in combat."

took Master Hopkins's rapier and measured it with the one Dotey held.

"No, no one."

" Francis Billington has been spying about here, though," Dotey spoke evenly. " 'Twas while you were at the Captain's house. I sent him packing. But he may bring — "

" Ere any come, we'll be done with the work," Ned Lister interrupted. " Here, Miles, do you run up to the hilltop and lie you down in the grass. If you see any man coming upon us, whistle us a warning."

The grass, in the glare of the sun where the trees had been felled, was a dazzling green, and the slope was very steep. From the summit of the hill where he lay down half-hidden, as they bade, Miles could see the blue harbor and all the sunny street of the town, so deserted that he ventured a glance back over his shoulder. His eyes were fastened there, for he saw the two young men close in combat; he heard the click of steel, saw the quick thrust and recovery, the bending and swaying of the struggling bodies. Then a cry rose up in his throat and choked there, for he saw the dagger fly out of Dotey's hand, and saw him slip upon the pine needles.

A clatter of feet on hollow boards made him look suddenly toward the gun platform, and he had an instant's sight of Captain Standish, who, clapping his hand to the railing of the platform, cleared it at a leap and ran headlong down into the pine thicket. Setting his fingers to his lips, Miles gave a shrill whistle, and right upon it heard the Captain cry, in a terrible voice, "What work is this?" Casting one frightened glance down the hill, Miles saw Ned lay on his side among the pine needles, and Dotey stood over him with one hand dripping blood.

The sky seemed to waver and the whole green world to stagger with the horror of what had happened. Miles crawled away through the long grass down the hillside, through the undergrowth, and never paused till he hid himself, terrified and sick, in the tangle by the pool in the hollow.

CHAPTER XIV

A MIGHTY RESOLUTION

THE sun had dropped behind Fort Hill, and long shadows darkened the soft sand of the street, when Miles at last ventured into the settlement. All the hot day he had lain hidden by the pool and watched the shreds of cloud skim across the deep sky and harked to the shrilling of the locusts, while he tried not to think, yet all the time was conscious of the awful thing that had happened, in which he had had a hand.

Disjointedly, from time to time, he had planned how he would act a part, would feign to be quite ignorant of the duel, and be amazed when he learned of it; but when the test came, when he found himself actually in the street of the town, his head whirled, and he felt that his guilt could be read in his very face.

From a dooryard some one called his name, whereat Miles's heart fairly ceased to beat; but it was only his friend, Jack Cooke, who came running to hang over his father's gate and speak to him: "Ah, Miles, where ha' you been? Have you heard talk of what happened?"   There was no time for Miles to stammer out a vague answer, before Jack ran on: "Ned Lister and Ned Dotey, they fought a duel, real cut and thrust, up behind the hill, and the Captain came upon them, and they've had them before the Governor and the Elder, and there's been such a to-do."

"Had them?   Then neither was killed?" Miles cried, with a momentary feeling that nothing could matter, if both men still lived.

"Nay, but Dotey has a great gash across the palm of his hand, and Ned Lister was slashed in the thigh so he scarce could walk.   I saw 'em when they were fetched down into the village, and they have locked Dotey up at Master Allerton's house, and Lister at Master Hopkins's."

"Wh—what are they going to do to them?" faltered Miles.

"Something terrible, to be sure," Jack answered happily; "the Captain and all are main angry. And Goodman Billington was for flogging Francis mightily out of hand, but the Elder said stay till to-morrow, when they would question all further."

"What has Francis done?"

"Why, he was with them; he kept watch while they fought.   That is, one of the lads lay in the grass and whistled them; the Captain had the least glimpse of him; but they found Francis prowling on the hill, so it must ha' been he. He says 'twasn't, but Francis is a deal of a liar, we all know."

Miles drew a long breath, and, turning from the gateway, went scuffing through the sand down the street. It was Francis, not he, whom they suspected, he repeated, but the next moment he told himself that it made no difference; since he was the culprit, he must come forward and take the blame. But when he saw Master Hopkins sitting by the house-door, his heart choked up into his throat, and his step faltered. After all, he would not speak to Master Hopkins yet; his share in the duel would be discovered soon enough.

With a feeling that he wished to propitiate every one, he trudged round the house to fetch an armful of wood, and there, by the pile, Giles was at work with an axe. "Well, Miles?" he said, pausing in his task, and then, as Miles came to his side, whispered him: "Look you, father thinks you were fishing with me all this day, that Ned sent you back to the house to be quit of you, and that you came home with me, but stopped at the spring. I told him naught; he just thought so and — I let him think so."

"Oh, Giles, you are right good," gulped Miles. "For I —"

"Hush now! I don't want to know aught." And Giles went back to his chopping.

No one would find him out, then; he was safe from the mighty beating he expected. Francis — well, since he was innocent, of course he would say so, and they would believe him and not punish him. Anyway, he had no thought of confessing, Miles assured himself hastily, as, on entering the living room, he met Master Hopkins's stern gaze.

The master of the house was in a gloomy temper that evening; a new sense of the gravity of that day's happenings came over Miles, as he looked on his harsh face. Mistress Hopkins, too, was silenced completely, and the young folk did not venture to speak while their elders did not address them, nor had they any wish to talk, with the two empty places at table confronting them. No word was uttered till the meal was nearly eaten, when Mistress Hopkins, after a swift glance at her husband, cut a thick end from the loaf of bread, and, setting it on a trencher, turned to Miles. "Fill a jug of water, and carry that and the bread to Edward Lister," she said sharply.

"Edward Lister may go fasting to-night," Master Hopkins spoke, in a grim voice.

Miles, who had slipped from his stool, stood shifting from one foot to the other, while he waited to see which he should obey.

"Do as I bid you, Miles," Mistress Hopkins repeated steadily, though one hand, which she rested on the edge of the table, clenched in nervous wise. "The man is hurt, and whatever he has done he shall not go hungry and thirsty. Either Miles shall take him food and drink, Stephen, or I shall do so myself." She rose, and, filling a jug from the water-pail, gave it to the dubious Miles. "Take it to him, there in the closet," she bade; so Miles, without waiting for Master Hopkins to prevent, stepped hastily into the little room and shut the door behind him.

The closet was very narrow, very hot, and very dusky, for the evening light came but sparsely through the little window. Just beneath the window, where whatever slight breeze entered the room could be felt, the old mattress was outspread, and on it Ned Lister lay. He had been resting his head upon his folded doublet, but at Miles's coming he drew himself up on his elbow; his face was white in the dimness, and he looked limp and sick and cowed.

"Here's bread and water, Ned," Miles began, as he crossed to him. "And — and I'm mighty sorry."

"I'm not," Ned answered, in a dogged tone. "I wish only that I'd killed him. Give me a drink." He took the jug from Miles and gulped down the water with audible swallowings; then, when he could drink no more, set it beside him. "They'd 'a' made

little more tumult if I had killed him," he went on.
" But I care not what they do to me."

" What — what do you think they will do to us,
Ned ?" Miles quavered ; the young man's prisoned
and unfriended state and desperate tone had dislodged
him from his last stronghold of security.

" They spoke of flogging us," Ned answered
hopelessly.

" A public flogging ? "

" Yes."

It was only a birching Miles had looked for.
A public flogging ! The horror and fright were
actual and overwhelming, for it never entered his
head that in punishment a distinction would be
made between the two principals in the duel and
their wretched little second. " Flog us !" he repeated dazedly. " Or — or perhaps they will hang
us ? "

" I care not if they do," Ned retorted, and, taking up the jug, drained out the last of the water.
" Fetch me another draught, Miley, that's a good
lad," he begged. " My throat is all afire."

It was darker now in the living room, so none
could note the expression of his face, and Miles was
glad for that. When he filled the jug at the pail
he slopped the water clumsily, so Mistress Hopkins
chided him. He could not seem to think or even
see, for, as he stumbled back into the closet, he

bumped his forehead against the door. "Oh, Ned," he whispered, as he bent over the injured man again, "they — they have accused Francis in my place, but I — "

"Why, that's well," Ned spoke, as he set down the jug. "I'm glad for't; you'll not be punished along o' me. I'll tell no word of you, Miley, you may be sure, and if Dotey will but hold his blabbing tongue — "

"But — but they'll flog him; I ought to tell — "

"Let him be flogged, the imp!" Ned growled. "But you, Miley — "

There was no chance to finish, for Master Hopkins, appearing in the doorway, sternly ordered Miles to come forth, and, when he had quitted the closet, bolted the door.

By now it was too dark for a reading lesson, and, even if it had been light, the whole routine of the day seemed overturned. Miles wandered out into the house-yard, but he had no will to seek the other boys; they might talk to him of Francis. Somehow, too, he did not wish to see Dolly or Mistress Brewster, who had told him how his mother looked for him to be a good lad. He went and sat down alone on the woodpile, where he harked to the distant frogs that were piping, and watched the stars come out over the sea.

So he was still sitting when at last Constance stole

out to him, and, putting her hand on his shoulder, whispered him he mustn't go away and grieve so about poor Ned. He shook her off surlily; he was tired and sleepy, and didn't want to talk, he said, and so rose and slouched away to his bedroom. There it was stiflingly hot, so when he lay down he pushed aside the coverlet, and even then he thrashed restlessly.

Presently Giles came in and lay down in the other bed that Dotey and Lister had shared; he did not offer to talk, but, settling himself at once to sleep, was soon breathing regularly. Miles counted each indrawing of his breath, and tried, breathing with him, to cheat himself into sleeping; and tried too, with the bed beneath him scorching hot, to hold himself quiet in one position. His face was wet with perspiration, and his head ached. Somewhere in the room a mosquito sang piercingly, so he must strike about him with his hands, and still the creature sang and the air was breathless, and he could not sleep.

Then he ceased the effort to gain unconsciousness, and deliberately set himself to face it all, and reason it out. He had done a wicked thing, and he should be punished for it. Francis was accused, but Francis was innocent and must be declared so. It did not matter though his comrades bade him keep silent; it was one thing for Giles not to bear tales of Miles, and another for Miles not to bear tales of himself; and for Ned Lister's way of thinking, it was not the way which Captain Standish would have counselled. What would the Captain think of him, when he knew him for a rascal who deserved whipping, Miles wondered miserably. Yet it was the Captain who had told him hard things must be done, not shirked aside; and by that ruling Miles realized that the only way for him was to let them know it was he himself, not Francis, who had borne a part in the duel.

Specious objections came, and he crushed them down; and there came, more stubborn, the promptings of fear. A public flogging, Ned had hinted; and Miles recalled a dull day in the market town, whither his father had taken him, a jeering crowd of motley folk, a cart with a fellow laughing on the driver's seat, and tied by the wrists to the cart's tail, stripped to the waist, a man who kept his head bent down and never winced, for all the great blows the constable was laying across his shoulders. Even now Miles turned sick at the remembrance of the red gashes the whip had made. But Francis had not earned such punishment, and he had earned it.

Miles rose from his restless bed, and stood by the window to catch a breath of air. The moon was up now, and a pale, hot glow lay on the fields to northward, but not a whiff of a breeze was astir. The

harbor, as he saw it from the window, lay glassy
smooth beneath the moon.   He put his weary head
down on his arms, and for a moment did not think,
only wished it were last night, when the duel was
yet unfought.

Then he lay down in bed, and turned and
tossed, and went his round of courage and fears
again.   He was not conscious that there had been a
period of sleep; he had no sense of restfulness just
ending, only of bitter dreams, but he found the room
alight and a faint, early-morning freshness in the
air, so he knew some time had passed and it was
day.

He did not remember in detail the thoughts of
the night, but the conclusion was the same, and still
clearer for him to see in the glare of morning.   Rising quickly, he dressed himself so hurriedly that he
was done before sleepy Giles had pulled on his shirt;
then went out into the living room.   Mistress Hopkins was lighting her fire with flint and steel, and
Constance was stirring up porridge for the breakfast; but he gave them no heed, for outside the
door he caught a glimpse of Master Hopkins.

"Why, Miles, are you ill?" Constance asked, as
she looked up at him.

Miles shook his head, and stepped out upon the
doorstone.   At the bench alongside the door Master Hopkins, in his shirt-sleeves, was washing his

face in a basin of water; he did not look up, but Miles, without waiting for his notice, plunged into the confession while his courage held. "Master Hopkins, I want to tell you —"

"What is it, Miles?" Hopkins asked curtly, as he began wiping his face on the big, coarse towel.

"It was not Francis, sir, it was I. The duel, you understand —" Miles's voice was faint and quavering, — "it was not Francis."

"What do you mean?" said Stephen Hopkins then, and lowered the towel from his face; the water-drops clung to his forehead, and his hair was all on end, but the very grotesqueness of his look made it the more formidable to Miles.

"It was not Francis," he repeated shakily, while his trembling fingers picked at a splinter in the doorframe. "I took the rapier out o' your bedchamber; I was in the grass and whistled to them." He stopped there, with his eyes on the toes of his shoes; he did not want to look at Master Hopkins's face, and he held his body tense against the grasp which he expected would hale him into confinement along with Ned Lister.

But instead there was a sickening silence that seemed to last for minutes; then Master Hopkins said slowly: "I marvel why that you, the son of a godly man, should have a hand in all the evil doings of the settlement. You must go tell this unto the Governor, so soon as breakfast is ended. And I shall myself speak more of it to you."

Mechanically Miles stood aside to let Master Hopkins pass into the house, and then he still stood a time, gazing at the gray doorstone beneath his feet. Presently he stepped down on the turf and slouched round to the corner of the house, where Trug was tied at night; though every one thought him evil, and they were going to flog him, Trug would still lick his hands lovingly. He untied the dog, and, holding to one end of his strap, went back through the yard; Constance, from the doorway, called to him to come in to breakfast, but, shaking his head, he walked on.

Outside the yard the street was quite empty, for the colonists were all at their morning meal. Miles trudged slowly through the sand up the hillside, and then turned down the path to the spring, which he judged at that hour would be deserted. Sure enough, the only moving things beneath the high bluff were the leaping waters of the living well, and the sunbeams that sifted through the branches of the encroaching alders, and sprinkled the trodden turf.

Casting himself down on the margin, Miles took a long drink of the water, that might have been brackish and hot for any good taste he had of it, then sat up and leaned against Trug, with one arm about the dog's neck. He had thought, so soon as he was thus by himself, he would cry, but he felt all choked inside ; his wickedness was too deep even for tears.

Suddenly two hands were clapped over his face. " Guess who 'tis," piped a treble voice, and, uncovering his eyes, Miles thrust up one hand and dragged Dolly down beside him, — a very brave Dolly, in a clean apron, with her scarlet poppet hugged under one arm. " I ran to the spring for Mistress Brewster," she explained, " but I cast away my jug when I saw you. Why are you here, Miles ? "

" Oh, Dolly," Miles burst out, " I have been uncommon wicked and helped fight a duel, and they are going to flog me through the streets, and maybe they'll hang me, and I would my mother were here." He mastered the inclination to screw his knuckles into his eyes, and, as he sat scowling at the hill across the brook, and blinking bravely, to keep a good showing before the little girl, a mighty new idea popped into his head and made him happy again. " But I shan't let them flog me," he said, grandly as Ned Lister himself. " You tell it to no one, Dolly, but I have it in mind to run away."

" Whither, Miles ? " the damsel asked, with interest, but no great amazement.

" I shall go into the woods and live with the

Indians," Miles said slowly, forming his plan as he spoke. "They're good, pleasant folk; and I'll build me a house of branches, and eat raspberries, and maybe kill birds with a sling, and I'll have Trug at night." It occurred to him that Trug would not be the liveliest of company. "Why, Dolly, say you come too," he cried. "We'll keep the house together, as I thought they'd let us when father died."

Dolly's face dimpled at the prospect, then grew sober. "But if we live in the woods, Miles, we cannot go to meeting of a Sunday, and that would never do. Let's build our house just over the brook —"

"Pshaw!" said Miles, contemptuously, "I might as well go back and let them whip me now. I'm going away into the forest. Will you come?" He rose and walked manfully toward the stepping-stones, but Dolly still sat hugging her poppet in her arms. "If you've no wish to —" Miles said, feeling brave and important, no longer a poor, trembling, little culprit. Then he turned his back on her, and gave his attention to leading Trug safely from stone to stone across the brook.

But, as he gained the opposite bank, he heard a cry behind him: "Wait, oh, wait, Miles!" Dolly, with the poppet in her arms, came slipping and scrambling across the stepping-stones and caught his hand. "Love Brewster says he does not like girls and went away to play with Harry Samson," she panted. "And you are the only brother I have, Miles, and I love you, and methinks I'd liefer go with you and be an Indian."

CHAPTER XV

ACROSS the brook the woods spread away to westward and to southward, — majestic oak trees, lulling pines, pale birches, besides the walnut and beech trees, and a host of others, the names of which Miles did not know. Thick though they stood in the forest, all were soundless now, and well-nigh motionless in the still air of morning. In all the wood the only active thing seemed the sunshine, which came sliding through the branches to mottle the turf or make the pine needles shiny.

An ardent sun it was too, even where it fell sparsely among the trees, and beyond the thickets, where the path led over unprotected hilltops, it beat fiercely through the breathless air till the heat fairly stifled the travellers. "Shall you go far before you build your house, Miles?" panted Dolly, when the roofs of the settlement were barely sunk from sight.

Miles explained that he held it best to push on to the river where he had gone eeling, so he might have plenty of fish in his dooryard. He thought to make his way directly to the place, but the journey through the heat seemed longer than when he tramped it in the springtime, and he could not find an easy path so adroitly as Squanto had found one. He had to bear away inland too, lest on the sea-coast he come upon some of the colonists gathering shellfish ; and inland, not only was the going through the undergrowth difficult, but the hills shut off the least whiff of coolness from the sea.

Soon Dolly gasped for breath, Trug lolled out his tongue, and even Miles found many pretexts to rest. Here amid the moss bubbled a spring, where the children delayed to drink and cool their hands ; there lay a muddy pond, covered with white lilies, which Miles, though he wet his feet, strove to get with a long stick ; and again and yet again they came on tangles of luscious raspberries, where they paused to eat their fill.

Miles had in his pocket a fourpenny whittle, his dearest possession, with which he stripped a great piece of bark from a birch tree, and, cleaving two sticks, shaped it into a basket, in which to carry away some of the berries "against dinner-time." But the basket proved an incumbrance to the way-farers, so, before they had wandered another mile, the two children sat down in a pine grove, and ate the berries they had gathered. They tied Trug carefully, a needless precaution, for the old dog, with as burdening a sense of responsibility as Miles himself, had no thought of trotting home and leaving those two foolish little bodies to their own protection.

By the position of the sun Miles judged it past noon, when they came at last to a brook, which he thought might be the upper waters of the stream he was seeking. He waded in first to try its depth; then, in gallant fashion, would have carried Dolly over, but little mistress wished the fun of paddling too. The alders, coming low to the brookside, cast a rippling shadow on the water, and the sandy bottom was firm and cool; so when both children once had waded in, they spent some time in splashing to and fro, while Miles set forth to Dolly how he had caught eels.

The shadows were beginning to lengthen when they climbed out on the farther side of the brook, and passed slowly up the next hillslope. Dolly now found she was tired, so Miles said they might as well build their house there as anywhere. Indeed, halfway up the slope they found a capital spot, where the hill, drawing back on itself, left a little level space, with sparse undergrowth and tall trees, the vanguard of the forest higher up, that cast a good shade.

To be sure, the exposure was northern, but that would make the place cool in summer, Miles set forth its advantages, and when winter came, they

could move round and pitch their camp on the
other side of the hill, to southward. "But I
shouldn't like to dwell in the wood when it snows,"
protested Dolly. "Let us go back and stay at
Plymouth, come winter."

But Miles, in his new independence, laughed at
the idea of return, and assured Dolly that he knew
how to make her a snug enough house for all
weathers. He would drive four forked stakes into
the ground; and then, from fork to fork, he would
lay four sticks; and across those, other great sticks;
and thatch all over with moss. He would drive
stakes into the ground to form the sides of the
cabin, and wattle them with elder twigs; and it
would be just the trimmest little house she ever
saw. Yes, he could drive stakes inside and divide
the space into rooms, and he would cut windows; the
only thing that troubled him was how to build the
fireplace, but he guessed he would think that out
presently.

About the time that the red rays of the sun
slipped under the lower branches of the trees, Miles
laid off his doublet and rolled up his shirt-sleeves,
ready for work. First, with his heel, he scored in
the dirt the lines of his house; they might as well
have a big one, he replied to Dolly's delighted
exclamations.

The little girl ran about within the four lines and

scored for herself the rooms which they would make.
" 'Twill be such sport, Miles," she chattered. " A
keeping room we'll have, and a parlor, and a great
hall." Down she set herself on the grass, between
the wavering lines that marked the hall, and waited
for her brother to build the house over her.

But, though Miles strode jauntily down into the
bushes and stayed a great time, when he came back,
he bore, not an armful of stakes, but two forked
sticks, very gnarled and crooked, and another stick,
some five feet long, without a fork. " What have
you been doing, Miles?" Dolly greeted him, in a
disappointed tone.

" Why, the wood is hard, and my knife is not
very big," the boy answered sheepishly, " so perhaps to-night, as 'tis drawing late, I'd best put up
just a little shelter. But I'll build the house to-
morrow, Dolly."

Then, because the little girl's face fell so grievously, he made haste to amuse her by turning to
such work as he could do that evening. With a
stone for a hammer, he drove his forked sticks into
the ground, and laid the other stick across them ;
that was the ridgepole, he told Dolly, and now, leaning other boughs against it, he would make a shelter
that would be quite sufficient on so hot a night.

But it was wearisome work, haggling off tough
boughs with his small whittle, and he was tired with

walking, and perhaps, he reasoned, as it was drawing on to sunset, he were best not leave Dolly alone by herself and go down into the dim thickets. So, after he had cut enough branches to go a third along one side of his ridgepole, he said vaguely that maybe he would get some more before dark, and so sat down close by Dolly.

In the west the sun had already sunk, and little pink clouds were drifting through the sky; the afterglow still lingered on the open land of the valley along the stream; but in the woods, as Miles glanced over his shoulder, the grim shadows lurked. It was awesomely silent too, till, on a sudden, a bird began warbling, and presently, fluttering near, perched on a branch above the children, where he trilled lustily.

Miles had some pebbles in his pocket, and, slipping off his garter, he improvised a sling; he would kill the bird for their supper, he told his sister, but Dolly protested; she would rather the pretty bird lived and sang than that she should eat him. So the songster finished his tune and flashed away into the darkening sky, and Miles felt as warm a glow of self-gratulation at giving in to his sister as if he had been quite certain of fetching down the bird with his sling.

" But we've naught for our supper now, Dolly," he sighed presently. " To-morrow, though, I'll find my way to the shore and take us some clams, and, in any case, we'll gather plenty of berries when it's daylight.   And you do not mind going supperless now ? "

" N — no," Dolly assented faintly; since the twilight came on them, she had grown very quiet.

" I wish Ned Lister could 'a' slipped away with us," Miles resumed.   " If he were here with his fowling piece and his fishing line, he'd take us all the victuals we'd want.   And he'd be good company, too."

Then they sat in silence a time, very close to each other, with the dog at their feet.   Over in the west the bright stars twinkled through the last waning flecks of the sunset glow, and somewhere in the dark the frogs were piping.   " Miles," whispered Dolly, " aren't you lonely ? "

" To be sure not," he answered stoutly.

" Do you not think — perhaps we could walk back home ?   I'm not weary now."

" I've come hither to stay," Miles said crossly; " you can run back if you will ; no one will flog you."

" You know I cannot go alone," whimpered Dolly.   " And maybe there are Indians and lions will get us.   Hark ! "

Miles sat erect and listened, every nerve tense, but he heard only the snap of a branch, yonder among the black trees. "It was naught, Dolly," he said more kindly, "and you needn't fear; I can take care of you. Come, let's lie down in our shelter, and to-morrow in the daylight we'll build our house."

They crept in behind the screen of branches slowly, for Dolly had hold on Miles's hand and would not let go; but at last they were settled, side by side, Dolly next the leaning roof, and Trug close against Miles. "The leaves tickle my nose," protested the little girl, "and there are humps in the ground, and I'm sure that bugs will crawl into my ears." With a movement that quite disarranged her companions, she sat up and tied her apron over her head; then all three lay down once more. "It's — it's fearsome still," Dolly whispered once, and then no further words passed between them.

But, although he was silent, Miles lay long awake; his body might be weary, but his brain was very busy with what had befallen him in the last two days, and with the unknown happenings that were yet before him. When he forgot the strangeness of the place and fell asleep at last, he dreamed of berry patches and ponds full of lilies, and the fine, great house he meant to build next day.

Somewhere sounded a bewildering crash, as if a thousand cartloads of stone were emptied right beside him. Miles sat up, wondering at the sound,

P

wondering where he was, why his face felt wet, why Dolly clung sobbing to him. A blinding light for an instant tore across the sky, and showed the trees about him twisting in an awesome manner; then darkness closed in again, and, through it, deafened the appalling crash of thunder.

" Don't be frightened, Dolly, don't be frightened," stammered Miles, clutching his sister; he could feel Trug, with his whole great body a-tremble, crowding against his knee, and, through Dolly's terrified sobs, heard the beast whine.

A second flash, that seemed to rip the sky, lit up the black woods, and, upon the roar that followed, sounded the rush of downpouring rain. As if in bucketsful, the water broke through the frail little shelter; the ground beneath the children grew sodden, and their faces tingled under the smiting of the raindrops. " Come away, in among the trees," cried Miles, through the sough of the rain, and dragged Dolly to her feet.

" Back to Plymouth, oh, let us go back to Plymouth," she wailed.

Without reply, Miles gripped her wrist and stumbled up the hillside, where he remembered the thicker growth of trees began. Bushes tore his clothes and buffeted his dripping face; rain blinded him; the flash of the lightning dazzled out just long enough to show how unfriendly trunks beset

him, then flared away and left him, half stunned by
the thunder that followed, to bruise himself against
their harsh bark.

Still, blinded and beaten and breathless, he fought
his way onward and at his side haled Dolly, dumb
with the bewilderment of the storm. He had forgotten whither he hoped to go; he knew only that
there was about him a lurid darkness of overpowering
rain and rattling thunder through which he fled
away.

It had been several moments since the last clap
of thunder, he realized suddenly, and the rain that
yet pattered noisily among the leaves did not beat
upon him with the old fury. When the thunder
growled again, it was from far in the distance, and
the space between the flash and the crash was wider.
"'Tis near over, Dolly," he spoke subduedly.

The little girl fetched a tremulous, weary sob and
made a movement to drop down on the wet turf,
but Miles held her arm more firmly. "Nay, we
must keep walking till we be dry," he said, in what
he tried to make a brave voice. "Maybe we'll
come on some warm, sheltered spot," he added, for
his poor little companion's comfort.

Holding each other fast by the hand, and with the
dog close at their heels, they trudged forward into
the black woods. Though lessened in force, the
rain still descended in a steady drizzle, and each

bush against which they brushed drenched them
with an added shower. The ground was so slippery
and thick with mud that Miles began to fear they
had strayed into a swamp, and, when they stumbled
at last upon a thicket of close-growing evergreen, he
thought it safest to shelter there till daylight.

Crawling in beneath the low branches that half
protected them from the slackening rain, they cuddled close to the dog and to each other. "I'm glad
I remembered to save my poppet," Dolly sought to
find some comfort. "She'd have been frightened,
had we left her alone."

So Dolly dropped off to sleep in Miles's arms,
and, lulled by the drip of the rain, he, too, dozed a
time, and awoke very chilly and stiff. The branches
above him stirred in a gusty wind, and in the mottled
sky he could see some faint stars. He crawled out
from the thicket and, as he stood up in the freer air,
caught the smell of brine in the breeze, and saw that,
in the quarter of the heavens whence it came, the
night was paling. "'Tis eastward yonder and the
sea," he cried, delighted to find, for all his wanderings, he was not hopelessly lost. "Come, Dolly,
we'll walk to the shore."

Over hills and through thickets they trudged
bravely, in the exhilaration of knowing whither they
were headed, and that the dreadful night was past.
Slowly the darkness was waning; the sky faded from

black to gray, and in the wet woods a bird piped dolefully. Presently a still more welcome sound reached the ears of the travellers, — a long, mournful sough as of breaking waters. " It's waves ; we're near the shore," cried Miles, and added a feeble hurrah, whereat Trug, judging all well, leaped and barked.

There was yet a wide stretch of bare uplands to cross, and the morning had broken in earnest before the children clambered down the low bluff to the sandy beach. The tide was out, and the brown rocks, like dead sea beasts, lay uncovered ; but Miles and Dolly gave them little heed, for just then, right in their eyes, the sun burst forth in the east, and made a path of yellow ripples on the water.

Forgetting her weariness, Dolly almost ran down the hard sand to the water's edge. " I thought maybe I could see Plymouth round that point on our left," she told Miles disappointedly. " We can walk thither, can we not, along the shore ? "

" We'll eat breakfast first," said Miles, who had found a great shell upon the sand. " I'll wade out and dig clams, while you fetch seaweed for the fire."

He had not yet made up his mind about the return to the settlement ; to be sure, he was very wet and hungry, but it did not rain every night, and with the thought of Plymouth came the dreadful vision of the public flogging. Besides, now it was daylight, it was good to be his own man and get his own breakfast; so he paddled about bravely, and did not complain, for all the mud and water were cold and the clams few, and his back ached with stooping to dig them. A dozen were enough for two, he concluded, so when he had that number disposed securely in his doublet, which he had twisted into a bag, he splashed shoreward.

Dolly had patiently fetched a mass of slippery seaweed, and, while he drew on his shoes and stockings, she arranged stones with the clams on top, and the seaweed all about them.

"And now I'll light the fire," Miles said soberly, as he rose up and stamped his feet in his wet shoes. Taking a smooth stone, he knelt over the seaweed, and, striking the stone with his whittle, sought to get a spark. But it seemed not a proper flint, for though he struck and struck, no spark came, and Dolly, cold and hungry, grew impatient, whereat Miles rebuked her sternly: "'Tis like a girl. I'm doing the best I can. Hush, will you, Dolly?"

Then he forgot his petty wrangling, for, at a growl from Trug, he looked to the bluff, and there, between him and the safe inland forest, he saw a little group of people coming toward him. The look on his face made Dolly, who knelt opposite him, glance back over her shoulder. "Oh, Miles," she gasped, "'tis the savages come for us!"

"'Oh, Miles, 'tis the savages come for us!'"

Miles stood up and held Dolly close to him with one arm, while he grasped Trug's collar with the other hand. "They're all friendly, Dolly, all friendly," he repeated, and wondered that his voice was so dry and faint.

A little up the sand the Indians stopped; several who kept to the rear were squaws, with hoes of clam-shell and baskets, but at the front were two warriors, who now came noiselessly down the beach. "Quiet, Trug," Miles said, stoutly as he could, and, as the savages drew near, greeted them boldly with the Indian salutation he had learnt of Squanto: "Cowompaum sin; good morrow to you."

They halted close to him, though evidently a bit uncertain as to the snarling Trug; they spoke, but he could make out no word of their rapid utterance. "I'm a friend," he repeated, hopeless of getting any good of his little store of Indian words, almost too alarmed even to recall them. "I come from Plymouth,—" he pointed up the shore where the settlement lay,—"and I want to go back thither."

He made a movement as if to start up the shore, when one of the Indians laid a hand on his arm and pointed southward. Miles shook his head, while dumb terror griped his heart; these were none of King Massasoit's friendly Indians, but people from the Cape, such as had fought the Englishmen in the winter. "Let me go home," he repeated unsteadily.

But without heeding him one loosed his arm from about Dolly's waist. Thereat Trug, with his hair a-bristle, gathered himself to spring, and the other warrior gripped the club he carried in his hand. "You shan't kill my dog!" screamed Miles, seizing Trug's collar to hold him back; and at that the savage, taking Dolly from beside him, lifted her in his arms.

The other Indian would have picked up Miles, but he dodged his hand, and, dragging Trug with him, ran up alongside the warrior who held Dolly. The little girl lay perfectly quiet, her eyes round with terror, and her lips trembling. "Don't be afraid, Dolly," quavered Miles, in what he tried to make a stout voice, "no matter where they take us. They shan't hurt you; Trug and I won't let them hurt you."

CHAPTER XVI

IT does not become an Englishman to make a weak showing before unclad savages; so presently Miles swallowed the sob that was fighting a way up his throat, mastered the other shaky signs of his terror, and put his whole attention to keeping pace with his captors. They were now well in among the trees, where the undergrowth, after the Indian custom, had been thinned by fire, so between the great blackened trunks opened wide vistas, as in an English park.

To Miles each open glade looked like every other one, but the Indians found amid the trees a distinct trail along which they hastened, single file, with the tall warrior who bore Dolly in the lead. Miles kept persistently at his heels, though the breath was short in his throat, and his whole body reeked with perspiration. The sun, all unobscured and yellow, was climbing steadily upward, and, by the fact that it shone on the left hand, he knew that they were going southward ever, southward into the hostile country.

About mid-morning they descended a sandy

slope, where pine trees grew, to a brook with a white bottom. Miles gathered his strength, and, making a little spurt ahead, flung himself down by the stream to drink ; he felt cooler for the draught, but, when he dragged himself to his feet, he found that, after his little rest, his tired legs ached the more unbearably, so he made no objection when the Indian with the club, lifting him unceremoniously to his back, carried him dry-shod through the brook.

Even on the other side, Miles made no struggle to get down; it would be useless, he judged, and then he was too worn out to tramp farther at such speed. He settled himself comfortably against his bearer's naked shoulders, and offered not half so much protest as Trug, who, trotting at the Indian's side, now and again looked to his master and whined anxiously.

As soon as he was a bit rested, Miles began to take closer note of the country through which they were passing, — a country of spicy pine thickets and of white dust, that powdered beneath the feet of the Indians. From his lofty perch he could pluck tufts of glossy pine needles as they brushed under the lower branches of the trees, and, hungry as he was, he did not find them ill to chew. Presently he tried to converse with his Indian. "Tonokete naum ? " he questioned. " Whither go you ? "

The savage answered in a pithy phrase, of which

Miles made out only the word Ma-no-met. That, he had a vague remembrance of hearing the men say, was a place somewhere to the southward; but, at least, it was not Nauset, where the Indians who had fought the English lived. In quite a cheerful tone, Miles called out to Dolly their destination, and, with something of his former confidence, set himself to watch for the town; he could not help imagining it would be a row of log cabins in a clearing, just like Plymouth.

But, for what to him seemed long hours, he saw no sign of a house, just the monotonous sheen of the pine trees where the sun struck upon them, and the dust that burst whitely through its sprinkling of pine needles. Now and again, through the branches, he caught the glimmer of sunny water, where some little pond lay; and once, when the trail led down into a hollow, sand gave place to the clogging mire of a bog, and the scrub pines yielded to cedars.

The slope beyond, with its pines thickening in again, was like all the rest of the wood, so like that Miles had suffered his eyes to close against the weary glare and the hot dust, when a sudden note of shrill calling made him fling up his head. They were just breasting the ridge that had been before them, and the trees, dwindling down, gave a sight of what lay at the farther side.

Unbroken sunlight, Miles was first aware of, —
sunlight dazzling from the hot sky, beating upward
from blue water, glaring on green pines that spread
away beyond; and then, as the dissonant calls that
made his whole body quiver drew his eyes to the
right, he saw in the stretch of meadow-land between
the creek and the ridge a squalid group of unkempt
bark wigwams. The smoke that curled upward
from their cone-like summits seemed to waver in
the heat, and for an instant Miles blinked stupidly
at the smoke, because he dared not look lower
where he must see the varied company of coppery
people who were flocking noisily forth from their
shelters.

Of a sudden, as if starting from a bad dream, he
writhed out of his captor's hold and dropped to his
feet in the sand. The Indian's grasp tightened
instantly on his arm; but in any case, whatever
they meant to do to him, even to kill him, it was
better to walk into Manomet than to be carried
thither like a little child. Where there might be
other lads, too, it went through Miles's head, even
in the midst of his sick fear.

Other boys there were, certainly, squaws and
warriors too, all thronging jabbering round him, so
that, with a poor hope that he at least might prove
friendly, Miles clung tight to the hand of the Indian
who had carried him. Wolfish yelp of dogs, shrill,

frightened cries of children, clatter of the curious squaws, — all deafened and bewildered him. Close about him he beheld crowding figures, — bare bodies that gleamed in the sunlight, swarthy, grim faces, eyes alert with curiosity, — and, overarching them all, the hot, blue sky that blinded him.

Along with their Indian masters ran dogs, prick-eared, fox-like curs, one of which suddenly darted upon Trug. Above the chatter of the curious folk Miles heard the currish yelp, the answering snarl; but ere he could cry out or move, the old civilized mastiff caught the savage cur by the scruff, and, shaking the life out of his mangy body, flung him on the sand.

Miles let go the Indian's hand, and cast himself upon his dog, while his mind rushed back to a dreadful day in England, when Trug had slain a farmer's tike, whose owner had threatened to brain "the curst brute"; people did not like to have your dog kill their dog, Miles remembered with terror; so, catching Trug by the collar, he buffeted his head, a punishment which the old fellow, with his tushes still gleaming, endured meekly.

The Indians, who had been pressing round him, had shrunk back a little, Miles perceived, as he paused for breath; they could not be used to big mastiffs. "The dog will not worry you," he addressed the company in a propitiating voice. "That

is, he won't worry you unless you harm Dolly and
me."

They could not understand his words, he realized,
but they could understand gestures, so with a bold
front he gripped Trug's collar, and urged the old
dog, still grumbling, along with him. He walked
bravely too, with his chin high and his neck stiff, for
all there was a fluttering sensation up and down his
legs. He was not afraid, he assured himself, while
he pressed his hand upon Trug's warm neck for
comfort, and fixed his eyes on the tall warrior striding before him who still bore Dolly.

Suddenly Miles perceived the press about him to
give way a little, and out from amidst the people an
old man came gravely toward him. He was a tall
old man, with a wrinkly face, and his dress was
squalid and scanty as that of the others, but by the
many beads of white bone that hung on his bare
breast, Miles judged him to be the chief of Manomet,
Canacum. So he made his most civil bow, though
he could not keep his knees from trembling a bit;
but he looked up courageously into the old Indian's
face, and, as he did not speak first, at length politely
bade him "Cowompaum sin."

He could not understand — indeed, apprehen-
sive as he was, he scarcely had the wit to try to
understand — what was said to him in reply, but
he knew the old man took him by the hand, so

in tremulous obedience he went whither he was led.

The blue sky was all blurred out, as he passed through the opening of one of the black wigwams; an intolerable smoky odor half choked him; and his eyes were blinded with the dimness all about him. But out of the dusk he heard Dolly call his name, and, stumbling toward the sound, he put his arms about his sister.

As he grew more accustomed to the dim light, he saw the old Chief, squatting on a mat at the back of the wigwam, and saw the shadowy gesture that bade him sit beside him. Almost cheerfully, since he held Dolly's hand in his, Miles obeyed; and for the moment, as Trug stretched himself at his feet, and Dolly snuggled close to his side, felt secure and whispered his sister not to fear.

There was no time to say more, for, amidst the confusion of folk that crowded the dusky wigwam, he now made out two squaws, who drew near, and, with their curious eyes fixed on him, set before him food — a kind of bread of the pounded maize and ears of young corn roasted.

It did not need the Chief's gesture to bid Miles fall to; he might be more than a little frightened, but he was also very hungry, for it was near eight-and-forty hours since he had tasted heartier food than raspberries. He now ate with such good will

that nothing was left of the victuals but the corn-
cobs, and he persuaded Dolly to eat too, though it
was hard work to coax the child to lift her head from
his shoulder. " I do not like to look on the Indians," she murmured tearfully, between two hungry
mouthfuls of corn. " I would they did not so stare
at us."

They were not over-civil, Miles thought, though,
after all, they scarcely stared at their white guests
more rudely than Miles himself had gazed at Massasoit, when the latter visited Plymouth. He might
not have minded their staring, if there had not been
so many of them, — squatting and lying all through
the wigwam, on the floor, or on the mats, or on a
broad, shelf-like couch which ran all about the
lodge, — and if the bolder ones had not been curious to feel of his shirt, — his doublet was left behind on the beach where he had taken the clams, —
and of his shoes, and of Dolly's gown, though no
one cared to put a hand upon the bristling and
growling Trug.

They chattered a wearisome deal too, till Miles's
head ached with the clamor, the squaws very shrilly,
and the men in guttural tones; the old Chief seemed
to be questioning the Indians who had found the
children on the beach, but presently he turned and
addressed Miles.

The boy fixed his eyes on the speaker's face and

tried to understand, but, while all things about him were so strange and ominous, it was hard to keep his thoughts on the hasty sounds. He did make out that the Chief asked him whence he came, and, answering " Patuxet," he pointed whither he judged the Plymouth plantation lay. " I should like to go back thither," he suggested, and endeavored, with signs and his few poor words of the Indian language, to explain that, if they took Dolly to the settlement, the people would give them knives and beads. He started to make the same arrangement for himself, but he judged it useless ; he doubted if Master Hopkins would think him worth buying back.

But, even in Dolly's case, no one made a movement to grant Miles's request, and though the old Chief spoke, for an Indian, at some length and in a civil tone, he did not mention Patuxet nor a return thither. Miles swallowed down a lump in his throat, and said bravely to Dolly that he guessed they'd have to spend the night with the savages, but they seemed kindly intentioned.

Through the low opening that formed the door of the wigwam he could see now that a long, gray shadow from the pine ridge lay upon the trodden sand ; the afternoon must be wearing to a close. Moment by moment he watched the shadow stretch itself out, till all was shadow and a thicker dimness

Q

filled the wigwam, and on the bit of sky, which
he could see through the smoke-hole in the roof,
brooded a purplish shade.   It was evening in
earnest, and it should be supper time, Miles told
Dolly; but Dolly, resting half-asleep against his
arm, made no answer.

Miles himself, for all his apprehensions, was
heavy with the weariness of the last two days, so,
whatever the morrow might have in store, he was
glad when, one by one, the Indians slipped away
like shadows, and he judged it bedtime.   He and
his sister were to sleep on the couch-like structure
by the wall, he interpreted the Chief's gestures, so
willingly he bade Dolly and Trug lie down; then
stretched himself beside them.   A comfortable resting place it was, very springy and soft with skins;
but, ere Miles could reassure Dolly and settle himself for the night, Trug began to growl, and the
great couch to groan, as what seemed an endless
family of Indians cast themselves down alongside
them.

"I — I wish I were home in my own bed,"
Dolly protested, with a stifled sob.

Miles hushed her, in some alarm lest the savages
might not approve of people who cried; but his
Indian bedfellows never heeded Dolly's tears, for
they were lulling themselves to sleep by singing in
a high, monotonous strain that drowned every

other noise.   After the little girl was quieted, they still droned on, and, when they were at last silent, there sounded the notes of swarms of mosquitoes that tortured Miles, for all he was so tired, into semi-wakefulness.

A snatch of feverish slumber once and again, and then, of a sudden, he was aware of the round moon peering in at him through the smoke-hole. That same light would now be whitening the quiet fields of Plymouth, and slipping through the little windows across the clean floor of Master Hopkins's living room ; Miles remembered just how the patch of light rested on the wall of his own chamber.

He sat up on his comfortless bed and hid his face against his knee. "I wish I hadn't run away ; I wish I were home — were home," he groaned aloud. But, save for the heavy snoring of the Chief of Manomet and his warriors, he got no answer.

CHAPTER XVII

A LITTLE daylight works a mighty change in the look of things. When in the morning Miles rose at length from the stupor of sleep into which he had fallen, the sky was clouded filmily to westward, but in the east, above the pines, hung a yellow sun. The river that curved through the meadow was half bright with the stroke of the sun, and, where the trees of the opposite bank grew low, half a lucid green; the strip of sandy beach shone white, and the coarse herbage of the level space all was gleaming.

Miles looked forth from the doorway of Chief Canacum's wigwam, and, sniffing the breeze with the tang of brine in it, decided that, after all, Manomet might prove a pleasant place in which to spend a day. He said as much to Dolly, but she held her poppet closer and shook her head. "There were fleas in that bed," she answered sorrowfully. "Let's go home now, Miles."

An easy thing to say, but to do it would have puzzled an older head than Miles's, for not only did leagues of forest stretch between him and the English settlement, but, even had he known the direct road to Plymouth, there was no chance to follow it, since, wherever he turned, the watchful eyes of the savages were upon him.

Now the first novelty had worn off, the warriors limited themselves to staring at their visitors as they sauntered through the camp, but the squaws and children still wished to press close, and feel their clothes and touch their hands. However, no one meant to harm him, Miles decided, though he only half realized how awe of their white faces and strange garments and of their great, ugly dog was protecting him and his sister; and, having once concluded he was to be left unhurt, he took pleasure in being a centre of interest; it was his first experience of this sort in all his much-snubbed life.

So, though Dolly would scarce look on the dark people about them, Miles sought presently to talk to them, just as he tried to talk to the Indians who came to Plymouth. So well did he impress it upon them that he wanted his breakfast, that one of the squaws, who had bright eyes, though her face was very dirty, led the children into her wigwam, where she brought them food, — roasted crab fish and bread. Miles thanked her and ate, and bade Trug and Dolly eat too, while the little Indians and the squaws, squatting in the sand about the wigwam

door, watched as if they had never before seen two
hungry children.

Presently, as he wished to divide a morsel with
Dolly, Miles drew out his whittle, whereat the on-
lookers crowded closer to gaze.   Miles showed them
his knife, though he took care not to let it go out
of his hands, and he exhibited the other treasures
he carried in his breeches pockets, — several nails,
a button or two, some beads, and an English farth-
ing piece.   Indians always looked for presents, he
knew, so, before he went out of the wigwam, he gave
a button to the squaw who had fed him.

With his Indian followers eying him the more
admiringly, he now went journeying through the
warm sand, past the dingy bark houses, to the farther verge of the camp, where, beyond a lusty patch
of rank weeds, the corn-field of the savages shim-
mered in the heat.   The tillage of the Indians
seemed to him of an untidy sort; they had cleared
away the trees with fire, never troubling to dig up
the roots, so blackened stumps dotted the field, and
here and there lay the greater bulk of a charred and
fallen trunk.   In between, the green corn straggled
up, and several squaws were tending it with hoes
made of great clam-shells.   They cast aside their
tools to stare on Miles and Dolly, but Miles stared
in return only a short space; he had seen corn-fields
before.

"Only to think, Dolly," he burst out, as he turned his back on the hoers, "there's no one to bid me weed or fetch water or aught else that displeases me. After all, 'tis a merry life the Indians lead ; I'm willing to dwell here with them."

"*I* do not wish to be a dirty Indian," Dolly answered decidedly, but in a whisper, as if she thought these attentive people must be able to understand her words. "Do you not think the men from Plymouth will come to seek us soon and take us home?"

"I do not want them to come," Miles replied calmly. "Maybe they would hang me for that Ned fought in the duel, and surely they would beat me for running away. I shall have to stay here always," he added cheerfully.

At this Dolly's lips quivered, but Miles, intent now on an Indian lad with a little bow in his hand, who had just come near, gave his sister no heed. "I'm minded to ask that boy to let me play with his bow," he spoke out, as they arrived once more within the lee of Chief Canacum's wigwam. "You sit here, and Trug shall watch you."

A protest or two from Dolly, after the unreasonable fashion of women-folk, but Miles, leaving her seated on the sand, walked away to the coppery lad he had singled out. For a time the two boys stared at each other gravely, then Miles, smiling affably,

touched the bow, saying, "Cossaquot? Nenmia,"
till presently the other yielded it into his hands.

Then they strolled away, with several other beady-
eyed youngsters, into the weeds on the outskirts of
the camp, where Miles tried his skill at shooting.
Though in England he had often handled a bow,
here the best showing he could make set the little
Indians laughing; and when the owner of the bow,
taking it from him, shot an arrow and fetched down
a pine cone from a tree many feet distant, Miles understood their merriment at his awkwardness.

But then he stepped up to a young sumach, and,
pulling out his whittle, hacked off a small branch in
a manner to make his new friends marvel; so, each
party respectful of the other's arts, they were speedily on a sound enough footing to race away together
to the river bank.

On the shore, half in water and half on land, lay
three Indian boats, light, tricky things, all built of
birch bark.   Miles had never seen such craft, so he
set to examining them, but his new comrades splashed
into the water.   On the sunny beach it was hot, but
across the stream, whither they swam, the trees that
pressed close to the margin darkened the shallows
with a deep green, so cool and tempting that Miles,
dusty with travel, longed to bathe in it too.

In the end he flung off his clothes, and prepared
to join in the splashing, when his Indian acquaint-

ances paddled shoreward to study his garments. Miles suffered the youngster who had lent him the bow to try on his shoes, whereat all grew so clamorous he feared a little lest his wardrobe disappear among them, for he remembered how Thievish Harbor took its first name from the pilfering habits of the Indians. Fortunately Trug, forsaking Dolly, arrived just then, and when he stretched his great bulk on his master's clothes, none cared to disturb them.

With his mind set at rest, Miles plunged into the tepid water, where he frolicked about with his new comrades, who swam like dogs, paw over paw, and dived in a way that bewildered him. But speedily he was doing his share in the ducking and splashing and whooping, till, before he knew it, the afternoon was half spent, and his shoulders smarted with the burning of the sun.

The little Indians followed him, when he spattered out of the river, and, with no more than a shaking of their ears, like puppies, were ready to run about, but Miles, as a penalty of civilization, had to stay to drag on his clothes. He felt chilly now, he found, and hungry too, and he guessed he and Trug were best go seek Dolly.

But when he came into the lee of Chief Canacum's wigwam, he saw there just scuffled, empty sand, so, with a big fright laying hold on him, he ran out into

the straggling street and called his sister's name
aloud. Just then Trug's bark told him all was
well, and, hastening after the dog, he found, in the
shade of a distant wigwam, a squaw weaving a mat
of flags, some children sprawling, and Dolly herself,
who was eating raspberries from a birch bark basket.
" Why did you run away and frighten me ? " Miles
demanded crossly, as he flung himself on the ground
beside her.

" I may go away and make friends as well as
thou," Dolly answered loftily.   " But you shall
have some of my berries, Miles.   They fetched me
them, and I can eat these — " her voice sank — " because they must be clean.   But their other victuals
are not, I know.   I watched, and the women do
never wash their kettles."

Miles had no such scruples of cleanliness, so
when, some two hours later, he scented the odor
of cooking, he rose eagerly and, thinking on supper, sought Canacum's wigwam.   There were four
dark boats upon the white beach now, he saw, so
he judged that a fishing party had come in.

When he passed through the low door into the
wigwam, he found a fire alight and a great pot of
clay hung on small sticks that were laid over it.
Into the pot the drudging squaws were putting fresh
fish, and acorns, and the meat of squirrels, and
kernels of corn, and whatever else they had of

edibles, — "a loathsome mash," Dolly whispered Miles, but he was so hungry that it did not take away his appetite.

So soon as the broth was done, near half the village squatted round the pot, the men in an inner circle, while on the outskirts, eager for any morsel their masters might fling to them, waited the poor squaws. But Dolly, because she was a little white squaw, was suffered to sit down with her brother beside the old Chief, who scooped up pieces of the fish and hot broth in a wooden bowl and gave it to Miles.

Dolly looked askance at the food, but Miles and Trug ate ravenously; neither his queer table mates nor their queer table manners troubled the boy, since he himself was licking his fingers and wiping them on Trug's fur contentedly. "I like to eat with my fingers," he chattered to his venerable host. "At home they make me to eat tidily with a napkin, but I like it better thus."

But, even at his hungriest, he could not match the Indians in trencher work; for, long after Miles had done eating and lain back against Trug, the savages still champed on, till nothing but scattered bones was left of the fare. By then the sun was quite down, so the lodge was black, save for the flashes of the sinking fire. Out-of-doors an owl hooted, and speedily the Indian guests withdrew to their own lodges, and the Chief's household went to their common bed. Little comfort did Miles and his two companions find there, for the singing Indians and the mosquitoes pestered them as on the preceding night.

"I'll not endure this a third time," Miles fretted, when he awoke in the chilly morning. "Look you, Dolly, why should I not build us a little wig-wam? I make no doubt they'll suffer us go sleep there by ourselves."

Full of this new plan, he bustled forth from the wigwam, but outside the doorway halted in surprise. He could see no river nor more than the tips of the pines for a thick white fog that drifted through the village and struck rawly to his very marrow. For a moment he had a mind to slip back to Dolly in the close wigwam, but, spying his Indian allies, he kept to his first manly resolve and began chatting to them of his intentions. Though they could understand nothing of his talk, they came with him readily, through the clammy fog, out beyond the camp, where the sand, sloping up to the pine ridge, offered, as Miles remembered, a good location for a wigwam.

The Indian houses, so far as he could judge, were built by bending over young saplings and securing both ends in the ground, then covering the frame with mats or great pieces of bark. Miles decided that poles, bound together at the top, would serve him as well, so he went to cut them in a growth of young oaks at some distance from the camp. The trees, all laden with fog moisture, drenched him as he worked, and the task took him a long time with his small whittle, — would have taken him longer, had not the Indian boys helped him to break the poles.

They were all intent on his proceedings, and, when he returned to the site he had chosen, settled themselves in the sand to watch him, an action which pleased him little. For, when he stuck his poles into the sand, at the circumference of a rough circle, and bent them all together at the top, the ends that were thrust into the sand would fly up, and 'twas annoying to have other people see his failure. It took him some minutes to make all secure, and by then he was so breathless and tired that he was glad to run tell Dolly of his progress, and, at the same time, rest a bit.

Spite of the fog, he found his sister had come out from the choking atmosphere of the wigwam. She was sitting a little up the pine ridge, behind the lodges, on a fallen tree trunk that was all a-drip; the sand, too, Miles noted, when he lay down at her feet, was damp and sticky to the touch.

"They have left us alone, haven't they, Dolly?" he said in some surprise, as he glanced about him and saw no Indians near. "But Trug, he has not followed; very like they think we'll not run away and leave him behind." Then he perceived that his sister's arms were empty. "Where's the old red poppet?" he cried.

"My poppet Priscilla," Dolly replied seriously. "I did put her away carefully. For 'tis the Sabbath to-day, Miles."

"Is it?" the boy questioned, with some misgivings. "I'd lost count of the days. Why, I have been cutting poles and begun my wigwam —"

"Then you are a Sabbath-breaker," Dolly said relentlessly. "If you be so wicked, I doubt if ever God let us go back to Plymouth. And I've been praying Him earnestly. Miles, have you said your prayers o' nights?"

"N— no," the boy faltered, "last night I forgot 'em, and night before I was weary."

"Come, we'll say them now," Dolly announced, and fell on her knees in the wet sand.

Miles obediently knelt beside her; his father had looked somewhat askance at this practice, but Miles's mother had first taught the children to say their evening prayer on their knees, and, for her sake, the boy held obstinately to that usage.

The thought of her came clearly to him now, and how she had bidden him be good to Dolly, so, when he had prayed "Our Father," he added an extemporaneous appeal, that the English folk might soon come in search of them. "Not for my sake, O Lord," he explained carefully, "but Thou knowest Dolly is but a wench and were better at Plymouth, perhaps. And, O Lord, I'd near be willing to go thither myself, if Thou wouldst put it in their minds not to flog me."

Indeed, as he prayed, his heart grew very tender toward the tiny settlement; he would have liked well to open his eyes and see the sandy street of the little village stretching away up the hillside, the ordered cottages, the grave men about their tasks, even Master Hopkins — perhaps.

Rather subdued, he set himself by Dolly on the wet log. "Now I'll tell you somewhat out of the Bible, since there is no one to preach us a discourse," he said, and set forth to her what he remembered of the last portion of the Scriptures which Master Hopkins had made him read. It was all about how Moses let loose the plagues upon the wicked king of Egypt, flies and boils and frogs, — Miles was not quite sure of the order of events, but he detailed them with much gusto.

"I do not think there is a great deal of doctrine therein," Dolly commented, with a mournful shake of the head. "Elder Brewster, he did not discourse thus; and Mistress Brewster and Priscilla and the boys will have bread for dinner to-day, and maybe butter, and lobster, and, if I were home, I should sleep in my own bed with Priscilla, and put on a clean gown in the morning. I wish I were home now."

Miles squeezed Dolly's fingers, and sat staring away from her into the fleecy fog that still shivered through the camp. So intent was he on gulping down his home-sickness that he started in surprise when a hand was laid on his shoulder, and he looked up into the face of one of Canacum's warriors.

He was to come to the Chief's wigwam, he interpreted the Indian's signs, so he rose and, leading Dolly, followed his guide down the sandy slope. "Maybe 'tis that they have meetings too on the Sabbath," Dolly whispered him.

Inside the lodge, where a fire smoked, many warriors were gathered, true enough, but no one preached to them. Instead all puffed at their pipes and, with long pauses, spoke together, till Miles, sitting with Dolly by the Chief, grew weary. Understanding nothing of their talk, he thought on his new wigwam and scarcely heeded them, till a warrior, whom he had a vague idea he had not seen before about the camp, rose up and, coming to him, lifted him to his feet.

"What will you do?" Miles cried, with a quick pang of fright as he found his arm fast in the other's grip. "Are we to go with you?" And then, with a sudden, overwhelming hope, "To Patuxet?"

"Nauset," grunted the imperturbable Chief.

"They set upon the English there!" gasped Miles. "I will not go, I will not!"

After that, all passed so quickly he remembered nothing clearly, just the confusion of bronzed figures in the smoky lodge, the choking odor of the fire, the sight of Dolly's blanched face, as one of the Indians drew her back from him. He had a scattered remembrance of crying out that they should not dare take his sister from him, Captain Standish would punish them for it; and then of a helpless, childish struggle, wherein he kicked and struck unavailingly at the savage who held him.

The chill fog stung against his face, as he was dragged forth from the wigwam. He seemed to come to his senses again, and, ceasing to struggle, called over his shoulder to Dolly not to be afraid, no one would dare hurt her. Something pressed feebly against his knees, and he looked down at Trug, with a broken thong hanging at his neck and his head bleeding. He caught the old dog by the collar. "Go in unto Dolly, sirrah," he bade in his sternest voice. "And guard her, guard her!"

He had a last glimpse of his sister, crouching in the door of the wigwam, with her arms clasped close about the mastiff's neck and her frightened

eyes fixed on him. Then the grasp on his wrist
tightened, and stumblingly he followed along with
his new captors, past the dripping wigwams with
their staring people, past his own unfinished lodge,
and into the chill silence of the moist woods.

CHAPTER XVIII

EASTWARD of Nauset, unchecked by head-lands, as was Plymouth Harbor, but sweeping away into the very sky line, lay the ocean. The tide was now rolling in; far out at sea the water all was ridged, and, as the waves pressed shoreward, their crests, heaving up, burst into white foam. With each inward swell the water crept nearer, till now it reached the bare rock where Miles Rigdale, his knees level with his chin and his arms cast round them, was perched.

Overhead, Miles knew the sky was bright, and the dazzle of the water was ever present to his eyes. He strove to think on naught but the barren glare before him, yet beneath, in his heart, he was conscious all the time of an aching weight of misery and sick fear. For this was Nauset; he had but to turn his head, and, far up the sandy beach, where the storm-swept pines began, he could see the cluster of wigwams, and, nearer, squatting upon the shore, the stolid Indian folk who had dogged him thither.

Only that morning he had reached Nauset. There had been more than four and twenty hours of journeying, through unknown villages, and by sea in a frail bark canoe, the pitching of which, under the stroke of the waves, had frightened him sorely. All, indeed, had been fright and confusion and the wearying effort to hide his terror. For the Indians of Manomet doubtless would beat Trug over the head again till he was dead, and they would send Dolly far away, as they had sent him, perhaps do worse. Miles buried his face against his knees, and bit his lips hard.

Of a sudden, he was lifted bodily from the rock where he sat. The white water eddied all round it, he noted, and the warrior who held him had stepped through it to fetch him ashore. For a moment after he was set upon his feet, he stood staring out upon the dazzling sea, then turned and passed slowly up the sand, through a patch of sparse beach grass, to the village.

Slowly though he loitered, he came at last to the sunny cluster of wigwams; in their scant shadow the men — the warriors of Nauset, and those who had fetched Miles hither — lay smoking, and, liking their surly looks little, he stepped presently into the Chief's great wigwam, where the squaws were cooking.

He was hungry, for he had not eaten since last evening, so he stood waiting and watching the women, though he no longer sought to talk to them. For they did not show a friendly curiosity, such as the squaws at Manomet had shown, but rather scowled upon him, as if they already knew enough of white folk. It was from this place that the trader Hunt, who stole Squanto, had kidnapped seven Indians, and it was here — Miles remembered only too clearly every scrap of his elders' tales — that only the last summer, in revenge for Hunt's dealings, three Englishmen trading thither had been slain.

So the heart within him was heavy indeed, when at length he set himself down amongst the warriors at the noon meal. His place was next the chief of the village, whom men called Aspinet, just as it had been at every village where he had sat to eat, but this chieftain was not friendly, as the others had seemed. What few gutturals he uttered were directed to his warriors, not to Miles, nor did he offer to give the boy food.

Of necessity, Miles imitated the others by thrusting his hands into the kettle and laying hold on the great claw of a lobster; it was so hot it burned his fingers sharply, but, mindful that he was watched, he held it fast till he could lay it on the trampled sand at his side. His fingers smarted, and he dared not raise his eyes from the lobster, lest the tears of pain that were gathering in them be seen.

Fumblingly he drew forth his whittle and was making a clumsy effort to dig the meat from the shell, when a dusky hand suddenly closed on his wrist, and the whittle was wrenched from his grasp.

For one nightmare-like instant the world seemed struck from under him ; then Miles was aware of the reality of the smoky walls of the wigwam and of those grim-faced savages who sat round him. He stood up slowly, with his knees a-tremble, but he thrust out his hand bravely, and, in a stout voice, spoke to Chief Aspinet : "That whittle is mine. Give it back to me."

A moment he stood fronting the Chief and his warriors, then, with a sudden feeling that for sheer alarm he would presently burst out crying, he turned and walked slowly from the circle of the feasters. "I shall not eat of your food nor come into your house till you give back my whittle," he flung over his shoulder in a quavering voice.

With that he passed out at the doorway and set himself down cross-legged in the deep sand in the lee of the wigwam. The sun of early afternoon poured scorchingly upon him, and the sand, as he sifted it between his fingers, was warm. Out above the ocean he could see a great white gull that flashed in the strong light.

A little shadow from the wigwam fell upon him, and bit by bit broadened, while he stupidly watched the strip of dark advance across the white sand. It must be mid-afternoon, he reasoned out, when the warriors, crammed with food, sauntered from the wigwam, and several came leisurely to squat in the shade close by him.

Among them was Aspinet himself, Miles's whittle thrust defiantly in his leathern girdle, and the sight of that braced the boy's resolution in soldierly fashion; he must not seem afraid or willing to bear an affront from a savage, he knew. So, with a steady face, he addressed the Chief again, seeking this time to find the Indian words: "When your people come to us at Patuxet we do not rob them. And you were best not rob me, else Captain Standish will burn your wigwams."

For an instant the Chief puffed slowly at his tobacco pipe, and impassively eyed Miles's face; then he spoke, with some broken words of English and his native words so slowly uttered that Miles could half comprehend the import of his speech: "We do not fear the coat-men. Thus did we to them. There was a ship broken by a storm. They saved most of their goods and hid it in the ground. We made them tell us where it was. Then we made them our servants. They wept much when we parted them. We gave them such meat as our dogs eat. We took away their clothes. They lived but a little while."

Miles's eyes were wide and his lips parted with frank horror; only for a moment, then he recalled the hint of such a happening that had drifted to Plymouth, and the very reiteration of the story made it a little less shocking. "That was a French ship, and they are a different race from us," he said slowly. "An Englishman would not 'a' wept for you. And *I* shall not." He drove his hands hard into the sand and blinked fast; the rough dirt hurt his burnt fingers, and he did not doubt the English folk, even the Captain, were so glad to be rid of him that they would leave him there forever, to the mercies of Chief Aspinet.

Squalid though the Indian wigwams were, he was faintly glad when the shadows had so lengthened on the land and so darkened the sky and sea that it was time to go to rest, for at least the blackness would screen his face from the peering eyes of his captors. It was to Aspinet's wigwam they led him, but the courage to refuse the Chief's dubious hospitality no longer endured in Miles; he would forgive their taking his knife, if they did not use him as they had used the luckless French sailors.

Obediently he snuggled down in one corner of the bed that ran round the wigwam, crowded and comfortless as was his bed at Manomet, but here neither Trug nor Dolly lay beside him. The sound of the sea, too, was strange; out-of-doors he

could hear it, — the slow crash of the incoming tide
that grew fainter and fainter.

Dolly and Trug, taken from him, he knew not
to what, and the safe little town of Plymouth
whence he had fled, — all were present to him. He
thought that he and Dolly, with the old dog beside
them, were trudging up the path from the landing,
only there were trees all along the path, like the
limes along the church lane at home in England,
and the houses were not log cabins, but English
cottages. He knocked at the door of Stephen
Hopkins's house, and at the same time it was the
English farmhouse where his father had dwelt, and,
when they opened the door to him, it was his
mother who, coming across the hall, took him in
her arms and drew him in.

The blackness of the wigwam and the heavy
breathing of the savages came once more to his
consciousness. He dragged himself wearily up on
one elbow. Through the opening in the side of the
wigwam he saw the sky quite dark, and he heard
the receding swash of the ebbing tide. Yonder
was the ocean, and a few miles westward lay Cape
Cod Bay, and across it snug Plymouth. If he only
walked along the shore, followed the coast line, he
would come home.

There was no plan, scarce any hope in him, only
he knew the English had forgotten him, and he

could not endure it longer with a stolid face among the Indians. Almost ere he thought it out, yet with instinctive precaution, he slipped off the bed, and, holding his breath, crouched listening on the floor.

Slowly and carefully, with the trodden dirt firm beneath his hands, he writhed his way to the door-opening. The morning air struck coldly on his cheeks, so that for an instant he shrank back, but there was in it something free that emboldened him to press on.

Out through the door into the chilly morning, which to his more accustomed eyes seemed so pale, he felt detection was certain. But no cry alarmed him, no motion betrayed him. The soft sand deadened every sound, as he crept through it, hands and knees. The débris of twigs, higher up at the verge of the pine woods, pressed cruelly against his palms, but, for all the pain, he still crawled on, till darkness thickened about him, and above him the pine branches stirred.

Springing to his feet, Miles ran forward, fast as two frightened legs could bear him. Brambles that plucked at his tattered sleeves made him halt, with heart a-jump; tougher young shoots near tripped him; but pantingly he held on his way. Through the branches he could catch a glimpse of the dull sky and one very bright star that he judged shone in the west, so he headed toward it.

Little by little the star faded from before his eyes, and the sky lightened, whereat Miles ran the faster. A swamp, thick with juniper, barred his course, and fearfully he turned southward to pick his way about it. When once more he turned westward, the sky was pale as lead, and the birds were beginning to sing. But though the coming of dawn might well alarm him, he did not heed it now, as, through the trees before him, he caught the pounding note of waves, and, a little later, broke forth upon a broad expanse of meadow, beyond which rumbled the great sea.

Yonder, very far to west, lay Plymouth, Miles told himself, and, with a foolish happiness springing in his heart, he stumbled briskly along through the sparse growth at the edge of the wood. The morning light now was sprinkling the sea on his right hand, and the sky was changing from lead-color to clear blue. Out from the forest a brook, all awake with the dawning, came gurgling, so Miles stopped to drink, and tarried to empty the sand from his shoes; he guessed he must have run leagues, for he was very tired.

But up he got and tramped on pluckily at his stoutest pace, through the coarse grass of a great salt marsh, where the new-risen sun struck hot upon him. At the verge of the marsh an arm of the sea reached into the land, so Miles had no course but to wade in, shoes and all. The water was cold as the sun before had been hot. He clambered forth on the far side all a-shiver and, with his head bent, began to run for warmth's sake, across another bit of marsh and up a little wooded slope of sand. Headlong he plunged down the opposite slope, and there, in the hollow, by a brookside, unmoved as the pine trees themselves, stood two of the Nauset Indians.

He trudged back to the camp with them, — there was no other way. One of them, when they came up to him, as he stood numb with the surprise, uncertain whether to run or front them boldly, struck him a buffet in the face, but the other, catching his arm, muttered something that made him desist. So Miles stole round and walked beside the second Indian on the trip back. They did not offer to carry him nor to slacken their pace, and he feared to vex them with lagging behind. His shoes, where he had waded through the salt water, were stiffening, so they hurt his feet sorely; by the time he came into the camp he was fairly limping, yet that was but a little pain beside what might be before him.

Yet no one did him hurt. A throng of people gathered scowlingly about him and talked among themselves, while he waited, with his flesh a-quiver, but his chin thrust bravely upward. But, in the end, they only hustled him into a wigwam, where they left him with two squaws who were pounding corn. Miles flung himself upon the couch, in the farthest corner, and hid his face in his arms, but rigidly he held himself from crying. The stone pestles that ground the corn went thud, thud, till his head so ached it seemed as if they beat upon his very temples.

He had come to count the rhythmic strokes in a sort of stupor, wherein he knew only that the pestles beat, when suddenly they ceased. Out-of-doors he heard a whooping and a scuffling of many naked feet in the sand. He pressed himself closer against the wall of the wigwam; they were coming to deal with him now. He shut his eyes tightly and buried his head deeper between his arms.

They had come into the wigwam. He ought to stand up and show them he was not afraid, but he could not, and, when some one grasped him by the arm, spite of himself, he cried out in nervous terror.

"Me friend. You not know Squanto?" grumbled a voice he remembered.

Miles sprang to his feet. The lodge was full of savages, Aspinet and a score of other hostile faces, but he gave them no heed, for over him stood his old Plymouth acquaintance, the interpreter Squanto. With a great cry of relief, Miles flung his arms about him. "Oh, Squanto, take me home, quick, quick!" he begged; and in the next breath, "Where's Dolly? You must find Dolly."

The little squaw and the puppy dog were safe, Squanto explained leisurely; the Captain and his warriors had come in the big canoe and taken them, and now they waited yonder for Miles himself. "I'll go to him straightway," cried Miles, with a laugh that caught in his throat.

But, like it or no, he must wait yet a time, for Chief Aspinet and his warriors would feast Squanto and the Indians who came with him, and the savages ate long and deliberately. Miles, unable to swallow a morsel, sat between his friend Squanto and one who came with him called Iyanough, the Sachem of Cummaquid, a young Indian with so gentle a bearing that the boy felt near as safe with him as with an Englishman.

He could not help a little movement of repulsion, though, as they rose from the feast at last, when Aspinet came up to him, but the Chief was in a humble mood now and merely handed back the whittle, which Miles clapped promptly into his pocket. Aspinet would have put round his neck a chain of white beads too, but Miles shook his head disapprovingly; he wanted no presents of the uncivil Chief. Yet when Squanto said, "Take um," he thought well to obey the interpreter.

They came forth at length from the wigwam,

"Miles made out the figures of the men in the shallop."

under a twilight sky, and, in some semblance of order, the whole throng of Aspinet's warriors took up their march across the Cape. One of them lifted Miles in his arms, and, though the boy would have preferred some other bearer than a Nauset man, he contented himself, since Squanto and Iyanough walked close by.

At a good pace they passed up into the scrub pines of the sand hills, and turned westward, where, in the dull sky, the restful stars were beginning to show, just as Miles had seen them come out above the piny hills of Plymouth. The branches bent noiselessly apart, as the swift train pressed forward through the woods. The moon was up now; Miles, glancing back, saw it gleam amid the boughs, and at first its staring light startled him. Then they came through the trees out on broad sand again; the tide was far down, and out yonder, where the line of moonlit water began, lay the English shallop, with its sails all white.

Down the beach the naked feet of the Indians pattered; now the water splashed noisily beneath their tread, knee high, waist high. Clearly and more clearly Miles made out the figures of the men in the shallop, erect and musket in hand, the gleam of the corselets and helmets, their faces almost.

It was Captain Standish himself, who, slipping his ready musket to one hand, reached over the gunwale and, grasping Miles by the waistband, dropped him down into the bottom of the shallop. As he did so he uttered something that sounded like a fervent " Thank God ! "

Miles neither heard nor heeded that, but he did remember of a sudden that he was a wretched, little fugitive criminal, now delivered into the hands of English justice, and even his hero, who had been his friend, had thought fit to take him up roughly and drop him down against his boots.   He rolled a little out of the way, and, crouching against the side of the boat, buried his face in his arms.

CHAPTER XIX

AT last the shallop had put off from the Nauset shore. The babel of clamorous Indians sank down, and, in its stead, sounded the thud of muskets laid by and the clatter of sweeps fitting to the rowlocks. Sharp English commands Miles heard too, but still he did not raise his head, till some one lifted him to his feet.

All about him gleamed the hard whiteness of moonlight, under which the idle sail looked vast and ghostly and the faces of the men around him seemed unfamiliar. But he heard Captain Standish's voice: "Come, Miles, clamber forward with you. Your sister is fair sick for the sight of you."

He saw it was the Captain who had lifted him up, and he caught the arm that held him. "I'm sorry, sir, oh, I'm mighty sorry; I won't fight another duel nor run away," he whispered huskily.

"Don't cry, my man," the Captain spoke hurriedly. "It's well over and you're safe with us now. Here, Gilbert Winslow, help him forward; and,

Stephen Hopkins, draw you nearer; I've a word to say."

Dumbly obedient, Miles clambered forward over the thwarts. Young Gilbert Winslow, one of the rowers, put out a hand to steady him, and, to the boy's thinking, grasped his arm roughly. They need not begin punishing him at once, he reflected miserably; he was sorry for all he had done, but when he tried to tell them so, even the Captain had thought him whimpering because he had been afraid.

Then for a moment he forgot his wretchedness, as he reached the forward thwart where Alden sat, and from beside him heard Dolly's voice pipe up. Miles slipped upon the reeling bottom of the shallop, and, stumbling closer to his sister, put his arms about her. "You're here, Dolly?" he asked, in a whisper, half afraid to let his voice sound out. "You're safe, you and Trug?"

Such a ragged, tousled Dolly as she was, half hidden in the folds of Alden's cloak, and almost too weary even to talk. She was quite safe, though, she found energy to tell him, and Trug was there behind her, tied in the peak of the bow. He was sore with his bruises, but Goodman Cooke said he would live, for all that. The Indians of Manomet had done neither of them further hurt, but had sent them to the Sachem Iyanough, who was a good man and had delivered them to the English that very morning. So it was all well, but for the poppet.

"Did they take it from you?" questioned Miles, mindful of his own experience with the whittle.

"N — no," answered Dolly, beginning to sniffle. "I — I did give her to a little maid at Manomet. Because she ground the corn and fetched wood all day, and she had no poppet. I gave it to her, and — and the bad old Chief, he took her away from the little maid — he did tear her up and make red cloth of her — and he tied her in his hair, my poppet Priscilla." Dolly curled herself up against Alden's arm and wept wearily.

"Very like Priscilla Mullins can make you another," the young man suggested kindly, though his face, in the moonlight, looked amused.

"'Twould not be she," wailed Dolly, provoked at such stupidity, and went on to cry as only a very tired little girl can cry.

But Miles, quite tearless, leaned back against Alden's knees, and, without daring to look at the men about him, gazed up into the shimmery sky. All the time, though, he was conscious that yonder in the stern sat Master Stephen Hopkins, and he thought of him and tormented himself with wondering what punishment he would inflict till he felt it almost a relief, when at last his guardian came striding across the rowers' seats toward him.

He came, indeed, but to help Alden unfurl the sail, for they were now well out from shore, and the breeze, though of the faintest, was worth calling to their aid. But when that task was done, Master Hopkins set himself down on the thwart by Alden, and presently spoke to Miles, who started guiltily, for all nothing worse was said than, "Take my cloak here, Miles Rigdale, and wrap it about you."

It was chilly, now they were out on the open bay, as Miles, in his torn shirt, knew, but, without looking at the speaker, he shrank away, muttering: "I wish it not. I am not cold, sir."

"Take the cloak as I bid you," Master Hopkins repeated, in as stern a voice as if it were a dose of poison he were pressing upon Miles. "Let me have no more of this sullenness."

He spoke so sharply and loudly that every one must hear; Miles thought to feel the indignant eyes of the company turn toward him. "I — I want to go up in the bow beside Trug," he whispered Alden, and, eager to put as much space as possible between himself and Master Hopkins, clambered over the thwart into the peak. There he crouched close to the battered old dog, who licked his hands, and lay so covered by the cloak that he could see only the blank moon rolling through the blue-black sky.

But, though he did not look on his companions, he could hear their voices distinctly. Alden it was who spoke first: "We are not heading for home the quickest way, are we, sir? We follow the shore —"

"'Tis that the Captain holds it best that we stand in to land and get fresh water," Hopkins made answer. "After that we are to hasten our shortest way unto Plymouth. For there's ill news astir at Nauset."

"What might that be?"

"They tell us the Narragansetts, that fierce tribe to southward, have risen and spoiled some of Massasoit's men and taken the King himself prisoner."

There was an instant's silence, during which Miles listened strainingly, then Alden spoke in a different, slow tone: "And after they have dealt with Massasoit, should they attack Plymouth because it is allied to him —"

"The pick of our fighting men are here in the shallop," Hopkins answered deliberately.

Miles felt something press against his legs as he lay, heard a sleepy whimper from Dolly. "Let your sister rest by you, Miles," spoke Alden, bending over him. "I'm going to aid at the sweeps."

"And you, Miles," added Master Hopkins, "were best give your thought to praying unto God that your mad prank may not prove the means of drawing the men from Plymouth at her greatest need."

Once more there was silence, save for the steady creak, creak of the oars against the thole-pins, and now and again the flap of the listless sail. Miles lay quite still and stared at the round moon, yet did not see it, for before his eyes loomed only the un- guarded cottages of Plymouth, white under the moonbeams, and, crawling toward them from the black pine hills, the slinking forms of the Narra- gansett warriors. Even when he shut his eyes and, at last, for sheer exhaustion, slumbered, he saw in his dreams the sleepy little settlement, all uncon- scious of the danger crowding close upon it, and the horror of this that his own folly had made possible startled him into wakefulness again.

He saw the mast sway blackly against the dull heavens, whence the moon had dropped, and, with something of comfort in their mere presence, heard the men grumbling inaudibly, as they tugged at the sweeps. A dead chill was in the morning wind, so gladly he huddled the cloak more closely about him and drowsed once more. But the same vision of leaping savages and blazing cottages burned before his eyes, till, with a half stifled cry, he started up, as through his dreams rang an Indian whoop.

All about him yellow sunshine rippled on the water; English voices sounded cheerily, and with them mingled the clatter of Indian tongues. So much of his dream was true, yet it could be no attack upon the shallop, for Dolly, quite uncon- cerned, sat gazing down at him from the nearest thwart.

"You are to get up," she greeted him gayly. "We are at Cummaquid to eat breakfast with Sachem Iyanough; the Captain and some of the men have gone ashore unto him, and they have sent us roast fish hither, and there is clean bread from home. And you are to rise and eat with us, Master Hopkins says."

At that name Miles, still half dazed with sleepiness, sprang to his feet. Near at hand, across the noisy blue water, gleamed the green shores of Cummaquid, where he could see a swarm of dusky figures, and in their midst the glitter of the armored Englishmen. But nothing of the shore or even of the folk about him was quite real, save the voice of Master Hopkins; Miles did not look at his face.

Creeping into the stern sheets, as he was bidden, he choked down the food that was given him, good bread and fish, that seemed to him gall and ashes. For the men about him spoke anxiously of the need of getting speedily to Plymouth, till Miles, heavy with the sense of guilt, scarcely dared stir or breathe, or even think. Only when Master Hopkins rose from beside him did he venture so much as to shift his position; then he swung about stealthily and leaned his head upon one arm that rested on the gunwale. He let one hand droop into the water, and, watching the ripples slip between his fingers, thought only of their flow and fall.

So he was still sitting, in what looked a sullen fit, when a good capful of wind came ruffling it along the water, and the Captain and his squad splashed noisily from the shore. Miles heard about him the clatter of their embarkation, the creak of the hoisted sail, the brisk voices of the men, and he longed to slip back to his old place in the bow, away from them, but he durst not venture it. He stared down into the blue water, that now began to press more swiftly through his hand, and, when he lifted his eyes, the green shore was fading in the distance.

With a creak of the cordage, the shallop came about on a fresh tack, so only dazzling water that made his eyes ache now lay before Miles. Through the rents in his shirt he felt the sun hot on his bare shoulders, and involuntarily he made a restless movement. "What's amiss, Miles?" spoke the Captain's quick voice. Miles did not answer, but, feeling rebuked, sat silent, and studied the grain of the wood in the seat on which he perched.

But the Captain, sitting next him, began to ask him questions in a curt, matter-of-fact tone, as to what Indian villages he had entered, and whether he had noted signs of warlike preparation, to all of which Miles answered hesitatingly, a little frightened, because the men about him silenced their talk to hark to him.

Once he glanced sidewise at Standish, but the

latter's brows were puckered and his eyes preoccupied, so Miles, not knowing whether he was worried about the savages or angry with him, looked again at his shoes. But when the Captain relapsed into grave silence, his fear grew greater than his shame before rebuke; so at last he plucked the Captain's sleeve and whispered him: " Is there any chance, sir, — maybe shall we come to Plymouth ere the Indians kill all the people? "

" What set such a mad fancy in your head? " Standish asked, almost sharply. " There's not an Indian within six league of Plymouth. Don't worry yourself for that, lad; you'll find the village as you left it, and all the women ready to weep over you."

At these first comforting words he had received since he boarded the shallop, Miles plucked up heart and drew closer to Captain Standish. But speedily he took note of the anxiety that made the Captain forgetful of him, and, with a new sorrow, he told himself that to his hero he was no longer " Miles, my soldier," but a foolish boy, who, because he was little, must be spoken to gently, and not even let know the full extent of the evil he had brought about. For, spite of Standish's cheerful speech, he could see clearly enough that every man in the craft was troubled and longing to reach the endangered settlement.

But the wind blew lightly, in veering flaws, so the

shallop must make tedious long tacks, while the hours rolled out. The heat began to go from the air, so Miles was glad to wrap himself in a spare cloak, as the Captain ordered; and the sun, in the west, slipped behind gray clouds. The water darkened, and the twilight had fallen in earnest, when at last the shallop tacked in at the outer entrance of Plymouth Harbor.

At first the thickly wooded beach point screened the shore, but, as the little craft rounded it, the dim hills across the harbor were visible, and there, on the greatest hill, too low for stars, Miles saw sparks of light twinkle.

It was as if the men in the shallop all drew breath again, and Miles himself, forgetting his guilt and the punishment in store for him, cried joyfully: "They're safe!"

But in a moment half the joy went from him, for, when Alden, in the bow, fired his musket thrice, with startling reëchoes, Master Hopkins told him grimly that the signal was to let the people yonder know he had destroyed neither himself nor his sister by his sinful foolhardiness. Miles hung his head sorrily, and, for all Captain Standish presently clapped him on the shoulder and bade him look how the people flocked to the landing, did not glance up till, with a splash of oars in the quiet water, the shallop lay to, by the dark rock.

In the thick twilight the faces of the people gathered thither could not be made out, but all the colony was there, Miles guessed by the babel of voices, and, after they had lifted him ashore, he knew it was Priscilla Mullins who hugged him undignifiedly, and he thought it was Mistress Brewster who cried when she spoke to him. But he had no time to make certain, for just then Master Hopkins grasped him by the arm and led him away up the hill to his house.

Within the familiar living room a candle was alight, that set Miles blinking as he was brought in from the darkness, but he made out Mistress Hopkins, with an anxious scowl on her brows, though, for all Miles's torn shirt, she did not scold one word, and he saw Constance, with her eyes red, and Giles, who had tramped in after him, and Dotey and Lister. "Then they didn't hang you?" Miles cried to the latter, too weary to be civil.

"Hang who?" asked Ned, pretty sheepishly, as his master's eyes were upon him.

"You said they were going to hang you — "

"Not I, never," vowed Ned, with his face flushing, and, slouching off into the bedroom, rattled the door to behind him.

Miles followed him thither speedily, — he was not to be coddled by two soft-hearted women, Master Hopkins said, — and Giles and Dotey came

too. They questioned him eagerly of his adven-
tures, but Miles, unflattered even by such attention, would not speak of Indians or of birch
canoes, just poured forth his woes in a weary voice
upon the verge of tears: he would surely be
soundly whipped, and Ned had said they would
be hanged and they hadn't been, and if Ned hadn't
said it, he wouldn't 'a' run away.

"I am right sorry, for your sake, I was not dealt
with less mercifully," Lister said bitterly, and Miles,
glancing up at him, was checked in his lamentation;
truly, Ned looked miserable, with his face white and
a noticeable limp in his gait, and Dotey, too, had
one hand bandaged, but, most awe-inspiring of all,
Miles noted, as Ned unfastened his shirt, a vivid
red mark about the base of his neck. "What was
it they did to you, then?" he asked, but neither
of the Edwards seemed eager to explain.

"They just tied 'em neck and heels," Giles volunteered presently, as he began undressing. "And
before they'd kept them so an hour, they promised
amendment and — Hey, Ed Dotey, make Ned cease
throwing shoes at me."

With a wrangling word or two peace was restored,
and the young men took themselves to rest; Miles
noted that the ex-duellists drew the line at sharing
one bed, for Ned Lister lay down beside him, while
Giles and Dotey slept together.

How quiet and clean it seemed in the little chamber, Miles thought; and how blessed it was that the Indians had not fallen on Plymouth! Involuntarily he sighed for very peace and happiness, then lost all sense of comfort at the recollection of the morrow and the punishment deferred that yet would surely come. "Ned, O Ned," he began, and shook Lister, who was lying with his head between his arms. "Tell me, Ned, how greatly does it hurt to be tied neck and heels?"

"Um-m-m!" groaned the exasperated Lister. "Miley, if you say 'neck and heels' to me again, I'll wake up and thrash you."

CHAPTER XX

MILES was not fated, however, to learn by experience how it felt to be tied neck and heels; for all his double sin of abetting a duel and running away from the settlement, he suffered no unusual punishment. Instead, next day at noon, when Master Hopkins returned from the fields, he ordered him into the closet, and there gave him as thorough a flogging as even the boy's tormented fancy had conjured up.

Miles came out, with his shoulders quivering, and, not staying for dinner, slouched away through the fields to the shore, where he stood a time blinking out to sea. He had been bidden go present himself to the Elder and be admonished for his sins, but he did not hold it necessary to go just yet.

At last he had himself tolerably in hand, and, with no great heart for what was before him, was loitering along the shingle to the village, when a shrill voice hailed him, and, looking up, he saw Jack and Joe and Francis running toward him. So Miles put on an unconcerned bearing, and, making the pebbles clatter beneath his tread, swaggered to meet them.

Oh, yes, he could tell them brave tales of how he had lived with the Indians, he bragged, but not now; he had to go now and be admonished by the Elder, he explained, as if he took pride in such awful depths of iniquity.

" And Stephen Hopkins has admonished you ere this, I'll warrant," chuckled Francis. " How heavily did he lam you ? "

With melancholy satisfaction, Miles pulled off his shirt and exhibited his stripes to his admiring companions.

" Big red weals," quoth Jack. " I'm glad 'twas not I must bear such a banging. Here's more than one stroke has broken the skin."

Miles twisted his neck, in a vain effort to study his smarting shoulders, while his estimate of himself rose surprisingly.

" And for each whang Miles cried out, I'll be bound," added Francis.

" I did not open my lips," boasted Miles. " A' could not make me. You can talk, if you will, Francie. We know if you'd borne the half of this, we'd 'a' heard you roaring from the Fort Hill clear to the Rock. But I mind not a beating, nor aught they can do to me or say. 'Twas so brave a life I led among the Indians — "

There something in Francis's face made Miles glance over his shoulder, and right behind him, his step deadened by the sand, stood the Captain, who was gazing down at him with a look between contemptuous and amused, that made the other lads slip away, and set Miles scuttling into his shirt.

" Well, sir, you show a deep and edifying sense of the mischief you have done," Standish said quietly, but the very absence of anger from his tone made Miles's face burn the hotter.

He was glad that his shirt was over his head at that moment, so he could not see the speaker's look, and he dreaded to meet it. But when he had drawn on the garment and could glance round him, he saw, with an added pang of humiliation, that Captain Standish, not holding him worthy of further notice, had trudged on to the landing.

For a moment Miles stood gazing blankly after him ; then he turned and, kicking up the sand in half-hearted little spurts, plodded on up the hill to Master Brewster's gate. Beneath the bluff, on the shore of the brook, he came upon the Elder, laboring diligently among his green things, and told him in a listless tone why he had come thither. Master Brewster talked to him a long time and wisely, Miles had no doubt, but he only heard the words vaguely, for he was feeling the piteous smart of his irritated shoulders, and watching the flecks of light through the green bushes that shifted across the Elder's doublet, and harking to the loud purr of the fat cat Solomon, who was rubbing himself against the Elder's knees.

Yet he was dully sorry when the Elder dismissed him, for that left him free for some heavy thoughts. It would be a little comfort to speak with Dolly; so, rather uncertain what welcome such a rapscallion as he might hope for, he toiled up the bluff and faltered into the Brewsters' living room.

The wind from the sea stirred the curtain at the window, and in the full blast, industriously sewing at a small gown, Mistress Mullins sat alone. "So you've come to visit me, little Indian?" she greeted Miles, and put her hands to her brown hair that had ruffled in the draught. "My scalp is quite safe? You are well assured you have no tomahawk about you?"

Miles shook his head in crestfallen fashion; he only wanted to see Dolly, he murmured.

"She is in bed, poor little one! till I make her some tidy clothes to put on," Priscilla answered. "Stay and talk with me, Miles, like a gallant lad. Come, if you'll look merry again, I'll show you something rare. 'Tis a humbird."

She led him to the western casement, where on the window-sill rested a little cage of paper, in which fluttered a shimmery atom no bigger than a bee.

T

For a moment, because Priscilla expected it of him, Miles gazed at the tiny whirring wings, and touched the cage gently, but in so listless a fashion that the young girl asked abruptly: "What has gone wrong with you, Miles?"

"Naught."

"Then you are an uncivil youth to wear such a glum face. Come, tell me it all. Is it that Stephen Hopkins hath flogged you?"

"No!" Miles answered, with an angry sniff. "A beating more or less, 'tis nothing to a man."

Priscilla suddenly put an arm about his neck. "My poor little — man!" she said, and, for all she laughed, her voice was tender. "I know I am but a silly woman, yet mayhap I can help you, — an you let me. Is it that the Elder rated you grievously?"

Miles shook his head, then, spite of himself, blurted out: "'Tis — Captain Standish is angry and scarce will look at me. And he has ever been kind to me. But now he will have none of me. I had no mind to be so wicked; I did not mean what I said; I'm sorry."

"Why, you need not lay it to heart if the Captain has been round with you," the girl coaxed. "He must be so troubled now with all this ill news of the savages."

"But he — he thinks I'm not sorry," Miles

faltered, twisting the ends of the window curtain relentlessly between his hands. "And I am, but I can't go to him and say it, when he is angered."

"But I can go to him and tell him you are sorry, if 'twill comfort you," Priscilla answered coolly. "I have no fear of your Captain."

"Will you so?" Miles cried gratefully. "Sure, you're uncommon good. When I'm older I'll marry you, — unless Jack Alden does it ere then."

Whereat Mistress Mullins's face flushed pink, and she pulled Miles's ears, and, calling him a scamp, packed him into the bedroom to speak with Dolly.

So, when Miles ran home to supper, he was in an almost cheerful mood, which speedily ended, for Master Hopkins made him read a sorrowful chapter on the wrath of God against transgressors, and cuffed him because he could not pronounce the word "Zarhites." Mistress Hopkins scolded too, because she had labored all the afternoon to mend the shirt which Miles had worn upon his wanderings; moreover, she would have to make the troublesome boy a new doublet, to replace the one he had lost, and new breeches, for those he now wore were disgracefully ragged, so perhaps she had reason to be vexed on his account.

"But I did not tear them wantonly," Miles lamented to Ned Lister next morning. "Yet she says she is so busied she cannot make me new clothes for days, and I must wear my breeches all ragged for punishment."

"Hm!" answered Ned. "Half Plymouth seems to take its diversion in punishing the other half." He was on his knees between two rows of the rustling green cornstalks, where he was grubbing up those weeds that were so tough as to resist his hoe; his doublet was off, but he had so scrupulously turned up the collar of his shirt that no trace of the red mark about his neck could be seen.

It was so unusual for Ned to work that Miles was lingering to watch him, when suddenly the young man broke out: "Look you here, Miley, you were with me that day I made Dotey to fight me, and you heard all I said unto him, so I ought to tell you — 'twas not he bore tales of me unto Hopkins; 'twas the mistress herself."

Miles nodded his head. "I never had any liking for her," he said softly.

Ned weeded scowlingly. "Well, she made Hopkins go unto the Governor and beg that Ed Dotey and I be released after we'd been tied an hour," he admitted, in a grudging tone. "She might be worse, and so might Ed Dotey; he's no talebearer, though he is a self-sufficient coxcomb."

For several days this was the only bit of private talk which Miles had with Ned, for Master Hopkins, who said that Lister had already corrupted the boy sufficiently, took now a new course of keeping the two rigorously apart. While Ned was sent to work in the fields, Miles was bidden weed in the house-garden, or fetch and carry for Mistress Hopkins.

Master Hopkins believed, too, that Satan found mischief for idle hands, so he saw to it that one task followed another, till Miles, honestly wearied, looked back with fondness to his life among the Indians as a time of perpetual holiday. One morning, indeed, about a week after his return to Plymouth, when he was forbidden to help Ned dig clams, and ordered, instead, to fetch water and then weed in the garden, he voiced his rebellious wish: "I would I were back with those good, friendly Indians at Manomet."

Master Hopkins, who was busy at the delicate task of repairing the lock of his musket, looked up at the muttered words. "You wish to dwell among those shameless idolaters?" he questioned grimly. "Verily, Miles Rigdale, you are a son of perdition."

A very terrible name that was, Miles thought, but it was worse than the hard name, that Master Hopkins cuffed him till his ears tingled and his eyes watered.

Frightened at his own wickedness, and smarting with the blows, he hurried off to the spring, and, halfway thither, met with Francis Billington. Even Francis's sympathy would have been welcome just then, and, after all he had undergone because of his confession to save the boy, Miles thought he had some claim to it. But Francis stiffened up at his greeting and put on a surprising new air of virtue. "I'm forbid to have to do with you, Miles," he announced, with open delight. "Sure, I see not why your father ever need keep you so tenderly from my conversation. Why, you are yourself the worst lad in all the colony; 'twas Captain Standish himself said so to my father."

"I think you are not speaking the truth," Miles answered doggedly; he had a mind to fight Francis for such a story, but very likely if he fought, Master Hopkins would whip him. So he drooped his head under the other's taunt and plodded on to the spring. He didn't believe Francis, he repeated to himself, while he swallowed and swallowed in his throat. But there came the remembrance of the look the Captain had given him, there on the shore, and his contemptuous words, and, with a sickening fear that, for once, Francis had spoken the truth, he felt the lump in his throat swell bigger.

He did not care, though the water, as he scooped up his pailful at the spring, slopped over his shoes, but he did care when he heard on the pathway from the bluff the scatter of pebbles under a quick footstep; he could not let any one see him in so sorry a mood. Catching up his pail, he pressed into the crackling green alders at the farther side of the spring, and, as he did so, heard some one call sharply, " Miles."

It was Captain Standish's voice, Captain Standish who would want to rate him as the worst lad in the colony, who would never believe he was penitent. Miles put his head down and, crashing through the alders, never paused till the whole dense thicket lay between him and his pursuer. He could hear on the lifeless, hot air no sound save that of his own fluttering breath ; no one had offered to follow him, and he felt suddenly sorry that he had escaped.

But, without courage to go back to the spring and face the Captain, he crouched down beneath the bushes and sat a long time staring through the leaves at the bright water of the brook. Up in the street he heard eager voices once, but the dread of encountering Captain Standish made him stay quiet in his hiding place, till the street was still again. Then he clambered painfully up the steeper part of the bluff below Cooke's house, and, with a new terror growing on him of the mighty scolding he could expect for his delay, scudded home.

But no one had space to scold him. When he came to the house he found Mistress Hopkins, quite silent, and Constance, with a scared face, busied about dinner, and Ned and Dotey, with Giles to help, overhauling their muskets. "What is it has happened?" Miles questioned in amazement.

"War!" Ned answered cheerily, and Mistress Hopkins, with a grewsome sort of satisfaction, added that she always said they'd yet be slain by the heathen savages.

"It happened at Namasket, five league from here," Ned ran on. "Squanto and two other friendly copper-skins, Hobbamock and Tokamahamon, they went thither quietly to learn how much truth was in this talk of rebellion against Massasoit. And there was a certain Corbitant, an under-chief of the King's, who is in league with the Narragansetts, and he discovered them. Hobbamock broke from them and came fleeing hither, not an hour agone, but Tokamahamon they took and Squanto they've slain. So we are furbishing up our muskets."

Poor Squanto, who had fetched him from Nauset, was dead. That was Miles's first thought, and he was honestly grieved. But ere dinner was out he learned from his elders that there was other fearful matter to think on, for if Massasoit's men were rebelling and joining the Narragansetts against the King and his allies, it meant a dreadful danger for the settlement.

Quietly, but resolutely enough, the Englishmen made their arrangements to march against Namasket and punish the slayers of their friends. After a night of watching and half hidden fear, next morning, in the midst of a beating rain, a little squad of ten, with the Captain at their head, and Hobbamock to guide them, went forth to the attack.

From the western window Miles watched them go. He had hoped to be allowed to slip forth from the house and see them start upon their expedition ; at least get a last glimpse of Captain Standish, who, perhaps, in the confusion, would forget he was angry and say, " Good-morrow, Miles," as he used. So Miles fetched Master Hopkins's buff-coat, and helped Constance with the breakfast kettle, and mended the fire, and quieted Damaris, and waited and hoped, till he saw the last man of the column disappear over the bluff.

He could run out and seek a dry stick of wood from the pile now, when going forth profited him nothing. He slouched into the wet and the wind, and, in the pashy dooryard, met Ned, who was in a bad temper, because, when he asked his master to let him go on the expedition, he had been con-temptuously bidden by Hopkins to " stay home with the women and tend the disgraceful hurts he had taken in his godless brawl."

" If I'd not been such a Jack as to get myself

slashed, I might 'a' gone," Ned grumbled now to Miles, as he kicked his heels in the big puddle before the doorstone. "And they'll have some good fighting, I'll wager."

"Do you think surely some of our men will be slain?" Miles questioned, terror-stricken.

"A buff-coat does not make a man immortal," Ned cast over his shoulder, as he stamped into the house.

But Miles, standing in the pouring rain, gazed up the path by which the little company had gone. The sky was thick gray, and the rain, driven by the wind from off the harbor, fell in long, livid streaks. He took up a shiny wet stick from the ground and snapped it slowly in his hands. "The Captain may be killed," he told himself dazedly. "And he does not know that I be sorry."

CHAPTER XXI

ALL that night the rain fell steadily; harking to its slow patter on the roof, Miles thought on those who were tramping the forest, and wondered how they fared. Ned, stretched beside him, save for his regular breathing, lay like one dead, and yonder in the living room he could hear Trug, admitted to shelter from the rain, grumbling in his sleep.

A long, long night it was, and the day that followed, all blurry with faint sunshine, was well nigh as long. Little work was to do in the wet fields, so Miles fetched pails of water and tended the fretting babies, while, like every other soul in the colony, he waited for news of the Captain and his men.

A second night, sickly with warm mist, had closed in on Plymouth, before tidings came. Miles and Giles had gone forth together into the moist darkness to the spring, where they drank, before drawing a last bucketful for the house; the alders looked startlingly dense against the lighter black of the sky, and Miles kept close to Giles.

Even the elder boy was more alert than his wont, and jumped listening to his feet, when far up the Namasket trail sounded ordered footsteps. "'Tis father and the men returning," he cried next moment, and scrambled swiftly up the bluff, with Miles, eager yet half in dread lest ill had befallen, panting after.

Down through the dusk of the trail men were coming — the heavily armed Englishmen and in their midst some scantily clad savages. Giles, forgetful of reserve for once, pressed forward boldly to meet his father, but Miles, having no one to meet, stood back in the bushes, that touched his face clammily, and watched the little column, noisy now, as home approached, swing past. At its head marched a stocky figure that he knew, and, as if the Captain could see him even in the blackness, Miles shrank a little farther into the bushes.

Yet he joined himself to the very end of the column, for he had no will to stay alone in the dark. Goodman Cooke marched there, and, eager to have some friend in the party, Miles fell into step beside him. "You are all come back safe, sir?" he asked propitiatingly.

"Surely, yes," the other replied. "All sound, save three Indians we fetched hither to the Doctor. Best of all, we've Squanto here; we found him unhurt."

By this they had come down into the village, where all the people, it seemed, had hurried forth, and, hearing the news of their interpreter's return, showed no small joy thereover. Squanto, a figure of varying light and shade beneath the lantern glow, took such expressions of kind feeling stolidly, and profited from the good wishes of his white friends by asking for strong water. There was some merriment thereat among the Englishmen, — all were in good spirits, in truth, for the expedition had fared well.

In broken fragments Miles caught the story as he was hustled about among the returned soldiers and, with the other lads, stood staring at them under the lantern light: how the Englishmen, coming at midnight to Namasket, had beset the house of Corbitant, but found that valiant chief had fled at the mere rumor of their approach; how several of the Indians, trying to press forth in spite of their promises that no harm was meant them, had been hurt; how Squanto and Tokamahamon had been found alive; and how, after leaving for Corbitant a stern warning as to what he might expect if he continued to stir up rebellion against Massasoit and his allies, they had returned, successful and unscathed.

But the story was quickly told by the hungry men, and then they scattered to their houses. The

street was swiftly emptied, and even Giles, calling
to Miles to fetch home the bucket they had left
at the spring, trudged away with his father.

Miles turned slowly up the street; he had admitted it to no one, even to Giles and Ned, but the
last week he had had a fear of the black woods.
Spite of his boasts to the boys of his merry life with
the savages, he shuddered every time he thought of
Nauset, and he had a foolish feeling that if he ventured into the forest the Indians might swoop down
on him again. In the daytime he could laugh it
away, but at night, and especially after the anxiety
of the last twenty-four hours, the fear came on him
strongly, and it did not seem as if the courage was
in him to go down to the inky spring alongside the
stepping-stones that led to the woods.

He stood a time by Cooke's gate, in the hope that
he might see some one else bound for the spring, but
no one came. He went a few steps down the
street, but, if he returned to the house without the
bucket, he would be scolded, so, at a snail's gait,
he trudged uphill again.

Then it was that he noted the companionable
light that shone in the window of Standish's cottage,
high up the hillside, and, though he was afraid of
the Captain, yet there seemed a kind of encouragement in that shiny spark that made him cross the
street and loiter nearer. " Maybe John Alden'll be

going to the spring," he told himself. "Or maybe
—maybe I'll go, presently."

Just at the edge of the Captain's unfenced dooryard, he halted and stood gazing at the light. He
was not spying, to be sure; he would go in a
moment. Through the open window he could see
a corner of the living room, a table, with a rack
and three guns above it, and, as he gazed, Alden, a
big, black figure, strode into the bright corner and
set down two bowls on the table. Miles drew
a step or two nearer. "Maybe the Captain will
come into the light next," he told himself. "And
after I've seen him, then — "

And then some one took him firmly by the
shoulder, and right beside him spoke the Captain's
voice, "Well, Miles?"

"Oh!" the boy gasped, and then, in a panic-
stricken tone, "I'm going home; prithee, let me go
home, sir."

"Nay, you are coming in with me," Standish
answered, and, helplessly, Miles yielded to the
other's grasp and stumbled over the threshold.

Within, the living room was bare and martial, with
a rapier above the chimneypiece that caught a
gleam from the candle set below it, and the form
by the door and the rough stools standing stiffly as
on parade. On a shelf beside the fireplace there
were some pots and platters; Miles noted all very

accurately, and wondered that he should note them at such a time.

He started when Captain Standish spoke, for all his tone was amused: " Here, Jack, set a bowl for this gentleman I have fetched to sup with us.   And you, Miles, will you give me your parole not to attempt an escape, if I take my hand from your collar ? "

Miles eyed the shaft of candlelight that lay at his feet and ventured no answer.   He knew the Captain had loosed his grasp on him, and then he heard him ask, in a different, serious tone : " Are you afraid of me ? "

At that Miles tossed back his head, stiffly as if a bar of iron were run down his neck.   " No, sir," he said, boldly and untruthfully.

He could not slip away now, whatever might be in store for him, but stood rigid and unpretending, while Captain Standish flung off his buff-coat, and Alden, with a ponderous movement, lifted the soup kettle to the table.   Then he sat down on a stool, as he was bidden, and ate.   It was clam broth, and he was aware of the good flavor of it, just as he was aware, beneath all his alarm, of the honorable fact that he was taking supper with Captain Standish. He began to hazard long looks at the Captain and to listen to the talk of the two men, with some thought for their words, as well as for his own concerns.

" This is none of your cooking, Jack," said Standish, as he rose to refill his bowl.

" Mistress Mullins fetched us the broth," Alden replied, with a studious lack of interest. " She thought we'd have naught to eat in the house to-night."

" 'Twas very wisely thought. When you have eaten, Jack, best carry back her kettle. They'll not yet be abed at the Elder's house."

Somehow, after that, Alden made short work of his portion, and, summarily emptying the kettle into the Captain's bowl, gave it a perfunctory scrub and started briskly for Master Brewster's cottage.

The Captain, with his face sober all but his eyes, swallowed his broth in leisurely silence for a moment before he addressed his small companion: " I had speech with Priscilla Mullins several days since. What is this, Miles, that she tells me you had to say to me ? "

Miles crumbled the fag end of his piece of bread with one nervous hand. " Why, 'twas — 'twas — Captain Standish, is it true you think me the worst lad in the settlement ? " He looked up into the other's face, and something he saw there made him blurt out, " I doubt if you do."

" So that's why you ran away from me day before yesterday, is it ? "

Miles kicked his heels softly against the legs of

U

his stool. "Because I want to tell you I'm sorry," he murmured. "I shall never run away to the Indians again. I — I was but talking when I said those words unto Francis and the others."

"A 'miles gloriosus,' eh?" said the Captain, and smiled.

Miles saw nothing amusing in the words, but he took it as a sign the Captain was his friend again, so he smiled back. "I won't do it again, sir," he promised vaguely, and then, as Standish rose from the table, he slipped off his stool. "May I wash the dishes, sir?" he volunteered for "a girl's work" eagerly.

"If you wish it," the Captain answered, and then, about the time Miles had dropped the bowls and spoons into the nearest pail of water, broke out irrelevantly, "In the name of goodness, Miles, are those the only breeches you have to wear?"

Miles clapped his right hand over one knee, and his left over an ostentatious rift in the side. "She hasn't time to make me new ones; I'm wearing these for punishment," he explained.

"Indeed!" said Standish; he took his pipe from the chimneypiece and, filling it, kept silent so long that Miles finished his dishes and stole over to the hearth beside him. On the chimneypiece some books stood up from the miscellaneous litter, and, because they were the Captain's books, Miles raised himself on tiptoe to read their names. A "Bariffe's Artillery Guide" pleased him most; he was wondering if he could learn from that how to be a soldier like the Captain, when behind him spoke a familiar voice: "Well, Miley, do you have it in mind to sleep at home to-night?"

Miles swung round with a start; Master Hopkins and that bucket of water and the scolding to come, — he remembered all clearly, for there in the doorway stood Ned Lister, with his out of temper look. "The master sent me to find the boy," he explained more civilly to the Captain. "I've sought him all through the village. Come, Miles, Master Hopkins —"

Involuntarily Miles pressed close to the Captain. "Is he going to whip me, Ned?" he asked anxiously.

"Tell Master Hopkins I'll send the lad home straightway," Standish dismissed Lister curtly, then puffed a moment at his pipe till the young man's leisurely footsteps died out in the yard. "So Master Hopkins whips you often?" he questioned abruptly.

"He says I need the rod," Miles answered in a woful voice, wondering if the Captain would take his part. "He says I'm a son of perdition. I see not why 'tis right. When Ned Lister called Dotey a fool, he said he was in danger of hell fire, and, sure, son of perdition is a worser name than fool."

"Hm!" muttered the Captain. "And you're still good friends with that valiant duellist, Edward Lister?"

"I like Ned mightily, yes. But Master Hopkins does not suffer me work near him."

"That's for punishment, too, I take it?"

Miles nodded.

"At this rate you should prove the best lad in the colony, not the worst," the Captain said dryly; and then, "Say we walk down to Master Hopkins's house now, and see how that wounded Indian is faring."

A queer, vague hope that had risen in Miles vanished and left an amazing emptiness; the blackness of the lonely spring, and the whipping for that evening's tarrying came to his mind before he had crossed the room, and in the doorway he halted short.

"What's amiss?" asked Standish, with no great surprise, however.

"I — I take it, I'm afraid," gasped Miles, hot and cold with the shame of the terror he could not check. "I must go down to the spring, and 'tis dark, and I think I'll be whipped, and — and —" His lips were twitching childishly. "But I wasn't afraid at Nauset, not a whit, and I didn't cry there," he added piteously.

"I understand," the Captain said, with amazing kindness. "I'll go to the spring with you, Miles."

For the second time in his life, Miles stepped out into the night with the Captain, but there was small elation in his heart with the knowledge of his cowardice upon him. He felt a censure in his companion's silence, yet he dared not speak himself, only hurried forward as fast as possible to end the walk. They left the last cottage behind them, passed a menacing clump of bushes, and then, at the head of the path, Miles spoke out, almost in spite of himself: "Pray you, go back, sir. I'm not afraid. I won't be afraid. I'll go alone."

He called back the last, halfway down the path. The pebbles rattled with shocking loudness; there in the thicket, across the sullen brook, something stirred, he knew. With his eyes on the black ground, he stumbled toward the gurgle of the spring, groped for his bucket, fearing lest his hand touch something else, and, seizing it, filled it sparsely at the first dip, then, setting his teeth tight, made himself fill it again, slowly and carefully.

Behind him, as he rose, the bushes all were moving and alive, and something, he knew, pressed close at his heels. He could not hurry with the bucket in his hand, only clamber, step by step, with the breath choked within him, till he came at last to the black pathway above the bluff. Before he could cast a frightened look up the trail, the bucket was quietly taken from him. "You waited here for me?" Miles gasped, and then, "But I wasn't afraid."

"You will not be next time, Soldier Rigdale," Standish answered him, and, putting a hand on his shoulder, kept it there.

Before they were into the thick of the settlement, he spoke again, abruptly: "So you're not happy at Master Hopkins's?"

"I hate it there," Miles said under his breath, and then the hope that the Captain's former words had raised swept back once more, and he caught the other's hand. "Will you take me away from him, sir?" he asked hurriedly. "If I could live with Jack Cooke, anywhere else, I know I could be good."

"I know you could, too," Standish answered. "And I think your father and mother would wish it. But Master Hopkins is your guardian and your kinsman; I can do naught, only try my hand at coaxing, and I'm uncommon ill at that. My faith, I know not why I speak it out to such a babe as you, Miles, but you must say naught of this, remember. Only — if 'twill comfort you for your tattered breeches and the rest of your penances, — so soon as pretext is given me, I am minded to take you from Master Hopkins to live with me."

"With you?" Miles asked in the blankness of joy, and then he must hush, for the candlelight 'from Master Hopkins's window struck across his face, and an instant later they came into the living room.

Master Hopkins looked angry, of course, but his face relaxed at sight of the Captain, and he only bade Miles pack off to bed. " But he'll surely thrash you in the morning, Miles," Giles said, with a sober pucker of the brows. " What made you stay so long ? "

" I was with the Captain," Miles replied light-heartedly, and to himself he added, " And by and by 'twill be like this evening every day, for I'll live with him all the time."

CHAPTER XXII

CAPTAIN STANDISH must have spoken to Master Hopkins of other matter than wounded Indians, for, to his surprise, Miles got no whipping next morning. "Since the Captain needed you, I cannot punish you for your delay," Master Hopkins said curtly, a remission which would have overwhelmed Miles, if it had not been surpassed by the joyous fact of Mistress Hopkins's bringing out an old suit of his father's that afternoon and starting to make him new clothes.

In duty bound Miles went forth, and, seeking Priscilla, thanked her awkwardly that she had spoken for him to the Captain. He wasn't seeking Francis Billington, he would have declared, but somehow he sauntered to the shore, where Francis was likely to be, and, true enough, there he was, paddling in the water by the landing rock.

Miles halted on the beach and resumed the talk where it had stopped at their last meeting. "Hm," he sniffed at his old enemy, "I take it, Captain Standish has other things to do than gossip about

me to your father. You lied to me, Francis Billington, when you said he called me the worst boy in
Plymouth, and I'm going to thrash you for that
lie."

" I was but jesting," vowed Francis.

Miles, with his aggressive fists, smote the boy and
rolled him in the sand. " I'm jesting too, now," he
said grimly.

Francis fled howling home, and Miles, with his
shoulders well back, swung away to the corn-field.
" I *had* to beat Francis," he assured himself, " but
now I'll not fight nor run from labor any more, but
bear me well, because I am to go live with the
Captain soon."

But Miles's "soon" proved, after all, a long, and,
in some ways, a cheerless time. There were many
days still to spend in his guardian's house, where
Mistress Hopkins scolded at his carelessness, where
Master Hopkins bade him work when he had
thought to win an hour's playtime, and where more
than once, sorry to tell, Master Miles himself
strayed wantonly into mischief and was sternly but
justly punished therefor.

Nevertheless, now that he had a big, pleasant
hope to live forward to, he found it easier to bear
what was not to his liking in the present. After
all, when he tried, it was not so difficult as he had
thought to do Master Hopkins's bidding, Miles

told himself, and never realized how much easier it
was for him to perform his tasks, while Ned Lister,
still sulky and subdued from his public punishment,
was working fiercely and would not pause to idle
with him.

Thus in little, dull labors and the large pleasure
of looking forward, the muggy August days panted
out their course and the September twilights short-
ened. A long, secure time of peace it was for the
settlement, in which there fell but one incident, —
an expedition which ten of the Plymouth men un-
dertook far up the coast to the Bay of the Massa-
chusetts, where they traded for skins and made a
league with the Indians. Ned, who was one of the
company, — because, Giles Hopkins told Miles,
laughingly, he was held too much of a firebrand to
be left behind, — came home with something of his
old braggart manner, and told big stories that set
young Rigdale wild with envy. Why could not
he be a man at once, a full-sized man with a musket,
and go with the Captain to trade or fight with the
savages ?

But presently there was manly work in which
Miles shared, for with the rare October days came
the time of harvesting, when, as in the weeks of
planting, every man and boy in the colony must
bear a part. It was good weather to work, though,
with nothing of the sickly heat of the April days,

but a bracing air nerved every muscle, and the sky was deep and clear.

Miles liked the stir and freshness of trudging to the fields, one of the whole company, in the awakening cool hours of the morning. His task at first was to follow after the reapers in the barley field and gather the heavy stalks of the bearded grain into sheaves. Then after the barley, as the days grew shorter, they harvested the corn, a toilsome labor, that soon became irksome to Miles, whose part was to sit all day under cover, amidst the stiff stalks and rustling leaves, and husk the ears till his arms ached and his fingers were sore. By and by, when the corn was dried, he foresaw he should have to help shell the kernels from all those ears, and he sighed a little, as he watched the pile rise high.

Yet at heart he knew that, like all the others in the settlement, he was glad for the great heap of yellow ears. It had been a fruitful harvest; the pease, to be sure, had withered in the blossom, but the increase of corn and barley was so great that there was no fear lest the colony go hungry that winter. Men's faces were soberly elate, and even Master Hopkins relaxed his customary sternness.

But Mistress Hopkins had a mighty grievance, for Governor Bradford, after the harvest all was garnered, set apart a week as a time of special rejoicing. "That means in a community of men, even of the most godly, a week of feasting," she lamented. "And who is it shall prepare the food but we ten poor women and maids of the colony?"

To Miles, however, a week of feasting sounded pleasant; he only wished he were Ned Lister, for the Governor sent him and three of the other men fowling to get provisions for the merrymaking. In a day the four killed near enough to last the company a week,—a great, feathery heap of woodcocks, pigeons, quails, and plump wild turkeys. Miles shared in the work of plucking the birds, and, for the rest, he fetched wood, armful by armful, for the great fires that blazed out-of-doors, and he ran dares with the other boys, who should go farthest in among the blazing brands, till Goodwife Billington bore down upon them, and, chancing to collar her own son, cuffed him mercilessly.

He tugged buckets of water, too, for the endless boilings and stewings, till his back ached, but he minded it little, for this was holiday time. The October air was crisp; there was plenty to eat, — meat, and bread of the fresh corn meal; and, all the time, the zest of strangeness was added to the jubilation by the coming of hordes of Indians to share the English cheer.

The third day Massasoit presented himself, with ninety hungry warriors, whereat not only Mistress Hopkins but cheerful Priscilla Mullins was in despair. But his Majesty did his part in supplying provisions, for next morning some of his men went into the forest and returned with five fat deer, which he bestowed, as seemed to Miles most fitting, on the Captain and the Governor. They were, however, roasted for the behoof of the whole company, and on the last day of the feast, after the Captain had drilled his little troop before the King to do him honor, the Plymouth people and their guests ate of good venison.

The tables were spread in the fields, and Miles held it a notable distinction that he and Giles were bidden by the Captain wait at the one where he sat, with Massasoit and the Governor and others of the chiefs of the red men and white. Miles carried the platters of meat thither, with all the decorum of which he was master, and hoped that Standish might throw a word to him, so his happiness was final when, on his last trip to the table, the Captain called him to his side. He was sitting at the left hand of the Governor, where the light from the afternoon sun struck athwart his face, and over opposite him sat King Massasoit, greasy as ever, but now monarch-like in a great robe of skins.

It was to him that Standish spoke, in words of the Indian tongue of which Miles caught only one or two. But the Captain answered his questioning look: " His Majesty was pleased to crave a sight of you, Miles. Truth, you put him to stir enough last July. It was he who, when he got tidings from Manomet, despatched the order thither that no hurt should be done you, and sent us word where to seek you."

"Did he do so much, sir?" Miles asked, and, gazing at the stolid Indian, made him a grateful bow. "I should like to tell him 'thank you,'" he added. "If Squanto would say it for me, — or you."

Then he tramped back again to the fire to take his own share of the feast, a large turkey leg which Constance had saved for him, and, whether it were overmuch turkey or overmuch labor, he was too tired even to rise and witness the departure of the Indians after the board was cleared, for all he knew the musketeers would fire them a parting volley. 'Twas toilsome work, this merrymaking, he agreed with Priscilla, and, going weary and cross to bed, he was glad to awake to the Sabbath quiet of the little village, and, on the ensuing morning, drop once more into the ordered round of duties.

There was naught to do in the following days but to make ready against the coming winter, by mending the cottages till every crevice was secure, and fetching good supply of firewood from the distant hills. A hint of wintry weather now was in the chill air and the lead-colored sky, so, one

November afternoon, Miles spent hours in hunting for his mittens that had gone astray.

Together he and Constance and Giles opened, in the search, the little chest that had been Goodman Rigdale's; it gave Miles a dull pang to turn over the clothes his father and mother had worn, but somehow all that sorrow seemed to have fallen very long ago. "Yet 'tis not a year since we sailed into the harbor," he said softly.

"Just a year to-morrow since we sighted Cape Cod," answered Giles, and Constance changed Miles's thoughts by adding: "The other ship with our fresh supply should come now very speedily; in about a month I heard father say we might look for her. I hope there'll be cattle come in her; 'tis hard for the babies to have not a drop of milk."

"And no butter," sighed Miles, thinking of himself. "And if they bring oxen, 'twill be easier ploughing, come spring; and there'll be more men to fight — "

"There'll be two more next spring, in any case," Giles interrupted. "Captain Standish says that then Bart Allerton and I shall have muskets of our own and be enrolled in his company."

In the days since the landing at Plymouth, Giles had grown a responsible youth, but Miles, who had been so much with him that he held himself near as

old, was quite jealous at his last speech and wondered if no one would offer him a musket.

He took himself forth from the chamber into the
living room, where Ned Lister, who was cleaning
his fowling piece and was in a good temper, as he
usually was when he was busied over his weapons,
let him meddle in the work till his fingers were
blacked. "I'm going northward to-morrow morning, where Squanto tells me a flock of geese are
astir," Ned spoke further. "If Master Hopkins is
willing, I'll take you with me, Miley; 'tis months
since we've gone about any labor together."

Disappointingly, Master Hopkins was not willing, for, when he came to his supper, he had to
report an evil rumor, which one of Miles's old ene-
mies, the Nauset Indians, had just brought to the
town, that a great ship had been seen on their
coast. It might be some English trader, or it
might be a French ship of war, come to dispossess
the colonists, just as the English had driven the
French, at an earlier time, from their northern set-
tlements.

Still, even if 'twere a Frenchman, Ned argued,
men must eat, and must kill their food ere they
could eat it, so, at the last, his master said he might
go fowling, and even, if he did not roam too far,
take Miles with him.

Early next morning the two hunters set out in

lively spirits, in spite of the fact that the woods were sombre and the sky rough with clouds that looked, should they thrust a hand deep into them, as if they would strike something hard and cold. Already there had been bitter frosts, and the thick fallen leaves, on the northward trail, rustled crisply beneath the tread of the fowlers. Ned wore his red cap, which blazed out bravely under the dull trees, and his buff-jacket, too, which gave him the martial look he liked. Miles had no such warlike equipments, but Ned generously suffered him to carry the fowling piece, so he felt quite like a soldier. "I do but wish the French would come upon us now," he panted boastfully, as he shouldered the gun.

"There's small danger you'll find a Frenchman, unless you cross the water to seek him," Ned answered. "I'll do it, so soon as my time's out. Go into Bohemia and fight—" There he turned off into discourse on the joys of a life where a man never fetched and carried, but handled a sword like a gentleman, which lasted them for a mile along the bare trail.

By then they came from among the leafless trees of the level land to a thick piny growth at the base of a tall hill, that blocked off sight of the ocean. Ned was for climbing it out of hand, for, on the other side, by the shore, he thought to find the wild

x

fowl, so up he scrambled, quite nimbly, since he had long legs and tramped unburdened, while Miles toiled after with the fowling piece. A mighty steep hill, where the pine needles lay slippery, so Miles stumbled and near fell, and, when he came at last to the little barren stretch of the summit, where the lowering sky seemed to bend down to him, he could only drop flat and lie panting.

Ned cast himself down beside him, although he did not seem weary, and, half smiling at Miles's breathlessness, let his eyes at last turn seaward. Lying back, Miles, too, looked out upon the gray water, beneath the hill, that far away to eastward merged into the gray sky, and then a sudden exclamation made him glance at his companion.

Ned was sitting erect with his hand shading his eyes, and the lines of his face were sharpened with a sudden tenseness. "What d'ye see?" Miles began carelessly, but the other, springing to his feet, spoke to him in a curt tone: "Jump you up, Miles. Look yonder, if you see aught in the offing."

Ned's hands turned Miles's head eastward, but, though the boy yielded himself obediently and gazed whither he was told, he saw only dull water and brooding sky. Yet he was beginning to guess the meaning of it all, and, with the heart fluttering into his throat, he cried, "Ned, sure, you do not think — that French ship —"

But Lister, wheeling about, had reached in two strides a tall pine tree that spired from the summit of the hill, and, grasping its lower branches, swung himself upward from bough to bough. His cap showed very red against the green of the pine needles, and Miles watched it go bobbing toward the tree top, with a mind so suddenly dulled that he could think of nothing else, till at last the young man, holding fast by one arm, swayed at the topmost point of the pine tree.

A long minute Ned clung there, staring seaward with his face sober, then headlong slipped and scrambled from the tree. "It's a sail, true enough," he cried, and, as the words left his lips, came to the ground with a crashing fall that made the branches sway.

Before Miles could reach his side, Ned sprang to his feet, stood a moment, took a single step, and then toppled over again across the roots of the pine, with his face working in a manner that frightened his companion. "Are you hurt? What is it, Ned?" he cried.

"Naught but my ankle," groaned Lister, struggling to a sitting posture. "I've wrenched the cursed thing. Tut, tut, tut! Don't waste time here by me. Run to Plymouth. Tell them the ship's in sight."

"The Frenchman?" gasped Miles.

"How can I tell, when 'tis four league off shore?" snapped Ned. "'Tis a ship, and that's enough. Run along with you, briskly!" Then, spite of the pain, there came a sort of softening to his face. "You're not afeard to go back along the trail alone, Miley?"

"I've been in woods before now," cried the boy, indignantly. "But — but if I go, what will you do?"

"Sit here and take tobacco," Ned answered, in his swaggering tone, and, with his hand a little unsteady, drew his pipe from his pocket. "Give me the fowling piece near to me, and now run your briskest, d'ye hear? Off with you, heavy-heels, unless you be afraid!"

The taunt more than all else sent Miles plunging headlong down the hill. The needles slipped beneath his shoes, and his knees jarred with the steepness of the descent. Once he tripped, and, falling, rolled over and over, and rose up in fear lest he had hurt himself like Ned. But he could run well enough, he found, as he stumbled into the more level part of the trail. His briskest, and warn the Plymouth folk, Ned bade, and suddenly Miles's heart gave a great leap that he was to do so soldierly a part in the Captain's sight. He drew a big breath, and, bending his head, dashed down the trail.

The dry twigs snapped beneath his feet; a fright-

"'The breath came gripingly in his throat.'"

ened quail, with a startling whir, flew across his path; the branches, as he rushed by them, wavered and shook. Below him the ground reeled and the sky above was shot with black; the breath came gripingly in his throat, and a pain like that of a piercing iron bored into his side.

Downhill, where the ground seemed not to be beneath him, and in the hollow splashed a brook. He felt the chill of the water over his ankle as he thrust his foot into it, and, stopping a moment, he plunged his head, that ached to bursting, into the icy ripples, then, gasping, staggered up the opposite slope.

He was running heavily now, so it scarcely could be called running, swaying from side to side of the trail, but more than half, than three quarters, of the way was out. The trees dwindled about him; yonder were cleared fields; yonder the smoke rose from cottage chimneys. Now the stubble of corn was stiff beneath his feet; now he crashed through a little patch of brambles; and at last, thrusting his hands gropingly before him, he pitched up against the door of Captain Standish's cottage. "Open!" he called, but his voice came in a mere whisper.

Within, they heard him, however. The door was flung open; he fell against Master Winslow; and yonder by the table he had sight of the Governor and the Elder and Master Hopkins and the Captain himself, starting up from the conference he had interrupted. Miles reeled forward a step or two and caught Standish's arm. " Captain Standish," he gasped, " the ship — the French — we saw it from the hill — the French are in the offing."

Then his knees gave way and the room whirled round. A blackness was about him in which he heard faintly the questions and re-questions of the men, the clatter of the house-door, a calling in the street. Then thunderously, subduing all other sound, he heard the crash of the great gun upon the Fort Hill that called home from labor the men who should defend their settlement.

CHAPTER XXIII

LYING upon his own bed, whither Master Hopkins had carried him, Miles harked to the rattle of eager drumsticks in the street, the hurried rush of footsteps, the shrill calls of boys. Nearer, in the living room, he could hear Mistress Hopkins's frightened tones, and the clatter of swords as Master Hopkins and Dotey armed themselves.

Presently heavy footsteps came toward him, and Master Hopkins, with his buff-jacket half fastened, opened the door of the chamber to question him further of Ned. "He's hurt, and he made me to leave him," panted Miles. "And the Frenchmen will find him, and can you not send some one to help him, sir?"

"Unless Edward Lister's neck is broke, I'll trust him to shift for himself till we have space to look to him," Master Hopkins answered with a grim sort of chuckle, and just there the house-door banged open and upon it Miles heard Giles's eager voice, "Father, may I not carry Ned's musket, since he is not here?

Bart Allerton has one ; the Captain himself said all
who could fight should get under arms."

Miles struggled up, with head still dizzy. " I
can fight too," he murmured, but the older folk,
without heeding him, tramped forth with their
weapons and left him to Constance and her stepmother. But the women had terrified thoughts to
keep them busy, so busy they took no note when
presently Miles, quite recovered from his run, slipped
off the bed and darted from the house.

Out-of-doors the men were rallying in haste to
the shore, among them John Alden, whom Miles
hailed shrilly from the house-yard : " John Alden,
O John ! May I have your fowling piece to fight
with ? "

" Ay, take it," Alden called, without looking
round, and Miles, forgetting he was weary, scudded
his fastest up the hill.

He was to have a gun and fight, even if it was
no more than a fowling piece, he told himself, and,
in a happy flutter that set at naught the Frenchmen, he clambered on the table in the Captain's
living room and dragged down the fowling piece
from the wall. He longed to take also the rapier
from the chimneypiece, but he had no right, so,
contenting himself with the gun, he hurried forth to
do his part.

A gray day and a strange day ; high noon, yet

not dinner time, for the whole order of life was broken, and beyond lay — no one knew what. But Miles thought on the fighting, and, with his pulses leaping, clambered to the gun platform, where a squad was stationed, and, ready as the best of them, gazed out upon the ocean. There, sure enough, loomed larger and larger a speck of white.

Captain Standish had gone down to the other men on the bluff by the landing, so presently Miles ran after him. He carried his fowling piece over his shoulder valiantly, and he stopped at the Elder's cottage to call to Dolly not to be afraid, and he wondered at Mistress Brewster's alarmed face.

The men on the bluff, too, looked grave and anxious, and the Captain's voice was sharp and stern. But the boys who were allowed muskets, albeit their faces were decorously sober, looked very happy, and handled their weapons with such pride that Miles grew ashamed of his paltry fowling piece.

"You might let *me* have the musket a little time, Giles," he murmured to young Hopkins, who stood beside him on the northern slope of the bluff, where they were watching the horizon. "Surely, I could manage it, and 'tis Ned's, anyway, and he is my friend."

Giles preserved an elderly, careworn silence, and puckered his brows upon the ominous east, when suddenly from behind them shrilled a whistle.

Miles guessed who it was before he turned, so, though Giles and some of the others cried out in surprise, he thought it quite a matter of course when he saw Ned Lister coming across the fields to the bluff.

Ned walked at a leisurely limp, with his fowling piece over his shoulder, and his cap on one side; it was not till he came nearer that Miles saw, too, that his clothes were muddied and stuck with briers and leaves, and his face was white to his lips, that were set in a hard line. "Well," he greeted his fellow-colonists civilly, "did you think I meant to sit there in the bushes till you chose to come seek me?"

There he staggered a little, so Dotey caught hold of him, and just then Standish, striding through the thin ranks of his company, came up. "How did you get hither, Lister?" he asked, with whatever surprise may have been his well in check.

"I walked," Ned answered, and then, as he saw the Captain's eyes upon his muddied jacket, he began to laugh oddly. "That is, sir, sometimes I rolled and otherwhiles I crawled. For I did not wish to be gulled of the fight. And — Giles Hopkins, you thief! give me my musket."

"My father said I might — " Giles began, unruly for once, but there a sudden sound of cheering on the hilltop cut short the dispute. A man — Gilbert

Winslow, they saw — came running break-neck down the steep street, and, so far as he could be heard, called to them, "English, an English ship!" and then those on the bluff, too, took up the cheering.

It was the sailor Trevor, who, from the Fort Hill, had watched the ship grow larger till he vowed that he could make out that she was rigged in the English fashion. Still the Captain held his force together on the bluff till the stranger's nationality should be assured past doubt, and, meantime, he bade Dotey and Giles help Ned Lister to the house. "And see that he stays there," the Captain added dryly.

So Ned, turned limp and unresisting of a sudden, staggered away between the two, and Miles, though he would fain have watched till the ship should loom up round the beach point, thought friendship required that he should follow after with the musket.

When he returned to the landing place, many minutes later, there was no longer a doubt or a fear, for the flag of England fluttered from the vessel's mast. The ship *Fortune*, with the reën-forcements for the colony, that was not expected for a month more, was casting anchor in Plymouth Harbor.

That afternoon seemed all a hazy dream. With a feeling that he must be some one else, Miles watched the men make ready the shallop, saw it go dipping across the gray harbor, and lie to beside the great ship. He saw the first boatload of the newcomers pull in to the landing rock, and he gazed shyly and yet gladly at the faces of the men and women who were to be his townsfolk. Elder Brewster's grown up son came with them, and there were many other young men, and a few older, and several women, but there were very few children among them.

At last, however, Miles and Jack found among the newcomers a boy but little older than themselves, so at once they made up to him and found that his name was Thomas Cushman. And because he had looked on ships and sea till he was weary of them, they led him away from the harbor, and showed him the spring and the Fort Hill, and laughed at him because he was so certain he should see an Indian at each turning, and Miles bragged to him mightily of his experiences among the savages of the Cape.

It was near dusk when they came down again through the village, where the last boatload from the ship had just landed. The street seemed fairly thronged with folk, and out to sea a light sparkled on the quarter-deck of the *Fortune*, just as it used to shine upon the *Mayflower*.

Feeling secure and happy, Miles bade his new friend Thomas good night, and walked home to his supper. " Bring firewood; we've many people to eat with us to-night," Constance called to him from the doorway, so he trudged on to the woodpile, where he picked out a good armful of the piny logs, to make a brave blaze for the friends who had come from England.

His face, as he worked, was toward the west, where showed a smear of red, which the sun, struggling forth just ere his setting, had left behind. Miles gazed on the gay fleck, that yet was lonely in the wide sky, till a step near at hand startled him, and, turning, he faced Master Hopkins.

" Lay aside that wood, Miles; I have to speak with you," his guardian greeted him; and Miles dropped the wood and wondered what he had done wrong. " Pray you, sir, John Alden told me I might take that fowling piece," he offered his excuses.

" Am I always so severe that you look for naught but chiding from me, Miles?" Master Hopkins said sternly, yet with something half wistful in his tone. " I would but say to you that Captain Standish has long urged me to let you be one of his household, and I have as long withstood him. For all he is a brave gentleman, he is not of the faith in which your father lived. But he has urged me strongly this day, and you, too, Miles, you bore yourself fairly this morning; you have tried to bear yourself well these last weeks, I can see. 'Tis possible that you will not suffer Miles Standish to spoil you with lax discipline, and in matters of faith you cannot go very far astray in this colony. So I think it safe now to leave this matter to your own decision. You may stay in my house, or go unto the Captain."

Miles breathed quickly and cracked a bit of bark between his fingers. "Am I to decide now, sir?" he asked.

"Yes,. now. There is a kinsman of Mistress Hopkins's come on the *Fortune* who will take your place in my household if you go. But you need not go for that. As long as I have a house, there is a place for you therein, if you elect to stay."

It seemed an easy thing to say, he knew what he desired, yet when Master Hopkins stood looking gravely down at him and waiting for his answer, Miles found it hard to give. "I — I — You've been good to me, after all, sir," he faltered. "I'm sorry I've vexed you so many times. I —"

"In short, you wish to go to the Captain," Master Hopkins interrupted. "Very well, Miles Rigdale. Be it as you wish."

Then he walked away, and Miles, gathering up his armful of wood for the last time, wondered that, now he had his desire, he felt a half sorrow that it was granted him.

But when he entered the house, different thoughts

came to him. All was stir and bustle within, for
Mistress Hopkins was cooking supper for the men
with sea-appetites, who were to eat there that night,
and suddenly Miles felt it quite a part of the day's
upheaval that he should leave his old home. All
afire with the pleasure of it, he went into the chamber, where he tied up his few clothes in his cloak.

Ned Lister, who was stretched upon his bed,
pulled himself up on his elbow to watch him. "So
you're going to live with the Captain, Miley," he
repeated the boy's news. "Well, it's far better that
you should ; there'll be no one in his house to lead
you into mischief." Ned's face grew serious and he
was silent a moment, then broke out, "On my soul,
I have liked you, lad, and I shall miss you."

"I shall see you every day," Miles answered, setting himself down on the edge of the bed.

"Hm!" Lister retorted. "Your Captain doesn't
like me, Miles. Though he did trouble himself to
see how I was faring, when he came to speak with
Hopkins this afternoon; after all, he's a good fellow, though I've no liking for the punishments he
gives. But that'll change now. There's a pack of
jolly good fellows come in the *Fortune*, they say, will
keep him busy. Plague of this ankle! I might 'a'
gone out and made friends with them, and I'm sick
to have speech again with an ungodly rascal like
myself."

Just there Constance pushed open the door and came in to bring Ned his supper, so Miles gathered up his bundle to go forth. But Constance had to kiss him good-bye, right before Ned, and tell him to come back often. "I will," Miles promised soberly. "You've been good to me, Constance, and—and if 'twill help you, I'll come tend Damaris—once in a while."

"No, you shan't, dear, ever again," Constance said, laughing, and pushed him out of the room.

He took the Bible that had been his father's from the chimneypiece, and, while Mistress Hopkins was busy talking to her kinsman, a grave young man who found no opportunity to answer her, thought to slip quietly out of the house. But Elizabeth Hopkins spied him. "Where are your manners, child, that you cannot say 'God be wi' you'?" she assailed him. "After what I've borne from your carelessness, Miles, and I'm sure your clothes never will be tidily mended now, and—"

But there Miles got the door open and scampered away. Trug came leaping at his heels, and, fast as if Mistress Hopkins were likely to pursue him, he ran till he reached the Captain's very dooryard, and was quite breathless when he opened the door.

Inside, the candles were lit, the meat was on the table, and the Captain and Alden and four of the newcomers were making their supper and talking heartily the while. At the noise of the opening door they all faced about, and Miles felt shy and abashed. "If it like you, Captain Standish," he stammered, "Master Hopkins said I could come, so I came."

"And you are right welcome, Miles," Standish said quickly. "We looked for you to-night. Put down your bundle and come to the table. Let your dog come in, too."

Miles slipped into a cranny on the form between Alden and a black-haired young man named De la Noye. It was a roast duck they had for supper, and the men fed Trug right at table, and they talked a deal, of Indians and of hunting and of planting, and then, as the Captain and Alden guided the conversation, of the Parliament and of the Spanish influence and the war in the Palatinate, till, spite of the excitement of the evening, Miles's head nodded, and at heart he was glad when at length, long after the sober bedtime hour of Plymouth, the men cleared the table hastily and went to their rest.

The newcomers were bidden lie that night in the bedroom, since two of them still were weak with sea-sickness, but Alden and the Captain were to sleep in the living room, so Miles silently elected to stay with them, and he was glad when the chamber door closed behind the strangers.

"So you've a mind to share the floor with us,

Y

Miles ? " the Captain asked, as he threw off his doublet.

" 'Tis like a soldier to sleep where 'tis hard," Miles confessed shyly.

Standish smiled a little. " We'll surely make a fighting man of you, Miles, or you'll make one of yourself. 'Twas a pretty race you ran alone this morning, your friend Lister told me."

" Lister made a stout march of it, too," put in Alden, who had already rolled himself in his blanket and settled down on the floor.

" There's more mettle in that rapscallion than I judged," Standish answered thoughtfully, and then : " Lie you down, Miles. Eh ? No blanket ? Here, take my cloak ; 'tis ample enough for you."

Indeed, it was, and very brave and martial, too. Miles curled himself up in it, and liked the manly hardness of the floor beneath his shoulders. He closed his eyes and half dozed, then, hearing Alden's voice, roused up a little.

" Captain," the young man was speaking softly, " there's not an ounce of extra provisions in the *Fortune.*"

From the neighboring corner where Standish had stretched himself came a non-committal " Um."

" And half these young fellows are equipped with nothing but the clothes they stand in ; they gambled away their very cloaks, when the ship touched at

Plymouth in Devonshire." There was silence in the living room for a time, before Alden resumed, "We had enough to do in the colony before, sir; now what shall we do with these?"

"Why, some we'll set to ploughing and some we'll set to fight the Indians," said Standish. "And those that will neither plough nor fight, we'll pack home to England. We've no use for idlers here."

Then again there was silence in the living room, and the embers in the fireplace gleamed red, and once, leaping into flame, set black shadows fluttering on the wall. "We've no use for idlers," Miles repeated to himself. "But I'll work as mother would wish me to, now I am in the Captain's house."

He drew the Captain's cloak closer about him, and thought to amuse himself with pretending he was a true soldier, like the Captain, sleeping in his military cloak out under the stars, but the reality pleased him better than the fancy. He lay with his eyes wide open, smiling at the embers. "The Captain's house," he repeated. "And I shall stay here always."